HOYDEN BRIDE

Ash took her hand and she stepped over her clothes to face her lover, as if in the center of a bright cocoon, for the sun flowing through the curtains blessed as well as mocked them for this breach in the fabric of good manners.

"It is the middle of the day," Lark said, in a tardy effort to play the lady, but her rogue of a husband's wicked grin said he cared not a whit. She had daily evidence that the earl of Blackburne liked breaking rules as much as did his hoyden bride.

He slipped her shift up and over her head. Then he stepped back to regard her, like a connoisseur examining a work of art, assessing and delighting in the vision.

For the first time in her life, Lark felt . . . beautiful, at least in the eyes of another, in the eyes of the rogue who mattered most.

BOOK YOUR PLACE ON OUR WEBSITE AND MAKE THE READING CONNECTION!

We've created a customized website just for our very special readers, where you can get the inside scoop on everything that's going on with Zebra, Pinnacle and Kensington books.

When you come online, you'll have the exciting opportunity to:

- View covers of upcoming books
- Read sample chapters
- Learn about our future publishing schedule (listed by publication month *and author*)
- Find out when your favorite authors will be visiting a city near you
- Search for and order backlist books from our online catalog
- Check out author bios and background information
- Send e-mail to your favorite authors
- Meet the Kensington staff online
- Join us in weekly chats with authors, readers and other guests
- Get writing guidelines
- AND MUCH MORE!

**Visit our website at
http://www.kensingtonbooks.com**

A CHRISTMAS BABY

Annette Blair

ZEBRA BOOKS
KENSINGTON PUBLISHING CORP.
www.kensingtonbooks.com

ZEBRA BOOKS are published by

Kensington Publishing Corp.
850 Third Avenue
New York, NY 10022

All Kensington titles, imprints and distributed lines are available at special quantity discounts for bulk purchases for sales promotion, premiums, fund-raising, educational or institutional use.

Special book excerpts or customized printings can also be created to fit specific needs. For details, write or phone the office of the Kensington Special Sales Manager: Kensington Publishing Corp., 850 Third Avenue, New York, NY 10022. Attn. Special Sales Department. Phone: 1-800-221-2647.

Zebra and the Z logo Reg. U.S. Pat. & TM Off.

First Printing: October 2004
10 9 8 7 6 5 4 3 2 1

Printed in the United States of America

All my love
to the best Christmas gift ever,
Travis Austin Mullens,
born December 2, 2003,
truly our comfort and joy.

Chapter 1

London, March 1818

Ashford Blackburne, fifth Earl of Blackburne, did not care where he married and planted his seed, so long as he did both before Christmas, when his tyrannical grandfather's archaic ultimatum ran out.

Awash in the stale scent of incense, aware of a mortifying rigidity in his spine, Ash fixed his gaze upon the claret marble altar before him, and acknowledged, if only to himself, the unlikelihood of his bride's tardy arrival.

Given his first jilt six years before—due to his lack of funds—Ash thought surely today's bride would show, for he had paid her well to be here. But her absence proved her as greedy and dishonest as the rest. An actress of some talent—simply regard the way she'd taken his money and run—she might have played the role of loving wife well enough to satisfy even his grandfather's skeptical eye.

Now he so obviously faced a second jilt that none but a strangled cough dared pierce the weighty silence behind him, only to be trapped in the gothic eaves, like a fluttering ribbon of echoes in an unending wave of mockery.

Ash glanced about, as if for escape. Although his groomsman, Myles Quartermaine, Earl of Northclyffe seemed loath to speak, the portly, plum-cheeked cleric stepped timidly forward. "My lord, I . . . do believe that your bride—" The parson plucked at his strangling collar. "She must have—" He blotted his brow with a palsied hand and opened his mouth like a fretful fish.

Ash cursed and sent the vested craven scurrying from harm's way like a crab before the tide while the resonance of his expletive filled the rafters, and the craven turned crimson.

"Devil it, Ash," Myles whispered. "She has taken your money and run."

Ash firmed his jaw. At this moment, he'd rather fight another horde of bayonet-wielding Frenchies than face a one of his gossip-greedy guests. Nevertheless, he turned to regard the vultures. "There will be no wedding today," he said, and before the surge of speculation broke, he'd stepped through the vestry arch, twice-jilted and thrice as furious.

The warble-voiced vicar barely offered a blessing before Ash cleared the north nave exit, leaving Myles to the mercy of its ravening jaws.

As the two reached the front of the huge steepled edifice, Hunter Elijah Wylder, Marquess of Wyldborne, another battle-scarred rogue of the club, quitted the church and fell into step beside them.

In a gesture of impotent fury, Ash waved off his coachman and together the three strode down Piccadilly and straight through the rotting portals of McAdams's Pickled Barrel Inn. There they always ended when dissipation came to mind, and there they sat now to drink and forget the scandalbroth to come.

"McAdams!" Ash shouted. "Your best whiskey, and bring the bottle."

"Bring three," Myles said.

"Hell, roll the barrel over," Hunter added.

Larkin McAdams had seen him coming. Him—the man who'd filled her dreams since childhood, foolish, wistful, impossible dreams, who had dominated them since he lifted her from the floor, wiped her tears, kissed her scraped knuckles, and called her a brave little lady—the most handsome and forthright being ever created: Ashford bloody-beautiful Blackburne.

If only he were not of the lowest and most feeblebrained of God's creatures . . . a man. Practical to a fault, Lark sighed and admitted that for dreaming purposes, Ashford Blackburne's manliness did not seem so much a failing, as an advantage. His male shortcomings paled in comparison to his masculine strengths, as exhibited by her nightly fancies, in which he played a leading role.

Ashford—as she dared call him in her mind—sat now in his favorite chair at his favorite corner table from which he liked to survey the room at large. And she, on the far side of the enclosed stairwell behind him, sat on the bottom step, her temple against the rough wall board, as near to him as she dared to get without being seen.

If she closed her eyes, she could ignore the stench of ale and tobacco about her and remember the special scent of him that day eleven years before, like the most exotic of spices. And when she did recall it, a yearning for more than she could ever have overtook her.

As always, she fought the pull. Being so near the object of her fancies never failed to rush her blood and pummel her heart with the kind of wild sentiment she hated; yet at this moment, there existed no place on this earth she would rather be.

Her dissatisfaction with life would pale with his departure, she knew, and reality would return, however rude and unpleasant, though her yearnings never seemed to end.

Lark slid to the floor just behind him and stretched her arm as far as she could reach, far enough to touch the hem of his frock coat, bold unworthy creature that she was, and stroke its fine and fancy cloth between her callused fingers. Too greedy by half, and ignoring the risk such abandon wrought, she slid her hand into his pocket, and out as fast, for nobody picked pockets better, not even her da.

She palmed a silver snuffbox with curls that might be letters cut into it, a glove the color of wheat, and a perfumed lady's calling card. Lark's jaw set at the sweet, cloying scent of the card, but she brought Ash's butter-soft kid glove to her face, let the wash of his nearness shiver through her, and forgave him. 'Twas the spicy scent she remembered from that long-ago day mixed with a strong touch of . . . lavender, as if he'd crushed a sprig in his gloved hand.

Lark slipped the calling card between the stair treads and watched it disappear from sight with utter satisfaction. Ash was only a man, after all—human, weak, selfish, and self-serving, like the rest—but kinder than most, infinitely more honorable, and much, much better on a poor maiden's eyes.

Lark pushed the remainder of her bounty into her trousers' pockets and sat in the stairwell so long, her legs cramped. The drinkers, Ash and his two cronies, at first rowdy, then silent, then morose, in turn, called for three more bottles, then three more.

For a while dust motes danced in the slant of daylight piercing the grimy bay window near Lark's perch, then the light changed direction, lost its brilliance, and disappeared altogether.

Ash stopped swilling whiskey long enough to belch and grin, and Lark was glad he was coming out of his sulks. Something must have gone terribly wrong, for Ashford Blackburne could be a rogue of a charmer when the world went his way.

The friend he called Myles caught his mood, winked, and slapped him on the back. "You're running out of time to get you a bride, old boy."

Ash clutched his friend's neckcloth and pulled him strangling close. "No bloody fooling," Ash said with another belch and another charming grin.

"God's teeth," Myles said, pulling from Ash's hold and loosening his neckcloth. "If *you* cannot persuade someone to marry you—"

Ash growled at that and Myles reared from harm's way. "I *meant* . . . what the bloody chance do I have, I'd like to know?"

"Not a chance in Hades," said the third rogue— Hunter, Lark thought Ash called him—his whiskey induced grin somewhat endearing, she thought, if rather dangerous to the female population. "Though I do think your grandfather's ultimatum is rather absurd, not to mention, damned near impossible to achieve. At this rate, you'll never inherit."

"Stubble it, Hunter," Myles said to both the personal slight to himself, and the discouraging commentary on Ash's dubious future.

Hunter shrugged and returned his attention to Ash. "Devilish bit of bad luck, there, getting yourself jilted again."

Again? Larkin sat straighter, ignoring their banter as it escalated toward disagreement. Jilted? Ashford Blackburne had been left at the altar? More than once?

Were society women daft?

"Does the first count as a real jilt?" Hunter, with his whiskey grin, put in. "You ran off to fight Boney without a word, after all, and Ellenora was desperate to marry; we all knew that. She could hardly wait to see if you would survive, and Ames was a duke with a fortune as big as hers, so she *would* take him."

Ash leaned over the table, fisted a quick hand, and knocked the sot of a speaker on his arse. "Thank you for the patronizing reminder, but she took the man too bloody fast, if you ask me. She did not even wait two months and that I cannot forgive. Fact is, I'd rather run this pub than be stuck with the fickle likes of either jilt."

Whoever the women were, they must be lacking in wits, as well as eyesight, to jilt a handsome rogue like Ashford Blackburnee, Lark thought, ignoring the talk of trade and pub profits that ensued.

She would have waited for Ash, however long it took him to return, Lark admitted to herself, no matter the issue of low funds, for Ashford Blackburne would know how to treat a lady. Then again, she did not need much—a cot, a warm blanket, a monthly bath.

"Well now, I don't feature *sellin'* ye me pub, me fine lord, but I'd sure like a go at playin' ye for it."

With rude dispatch, and no small shot of panic, the warm haze of Lark's musings popped at her father's words. What? What had her da just said? Rat's whiskers, she wished she'd been paying attention.

"Name your stakes," Ash said.

Oh no. Lark sat straighter and peeked around the stairwell as Ash rubbed his clean, strong hands in glee, the fool. He'd had a great deal too much to drink, if he was thinking of playing her da for the Pickled Pigsty.

Lark sighed as her father called for Toby, his barman, to bring a "fresh" deck—properly marked, of course—and supposed she should be glad Da hadn't tried to add her to the pot.

"If ye win, ye get me fine pub," said her da, spelling out the terms and entertaining Lark with his wit. No doubt he'd also add his secret recipe for mystery-critter stew, and call it ambrosia. "If ye lose," he said, shuffling the cards fast enough to make the sots dizzy, "I get a thousand gold guineas. And just so ye don't go home empty handed," he added, generous as a lord, "I'll throw in me beautiful daughter for wife, as a consolation."

Ash gave an inebriated laugh and took another swallow of his whiskey, while Lark rose with a silent screech and made to leap to her own defense . . . but her father shot out with a right, and liked to blacken her eye.

She hit the floor behind Ash and scampered back into her stairwell as Ash looked up from his drink. "Did you hear that?" he asked no one in particular.

"Rats," said her da as he dealt the cards. "To keep the cats out." He shuddered. "Hate the mewling things."

Lark cupped her eye and refused to acknowledge

the sting. She had once seen her sister on her knees, weeping and groveling at the feet of a bloody cur, and vowed there and then that no man would see tears in Larkin McAdams's eyes . . . especially not the man who'd once called her brave.

Testing her vision, Lark saw Ash pointedly regard her father with speculation in his red, drink-dazed eyes.

Myles cleared his throat with authority. "The daughter of an innkeeper is hardly a suitable wife for an earl, old man."

No bloody fooling, Lark thought, but her father rose, as if in indignation. "Her mother was the daughter of a duke, I'll have ye know," he said in all truth, though he failed to mention that Mum had been born on the wrong side of the blanket.

Ash's laugh raised Larkin's hackles in an odd, unsettling way, as if she must prove her worth, when she knew bloody well she had no worth to prove.

"How old is this unexpected blue blood?"

"Twenty-two come May."

Ash choked on his drink. "A bit long in the tooth."

Larkin took offense, wishing she could fight for her aggrieved honor, for no one else would.

"Look at it this way," Myles said. "Win or lose, your problem is solved."

"I bleeding well wish he would lose for a change," Hunter said, retaking his seat and tossing a handful of coins on the scarred oak table. "Might as well throw my blunt in a cesspit."

Ash regarded his friend Myles with intoxicated bewilderment. "What problem will be solved if I win or lose, and how?"

"If you win the game, you win the pub, so you won't

need a bride, for you won't need your grandfather's blunt when you're turning a profit. If you lose the game, you get the bride you need to fulfill your grandfather's requirements. Either way, you win."

Ash seemed to ponder some thorny quandary, and after a stupefied minute, in which Larkin found herself holding her breath for some odd reason, Ash nodded, as if with respect for his friend's wisdom. Then without thought to the consequences of the shoddy solution, he returned his attention to the cards in his hand—a measure of his whiskey-soaked brain.

Why did a man like Ashford Blackburne not have brides clawing at each other to get him to the altar? Lark wondered.

Though Ash took her father's "gracious" suggestion to heart, that he "start the bloody betting," Ash's brow remained furrowed throughout the better part of the first hand.

"A consolation prize for wife," Myles repeated, his chuckle harsh in the deep silence. "Lose and you could have a woman with no choice but to marry you."

Ash cursed and Larkin's eyes widened, but even as she tried to work up the proper measure of indignation on his behalf, or imagine her hero losing at anything, a rather pleasant lethargy stole over her at the very notion.

Ashford Blackburne for husband . . . she should be so fortunate.

"Is she a virgin, at least?" her erstwhile hero asked, sending a shaft of fury through Lark, and lowering him mightily in her esteem, partly for the intimate nature of the question, and partly because he attended more to arranging his bloody cards than either her da's answer or the cheatin' glint in her sire's eyes.

Before he deigned to answer, the guinea her da tossed into the pot spun and rolled dutifully back into his lap with none the wiser. "Me daughter is as pure and virginal as me inn's snow-white bed linen," said he.

Chapter 2

Two hours later, Larkin knew that Ashford Black-burne, womanizer, spendthrift, card sharp, was as good, or as bad, as his colorful reputation painted him. He was like to win the game, hands down, despite her father's treachery, and the knowledge made her sweat.

She had started thinking of little Micah, alone in the country—no mother, save her, God help him, not that she managed to see him above twice a year, if that often.

What would it mean to Micah to be brought up in the home of a wealthy man like Ashford Blackburne?

With growing apprehension, and that thought in mind, Lark watched the game's every turn through the eyeball-sized hole she had bored between the planks in the stairwell over the years.

Only two players remained now—her father and Ash. The others had long since fallen into whiskey-induced sleeps—Myles with his head on the table and Hunter curled on the floor—the both of them snorting and snoring fit to rattle the rafters.

This last hand could decide Micah's fate, Lark realized. Until today, the boy might have spent his adult life on the streets, at worst, or running the Pickled Barrel Inn, at best, *if* her father ever relented and acknowledged his grandson's existence.

At seven, Micah was too young to care which sad future he faced, but Larkin cared. He was a good boy, living in a foster home without complaint, asking for nothing save a warm blanket and a daily scrap of bread, but Larkin wanted better for him.

The more she considered Micah's wretched prospects, the more she knew that this fool's game of chance might very well be his single hope for a decent life. If only she could tip the scales. . . .

Her da rose and went to nudge Toby, none too gently, toward the door, and Ash lowered his cards to take a left-handed swig of the inferior ale just poured him. The drunker her da's customers got, the lower the quality of drink he served, and Ashford Blackburne and his cronies were plenty damned drunk.

Larkin regarded the cards dangling from Ash's loose grip as something akin to a gift from the gods, and she had never been one to refuse a gift. With Micah's future in the balance, she reached over and plucked at the fabric of Ash's right sleeve.

His cards hit the floor and scattered.

While Ash blinked and looked about, as if to identify the sound, Lark replaced his ace with her father's two of hearts, the card Da had earlier switched for the ace up his sleeve.

Lark had originally pocketed the switched card as evidence of her father's cheat, with a thought to proving her sire's deception and setting Ash free. That she was now attempting the opposite, Lark considered minor compared to Micah's needs.

Later. Later, she would fix everything. She would

set Ash free, she promised herself, but not until Micah's future was secure.

When Ash gathered his pickled wits enough to retrieve his cards from the floor, and she knew there was no turning back, panic and remorse rose in Lark, until she reminded herself that her switch was no worse than picking pockets to keep a boy—a babe, really—fed and sheltered. She loved Micah enough to do murder, if she must, so what mattered a little fast and fancy card shuffling in the harsh game of daily survival?

When Ash crowed, Lark cowered and covered her head, certain she was caught and about to be trounced. Prickles raced up her arms and down her legs, but the blow never came. When she raised her head, and looked through the peephole, all Ash had done, as her father took his seat, was fan his cards on the table with a flourish. "Looks like I win," said the cocksure earl, brain addled and smile bright.

At her father's greedy-eyed behest, Lark watched her toppled hero focus on his "winning" hand with slow-dawning surprise. He scratched his head of dark mahogany, and examined his cards again. "I'll be damned."

"Damned or married, same difference," said her da slapping his own winning hand onto the table. "Arky!" he bellowed.

When Lark could not move a trembling limb, could not for the life of her believe what she had set in motion, her father's beefy fist appeared to drag her by the scruff of her neck into the morning light. "Behold yer bride, me lord. Ah, and here's the vicar, as fetched by me good man Toby."

"Wait just a bloody minute!" Ash rose like a venge-

ful god, no longer a victim, but the Earl of Blackburne
once more. He towered over the group with haughty
disdain, and looked ten times more glorious for it, in
Larkin's opinion.

All of a sudden, his alert predator's eyes, however
red-rimmed, were fixed upon her, as if he knew the
depth of her deception. Black and furious as thunder,
dangerous, Ashford Blackburne looked. Menacing.
And more handsome than a racing heart could bear.

Lark told herself she could stop this foolishness
now. Ash deserved better than a stinking, street-smart
pickpocket for wife, but for the life of her, she could
not make her throat work enough to speak the truth
and set him free. For Micah's sake, she dared not.

Ash could not collect his thoughts or gather his scattered wits. He knew he must terminate the twisted jest
at once, but could not seem to push an intelligent word
past his drink-furred tongue and muzzy brain.

He shook his head again to clear it, and damned
near retched, for his stomach had set up a furious roiling since the last tankard he'd drunk, and the taproom
dipped almost faster than he could keep his balance to
ride it. What had he brought himself to?

McAdams pushed a stinking gutter rat of a stable
boy in his general direction, a lad who swore like a
sailor, but with a shriek too high to vouch for even the
smallest set of ballocks. No. . . .

"Whatever it is, it smells," Ash said.

It swore as well, he soon learned, and had a spitting
aim that could win a trophy.

Ash echoed its vulgar profanity and planned to return the favor in the exact same way that he—she?—it

had expectorated on his own champagne-bright boots, but he could not bring himself to besmirch the smallest pair of mismatched shoes he had ever beheld.

Whatever "it" was—and Ash was almost certain it was not male—it skewered him with eyes of gold and green bearing as many facets as a gem-cut emerald surrounded by shards of topaz, tiger eyes that could see far deeper into a soul than a man cared to allow.

Ash regarded McAdams and attempted to focus him into one unwavering entity. "Who did you say this was?"

"Me daughter. Larkin McAdams. Arky. Yer bride."

Hunter snorted and grinned like the sot he was. "The Lady Arky."

Ash squinted in the girl-boy's direction, wishing his faculties were not quite so pickled, and holding the whiskey responsible for the horrendous sight before him. "A girl? Are you certain?"

Before Ash knew what hit him—and it hit hard—the smelly scrap of humanity the innkeeper called his daughter jumped the table and toppled him, chair and all, to the floor, and proceeded to try and beat him to a bloody pulp.

Hurling guttersnipe invectives at his head, she left him no choice but to give her the lead, while he evaded her every blow, for she was a girl, after all—she'd proved it, flat atop him as she lay—boasting a surprising number of curves in most of the right places.

Before Myles and Hunter managed to rouse themselves from their respective stupors to come to his aid, Ash felt as if she had blackened both his eyes and broken his nose in the bargain. In rising panic, he knew bloody well that she was trying to knee him where it mattered most, all the while cursing like a sailor.

When her knee did hit target, Ash took up her briny chant, stars dancing about his eyelids, stomach churning fit to cast up its accounts, and the knife-pain in his ballocks like to bend him over double.

When Myles and Hunter finally rose to the occasion to focus on his dilemma, the sots found it amusing that he refused to fight, but as a gentleman, what else could he do but try to survive the she-cat's onslaught? He had been taught never to strike a woman, though this might be the time to begin.

"Get off me, hellcat, or I'll turn you over my knee," Ash said at her ear, and when they held each other at bay, so that neither was able to move, her cat's-eyes boring into the fury in his own gaze, he upped his threat. "Stop now, or I'll bear your arse before the lot, I swear I will, and spank it crimson just for sport. Do not make the mistake of doubting me, for I am the man who can."

That made her falter enough for him to get the upper hand, which landed on a firm little bee sting of a breast, which went a long way toward healing Ash's manly pride, though it did nothing for his bruised ballocks.

Under something of a struggle to decide which of them won the battle, they tried untangling arms, legs, and sundry parts, while the reeking guttersnipe got in a bit more knee pressure, until Ash tried to match her might with a gentle, but unsatisfying nipple-flick.

Deafened by her screech, nonetheless, and with the help of his two former friends, Ash and the boy-girl rose, the two of them scrapping like gutter rats over

sustenance, her face as bright as a bleeding pomegranate.

Separated, finally, Myles and Hunter holding them
at bay, Ash tried to compose himself, to straighten his
screaming body, his torn and bloody clothes, and get
himself the devil out of there, while on the command
of the wily innkeeper, and to the sudden cocking of
four—count them: four—pistols, a scrawny, gin-sot
cleric opened his book and cleared his throat. "Dearly
beloved . . ."

"You need a special license for this kind of thing,"
Ash announced with all the haughty disdain he could
muster, despite his fight to remain upright with the
taproom turning about him.

McAdams laughed. "Hell, I've had me one of those
for two year now. Didn't do me much good, mind.
Haven't shed the baggage yet, but I guess this is me
lucky day. A thousand guineas, and her trussed like a
goose for the stuffing."

The innkeeper's grin revealed his rotting teeth. "I
guess me fine lord, you'll be the one doing the stuffing," said the fetid fellow. "But not, mind, 'til the vows
are spoke."

Ash gave up his scant veneer of refinement.
"Bloody hell, I am not going to marry this stinking
scrap of rags!" He called himself craven for picking on
the weakest of the lot, but hoped the filthy scrapper
might have some influence with her sire, if the
scoundrel were indeed her father.

Ash supposed the girl had been in on his fleecing
from the start, but she might change her tune, if she
got a sample of what she could be in for with him.

Despite the fact that one of McAdams's thick-
necked poltroons raised his pistol and cocked it Ash's

way, he dared to clasp the girl's arm and turn her
so as to force her to look directly into his eyes. "I'll
beat you," he said. "Every day before breakfast."

Bloody hell. She didn't believe him. That was when
he saw a spark that made him think for all the world of
. . . hope and . . . redemption, for he glimpsed a shim-
mer of something amazing in her eyes, yearning
perhaps, but for what? To be taken away from all this?
And who could blame her for that?

Ash shook himself, and her, physically as well as
mentally, and tried again to make eye contact, hoping
not to see anything more worthy than he wanted. "Call
them off," he said, more gently than he planned, and
sensed the desired effect, not as a result of his threat,
but of his tenderness. "Please," he added.

"Da," she said, now more than willing to comply, for
Ash had unfortunately caught a fast flash of raw,
naked fear in her eyes, not when he had acted the
beast, oddly enough, but when he had gentled his
touch, softened his voice, and pled for mercy.

What ilk of womanhood did brutality strengthen
and gentleness disarm? he wondered, but he had no
time to consider answers or causes, nor did he wish to,
for McAdams's henchmen were closing in, pistols at
the ready.

"Repeat the vicar's words, me girl," the innkeeper
ordered, "or me fine lord won't need him a bride, but
a pine box with a tight lid, and a deep hole in the
churchyard dirt."

Ash watched untold emotions transform that be-
grimed genderless countenance, made up of a
surprisingly aristocratic mix of gull-winged brows,
high cheekbones, heart-shaped lips, and a nose upon

which he counted three freckles and enough soot to keep a chimney sweep busy for a week.

Regret, he saw on that promising visage, dreams flaring to life one minute, taking flight the next. Hope and the death of hope. They all came and went in a blink and left behind them nothing save the ashes of regret, sorrow, and a loss the likes of which Ash could not begin to fathom.

While mired in confusion, Ash faltered in his resolve, until one of the innkeeper's flat-faced toadies stepped nearer still. The barrel of his pistol kissed Ash's temple and brought a rush of cool sobriety, but the depth of it was nothing to that brought by the cocking of its trigger.

"I, Larkin Rose McAdams," the guttersnipe said in a rush, then waited for toady to release the trigger, "take Ashford Edward Blackburne, Earl of Blackburne, as my lawfully wedded husband . . ."

Something in her voice—sweet, melodic, almost reverent—as she said his name, her concern for his safety, and her own name, Larkin Rose, of all the feminine appellations, all seemed to soften Ash's pickled brain.

How had she known his middle name? Why did he perceive some vague mirrored kinship in the lost-soul depths of her gilded verdant eyes?

"Fine," Ash said more or less accepting his fate, "but only because I am desperate for a wife."

His words brought a renewed surge of fury to his grimy bride's face, and he was forced to fight her to take one of her hands in his, then he found himself looking for something in the way of reassurance in her eyes. But when all he'd previously glimpsed now seemed closed to him, Ash called himself a fool and ran his thumb along her jagged fingernails to root himself to earth.

Her father relaxed, as did his toadies, and Ash knew if they could get away from here alive, married or not, they had choices, a future.

He could scrape the incrustation off her and see what he found beneath. He could get to know her and see what he found inside. And if she turned out to be as dreadful as she appeared, there was always banishment, or at the worst, annulment.

At the improbable best, he had himself a bride he could get with child before Christmas, which would fulfill his grandfather's requirements and save the estate for his mother. Revenge and repentance at the turn of a card, imagine that. Had he been offered as much when he quit his botched nuptials earlier, he might have accepted with gratitude.

Prodded and further sobered by a second kiss of the pistol barrel, Ash repeated his own vows with a slur he could not seem to shake and in a discordant voice that echoed as if it belonged to another.

Once the stipulations to his grandfather's will were fulfilled, if he and his bedraggled bride did not suit, he could set her up with a small house and an allowance. Either way, she would live better in the future than she had in the past.

However, if the depth of her hidden need, the sound of her voice, and her willingness to marry him to save him was any indication of what lay beneath the crust, then perhaps, with some effort on both their parts, they might make a decent night's work of this, after all.

Likely not, Ash cautioned himself, but devil it, alive

they could find a way to make it work. Dead, neither of them had hope at all.

"I now pronounce you man and wife."

The room swayed again, not so much from drink as shock, Ash feared. "Tell me this is better than being dead," he begged Myles . . . and Hunter belched.

Chapter 3

At the finality of the vicar's pronouncement, Ash and his bride seemed to pale as one, Ash uncertain as to which of them seemed more like to retch.

The cleric placed the parish register before them for their signatures, but McAdams shoved it aside to get Ash's signature first on his thousand-guinea voucher.

Ash wished his head was not so muzzy or his stomach so unsettled. If he had his wits about him, he might refuse this final step for a chance to think, but the pistols rose again, aimed again, and the thought of getting himself killed in this intoxicated stomach-sick condition did not sit well with him. He signed the voucher, then the register, vowing to God on High that he would never drink again.

After that was done, and his bride had made her mark—God help him—beside his name, the big-bellied innkeeper slapped his filthy apron, laughed, and offered a toast. When his henchmen lowered their weapons to get their share of life's nectar, Ash's former friends belatedly relieved the thugs of their weapons. Not that the pistol-wielding poltroons seemed to care any longer, for they seemed more interested in drinking now, than killing, and well, the harm had already been done.

After the parson filled his tankard, McAdams raised his own. "To my daughter," said he, "the Lady Blackburne."

Ash groaned and rolled his eyes as Myles and Hunter cocked the pistols they had confiscated—now that the bloody horse had escaped the bloody barn!

McAdams raised a brow at the sound, but he tipped his tankard back for a good long, greedy swallow. At length, when he finished swilling the stuff, and slammed his empty vessel on the table, he swiped his mouth with a grimy sleeve, belched, and nodded at the pistol-wielding pair. "No powder, no balls," said he with pride. "Empty as me till, those pistols. Worthless as the bloody pair of *you*."

Aiming at the ceiling, Hunter tested the revelation only to prove it correct. Myles and Hunter cursed as one, and Ash began to laugh. "This farce is over," Ash said, thinking the parson and the marriage might be as empty as the pistols, set to test the theory and see if he could escape after all.

"Thank you McAdams, for an interesting . . . exchange." Before donning his curly beaver, Ash tipped it to the "lady," picked up his cane, and headed for the door.

McAdams's roar behind him did not hasten his retreat, for he willed himself to remain calm. Not so, his inebriated friends, who quit the premises faster than stones shot from a boy's sling. "Mewling idiots," Ash said beneath his breath as he walked sedately on.

Then he heard a screech, a somewhat familiar sound now, and kept walking, not certain what to expect. When he cleared the door, Ash breathed a deep draft of fresh night air, felt almost sicker for it, but heaved a sigh heavy with relief at any rate. Perhaps he would be forced to suffer neither an annulment nor his guttersnipe bride's overripe scent a minute more, *if* she were indeed his bride.

His elation was short lived. No sooner had he stepped from the curb than McAdams's henchmen carried the screaming hellcat out the door, and deposited her in his path. And there she sat, on her arse, beside a pile of horse dung, his reeking, blushing bride, Countess Arky.

Ash shook his head, extended a hand to help her up, and she bit it. "Damnation! That will be enough," he shouted.

Catching his breath and scooping her into his arms, Ash carried her, surly as ever, hissing and fighting, mad as a wet cat, back to the pub, where he opened the door and threw her back inside.

Again, he departed, and again, he breathed a tentative, though more cautious, sigh.

"What the devil are you going to do with her?" Hunter asked as they made for Ash's carriage at a quickened pace.

"I just got shed of her, didn't I?"

"Don't look now, but she's catching up."

"Stuff it, Hunter," Ash said. "How the bloody devil should I know what to do with her? I can tell you one thing; strangling her ranks right up there with giving her a bath."

"I'm not deaf," Larkin snapped coming up beside him. "Nor am I stupid," she said. "He kicked me out then locked the door, by the way. I'm yours."

"You might have a sense of hearing, even a modicum of intelligence, I'll grant, but do you have no sense of smell?" Ash asked. "Because I damn well wish I did not. Stand back, will you, and give a man some breathing space."

"What, no perfumed hanky?" said she, throwing her hips out of line and mincing like a bleedin' fop. "I thought all the prancing dandies carried them."

"I do not prance. Nor am I a dandy. And the day I place a perfumed hanky under of my nose is the day I'm daft enough to bed you."

"Bloody hell," Myles said. "Don't tell me you're not going to?"

Ash stopped and his bride slammed into him. He turned, stopped her from falling and regarded his friend with a growl. "Not going to what?"

"Bed the wench, damn it," Myles said. "You can hold your breath and keep your eyes closed, can you not?"

"I *said,* 'I CAN HEAR YOU!'" Lark kicked Myles in the shin for his crude suggestion, and Ash jumped back in time to evade a similar fate, though it was her knee she was raising that time, and Ash's stomach that was churning for remembering the consequences.

Hunter stepped behind Ash, for safety's sake, and chuckled.

"You needed a bride, and now you have one," Myles said, as he hopped and tried to rub his shin. "Just get it done man."

"You mean, before she kills one of us?"

"For the love of God," Hunter said, "Myles, do not be an idiot. Ash has to clean her up first. The wench is a reeking disgrace."

Another screech, another wounded friend. Some days did not go the way you expected, Ash thought. Like wedding days. If this were, indeed, his wedding day.

"Parson, Parson!" Ash shouted to halt the man reeling down the street, a huge book beneath his arm.

The intoxicated cleric who'd performed the seedy ceremony turned and waited for Ash to catch up. Ash took five guineas from his pocket and held them palm up. "They're yours if you answer a question in God's own truth. Are you or are you not a man of the cloth?"

The parson shrugged. "An unworthy sot to be sure, but a man of the cloth all the same." He showed his closed book and there on the cover etched in gilt Ash read the words, "Parish Register, St. Adelbert Church, London."

"You are married in the eyes of God, my son, though I will regret my part in your downfall until I take my next drink, and forget you exist, and that's the sordid truth of it. I pray you will someday forgive me."

"If downfall I face, seek God's forgiveness, never mine." Ash opened the cleric's shaking hand and dropped the coins into it one by one. "For the poor box not the drink."

"You trust I will do as you say?"

"Inasmuch as I consented to my own marriage," Ash said, and though the parson flinched, he pocketed the guineas and turned to walk away.

Ash returned to his carriage. "I'll thank the two of you to wish us happy," he said to Myles and Hunter. Then he turned his bride toward his open carriage door and pushed her trouser-clad bottom up and inside, to her mortified screech and sailor's curse. He climbed in behind her and tipped his hat to his friends. "I'll thank you to stop calling my bride a wench."

Said bride's face filled with mottled fury, her posture poised to bolt, so Ash tripped her on her hastening way. By the seat of her trousers, he pulled her back in, and shoved her to the seat opposite. "Sit, wench, and shut up, while I decide what the bloody hell to do with you."

"You told them not to call me wench."

"But I can call you anything I choose. Brinks," Ash said as his coachman made to shut the carriage door,"home to Gorhambury, if you please."

For the first full fifteen minutes of the two-hour journey, Ash regarded his bride, and she him, with a mutually murderous rage. For the next half hour, they both looked away and out their respective windows, though Ash peeked her way at odd intervals.

Truth to tell, he'd needed a bride and now he had one. Problem was getting up enough courage to bed her. "Hunter is right. You need a bath," he said, regarding the unexpected fulfillment of his grandfather's maniacal will—the bloody devil of a bad night's work—hell, a bad life's work, more like.

Thank God for a closed carriage, he thought, for he would not want even a servant, to espy his consolation "prize" of a bride. Hair the color of . . . a dirty floor . . . though somewhat less tidy, and much less appealing— sooty of face, bruised of eye, though not his doing, much as he'd considered it—she stood nearly as tall as him. She stood reed-thin of body, but for a fine flair in her hips, which he'd discovered with his hands while rolling on the filthy taproom floor.

Her tiger eyes, he must admit, were amazing and possibly her best feature. Her heart-shaped lips, he thought, might be her best, though he would reserve judgment on that score until after her bath.

No wonder he'd thought her a boy at first glance, though suddenly he could barely mistake the curvaceous hips he'd so recently handled, the feminine arch in her brow, the tilt of her nose.

"Are you certain you're nearly twenty-two?" Ash asked, opening a window against the sweat and stale-pub stench of her before settling himself more comfortably against the squabs, trying to calm his roiling stomach even as he tried to catch a glimpse of her faceted eyes in moonlight.

"So *he* says."

"He, who?"

"Me da. Who else would know for certain?"

"Your mother?"

"Dropped me an—"

"On your head, I must conclude."

The way his bride narrowed her eyes made Ash cross his legs to protect himself from further attack.

She caught the move, however, and raised her chin, rather regally for a filthy urchin, while she pretended for all the world that another wash of pomegranate was not working its way up a neck that appeared suddenly swanlike. He must be drunker than he thought.

"I didn't know Tobe and Da had the pistols," she said, nearly beneath her breath, a dozen silent minutes later. Then she looked up, regarded him full in the face with so much . . . longing, Ash nearly blushed. "Guess I wouldn't be here else."

"You bloody well would not!" Good God, she must have rattled his brains with that right hook Jackson would applaud. Something around his heart ached, or got nudged, or prodded, perhaps. However he looked at it, she had managed to touch some chord that he bloody well did not want touched, or he had not, to his knowledge, until this very moment.

"You don't smell so good yourself," she said out of

nowhere. "And don't think *you're* such a bloody blue blood of an agreeable bridegroom, you selfish sot."

Ash realized then that he must have gone plain old daft, for he could swear that he was half-charmed by the worst mistake he had ever made in his life.

When he opened the other window to let in a cross breeze and dilute the stink, her curse on him and his descendents, in perpetuity, made him chuckle. "Take care, they could as likely be your descendents as well," he said, then he looked toward the heavens to beg almighty deliverance from that ghastly possibility.

He lived in a bleedin' castle.

Lark wished she had not tried to bolt when they exited his carriage on arrival, or she would now be walking beside her unfathomable new husband, rather than thrown over his shoulder like a grain-sack, an empty one for all the ease he made of it, though he teetered now and again and she feared she would get dropped. "I wish you would put me down. You are drunk as a lord."

"Am a lord."

A lord, stuck with her, she thought, amazed anew. After such a terrible deed as cheating him into marrying her, she had decided in the carriage to give him his freedom at first opportunity by disappearing immediately from his life. But not only had she failed when she tried to bolt, she had managed to turn him into a thundercloud.

Larkin sighed. She did not want Ashford to be angry. Idiot that she was, she wanted him to like her. How would it feel, she wondered, being his friend, viewing his handsome face over the breakfast table every morning, having the freedom to touch his hand, take his arm, brush that unruly lock of hair from his temple?

Lark shivered at the intimate thought, but she was too dirty for any of it, too dirty to lie in any of his pretty beds—not that she had seen them, but they must be special, judging by what she'd seen of his home so far.

From this vantage point, she examined a set of mulberry carpeted, bees-waxed stairs, and the bottommost portion of a gold striped wall, with a fancy mulberry-colored key design along its bottommost edge, and the most amazing railing ever imagined—all of it too good for her.

She stank, said he, as if she had not known this. He regarded her as if she were lowlier than dirt beneath his bright-polished hessians. As if she were . . . pig mud, infinitely lower than dirt, and exactly what she smelled of.

Lark wished she could see his face right now. As things stood, all she could see of him was—

She allowed her hand to fall into slapping his nether end at every step, almost by accident—and a fine and firm nether end it was. She took great delight as they climbed in this blatant, almost intimate act that he had forced upon her.

"Stop that!" he said, giving her own nether end a stinging slap.

Larkin screeched, and fought to be free, and he slapped her again. "Keep it up, Larkin Rose," said he, and I will slap you, every time you slap me."

She kept it up. He did too, slapping her harder than she could ever slap him, until she stopped, and he took to keeping his hand there, flat against her, bold as brass, if you please, his rising movement making it feel as if he were stroking her, there, on her private bottom.

Lark stopped touching him at all then, so he would remove his own hand, for his touch had started a kind of wild rebellion inside her body, an insurgence she did not take to the shivering likes of.

"Put me down," she said, with less command and more plea in her voice. "I do not like being up here, any more than you like having me here. I promise not to bolt again."

Ashford snorted. "Tell me another."

Being draped over the man who had been the center of her dreams for years gave new meaning to the word "intimate" as it had been imagined, once upon a time, as regards to Ashford, himself, and the role he played in her own secret world.

"You have no right—"

"As your husband, I have every right. You are my property now to do with as I please."

"As you belong to me," she said, taking a path that surprised even her, "according to the laws of God, and man, and that means all of you, including your hind end." She slapped his bottom again, hoping to get him to put her down.

"As every part of you is mine to slap, or beat, or stroke," he stressed, letting the word linger, though Lark was not as afraid as she thought she should be, but exhilarated and . . . cast as if afloat.

Panic and something more rose in her. Yes, her bottom was his to touch. As all of her was his to do whatever husbands were wont to do with their wives. If she knew what that was, precisely, and if she could be sure that a great deal of blood must not be involved, she might breathe easier again . . . or perhaps she would not.

Chapter 4

As she remembered the brutality her sister had suffered at the hands of the man she thought she loved, panic rushed Lark in bold strokes. She prayed that her faith in Ashford would be confirmed, no matter how dangerous he had appeared at several moments during the course of the evening just passed, and that he would not hurt her in the way her sister had been hurt.

Ash must have sensed her fear in some way, because he held her tighter of a sudden, almost as if with the reassurance of a protector.

No, she thought, denying her own foolishness, he held her in that way, only to keep her from sliding off his shoulder and down the bloody stairs.

Before another minute passed, he carried her into a chamber Prinny himself might happily occupy. The marble around the fireplace shone a tawny gold, a rich color that perfectly matched the veins in its cream marble trim. Did God create matching marble for the gratification of the wealthy? Lark wondered.

"Here we are, my gunpoint bride," he said with obvious resentment. "The master bedchamber."

Oh, she did not like his tone, Lark thought. "Why did you seek a wife if you do not actually want one?"

she asked, to turn her skittering thoughts from bed-chambers, especially his.

"My grandfather's money will not come to me unless I have a wife." He set her on her feet. "It appears as if destiny meant for you to take on that exalted role."

"Money," she said, with as much disdain as he had employed. "I should have known. There must be a great deal of it in the offing, then." She was thinking of Micah again, realizing he might now have a decent future. What would the boy think of this place? The main stair rail alone would make for some superb sliding, safe landing and all, carved as if to bow and kiss the floor.

"Money, yes, of which I have little at the moment," her bridegroom admitted. "Fortunately, however, I do have enough to purchase a nicety or two, like soap, praise be. Grimsley, good man," Ash said, as his valet appeared. "Have my big copper slipper bath filled at once."

His valet looked her up and down, and narrowed his nostrils, as if he could smell her from where he stood, though he was too polite to say so. "*Your* bath, my lord?"

"Do we have a problem, Grimsley?"

"No, my lord. That is to say, ah . . . of course not, but I would dare to offer . . . Cook or Mim? Either, could set up a bath in the scullery, say, or before the kitchen fire?"

"Here, said I"—Ash struggled against the spinning in his head—"and, here, I will say again. At once, whether you please or not. And bring the brandy." Ash regretted his swollen head, a remnant of his evening's entertainment, but what could a man do in such a case but raise his chin and scowl?

Grimsley regarded him as if he were daft, then he

regarded his bride, with no less horror, and gave up the fight. "Very good, my lord."

His bride, Ash saw, regarded her new husband as if he had sprouted wings and taken flight. She retreated as far as the wall at her back. "Had me a bath just last week," said she, with so much humility, he would be a fool to lower his guard.

"Nevertheless, you stink, and if you fight me on this, well, your clothes, I could throw on the fire, but you, I might be forced to drown."

"You cannot burn my clothes, you'll leave me without a stitch? What kind of depraved man are you?"

"I am the degenerate who married you at gunpoint. Have you never heard of a husband's privilege?"

"I do not recall hearing that wife-drowning was a husband's privilege." Lark dropped her arms to her sides in an expression of futility. "The stink-maker was Da's favorite sow. She got loose before you come today. Had to chase her all the way up Market Street. Lost her twice, before I got me a riding hold on her. Slippery, don't 'cha know. I don't usually smell so *terrible* bad."

"Only half so bad, then? Happy to hear it. You rode a pig, you say?" Ash coughed to hide his grin, cringed at the pain in his head, and knew he must still be sotted. "No wonder my eyes watered all the way up the stairs. We *will* throw your clothes in the fire."

His bride bit her lip, charming the muzzy bejesus out of him, while a swift swing of emotions—shock, awareness, curiosity—marched across her tri-freckled nose and furrowed her gull-winged brows. "I can hardly appear naked before the world."

Ash raised a brow, bringing that pomegranate stain to her cheeks in the process, and chuckled, while she took to tracing a fleur-de-lis in his carpet with the toe of a tattered slipper.

"You do know that you're wearing two different shoes, and that the rest of the world wears matched pairs?"

That brought her Scot's temper to the fore. "They're shoes, ain't they? They keep me feet warm, don't they? Try fighting a rag-picker and see how many matched pairs you come off with!"

"I'll buy you a dozen matched pairs," Ash said, surprising himself. He cleared his throat and shook his head free of the surge of sympathy that had overtaken him on her behalf. What cared he for the smelly schemer? "You can wrap up in a bedsheet for all I care, until I make other arrange—no, wait, I can spare a dressing gown."

At her look of gratitude . . . or adoration, Ash felt a burst of warmth that radiated outward, until he could hardly bear the burn. He moved a safe distance away and regarded her curiously. "What do you look like under all that soot?"

"My mother, I've been told."

As Ash made to reply, Grimsley and two maids arrived with buckets of hot water. "Fill my bath and be quick about it," he ordered, and his bride yelped and made for the hall. "Catch her, damn it!" Ash shouted, then he swilled the brandy Grimsley had poured and took chase.

After a lengthy dash around the third floor, and a side trip to the fourth and fifth, Ash carried Lark, screaming, kicking, and pummeling, down the hall and into his dressing room, where he unceremoniously dropped her, stinking clothes and all into a bath full of steaming water.

Ash knelt and tried to keep her there. "Quick, Grim, throw in as much soap as you can find. The way she's thrashing, she'll whip up a froth and wash herself, clothes and all."

Ash had never noticed before that Grimsley could not stand without swaying, or was it the room? Ash wasn't certain. The room, he thought, his stomach churning fit to rebel again. Drat the woman; she was already discomposing him. He was exhausted from chasing her and his head throbbed from the sound of her screeching.

Ash dunked her under, just for a moment's silence.

"You might be sorry for this night's work tomorrow, my lord," Grimsley dared as he dropped three bars of French milled soap into Larkin's bath. "If you do not mind my saying so, you are somewhat in your cups."

"Do you think so?"

"About which, my lord?"

Ash laughed. "I already regret it, Grim, but what can a man do? I married her you see."

Grimsley paled and Ash made to explain, until he realized that he'd nearly forgot to let Lark surface, and when he did, she rose like a vengeful sea goddess and knocked him flat on his arse.

"I have had a great deal of experience with the male of the species," she screamed like a fishwife, rising fully dressed, soaked and shaking with rage, "and you Ashford Blackburne are of the lowest variety!"

Ash met her head-on then ducked to evade the facer she tried to plant him. "I won her in a card game!" he shouted to his valet above her screech of indignation.

"I am no prize!" she shouted.

"Obviously." Ash pushed her back under.

"Good God," Grimsley said, clearly unsure as to

how he could extricate his master. "You won, my lord, and got that, er, her?"

She rose and tried to stand but Ash forced her to sit. "Uh . . . no, I lost. She's a consolation, of sorts." He held her by the shoulders to keep her sitting.

"What . . . what are you going to do with her?" Grim asked above her sailor's curse.

"Bathe her . . . to begin with."

"And send her away?" Poor Grimsley, he looked and sounded so hopeful.

"Ouch!" Lark had landed a blow to his jaw. In retaliation, Ash poured the remaining contents of the hot water bucket over her head. "I suppose I could, though I have need of her if you will remember. Here, help me unfasten some of these clothes."

His hellcat bride did not agree with the notion. Though thrice wounded, Grimsley nonetheless persevered and attempted to help, without success, so Ash sent him away.

For good or ill—ill more like—Lark was his wife, and in the event he actually succeeded in his current quest to rid her of her clothing, he would not be flaunting her in the flesh before another.

Grimsley, of all his staff, would never speak of this night's work. Loyal to a fault, Grim had been with him through his bloody days under Wellington's command. He'd evaded bullets and bayonets and helped Ash off the field after his horse went down, when he might otherwise have been left to perish. Loyalty was Grimsley's motto.

Ash attempted to strip Larkin himself, wishing he had a whip and a chair to hand, as he'd seen at Astley's back when he thought his worst problem was finding a bride, before he knew that taming one could be the death of him.

Him, wed to a guttersnipe, a smelly, foul-mouthed pig-chaser, a cardsharp's scheming daughter. On the other hand, a schemer might understand his scheme to win his inheritance, a schemer might be more than willing to strike a bargain.

He needed to fulfill the will. Would Larkin Rose McAdams—no Larkin Rose Blackburne now, God—help him? Would his new wife help him in his ultimate pursuit, he wondered, once she knew *all* the requirements?

Unfortunately, before he could inherit, he would first have to prove to his grandfather that he had made a good match, never mind getting his bride with child before Christmas, which stipulation said bride had yet to learn, and which blessed event would never take place if he could not bathe her before he tried to bed her.

He must also find a way to convince his bride to act the part of devoted wife, at least in the presence of his grandfather, if Ash decided to keep her, that was.

He stopped dunking her and tried to scrub wherever he could reach, which was impossible in the face of her struggle to get free, her screams, bites, kicks, and the occasional poke in the eye.

When soaping every available inch of her fully dressed did not work, Ash tried tearing her clothes off, which worked as regards to her socks and shoes, though her man's shirt was a bit trickier. When he finally pulled her second arm free of the shirt, and won the tug-of-war over that piece of clothing, he tossed it over his shoulder as she crouched low in the water.

The hiss and sputter from the hearth, and sudden loss of light, told him her wet shirt had snuffed the fire. "Bloody brat." Ash pulled her trousers over her hips. "These are miles too big for you," he said, tugging and pulling so hard, he dragged her under again.

Her head and shoulders emerged and she sucked in air.

"Another rag pick, I suppose?" Ash said, holding her trousers by two fingers, and she slapped the water with both hands and splashed him like a tidal wave.

"I have never laid an angry hand on a woman in my life," Ash said, wiping his face, "but in your case, I'll make an exception."

"Go to hell," said his blushing bride, then she screeched as his hand chanced upon something that felt like a band about her breasts.

"Fancy this," he said, learning the shape of it like a blind man. "Hiding our light beneath a bushel, are we?" He located the tucked end of the binding between her breasts. Thence began the fight to unwind her, and when he succeeded—though she tried to cover her exposed breasts at every turn—he found two handsful more bride than he expected.

"Perhaps tumbling you won't be so difficult as I supposed," he said, testing her breasts as if he'd be using them for two plump pillows, a pleasant surprise given her willowy structure. "You'll need fattening up, but not here," he said. "Here, you are amazingly perfect."

His bride took one of his happy hands from her breast and bit it . . . hard.

"Blast and damnation!" Ash pulled his hand from the jaws of death. "I think you've drawn blood."

"Good," said she, as she rose like a vengeful goddess, escaped her bath with a graceful leap, then ran naked through his bedchamber and out into the corridor. Hair in a wild, wet tangle, she knocked Grimsley on his arse, his pot of tea spraying the upper hall in puddling circles as it twirled like a dervish.

"Start the fire in the dressing room," Ash said on his rushing way by, realizing as he ran up the stairs that he should have helped his man up, though he couldn't spare the time.

He cornered his bride in a bedchamber housing two screeching maids, Nan and Mim, trying to cover themselves in their night rails. "What are you screaming about?" Ash asked. "The mistress of the house is more naked than you are."

That shut them up, for this was the first they'd heard of a mistress.

Ash had her now, cornered between a bed and a wall, and so he took off his shirt and threw it at her. She took it, half surprised, half haughty, and put it on, and then he lifted her into his arms and carried her out with all the dignity he could muster, given the fact that his chest was bare, his clothes soaked, and his temper near to exploding.

"I'm going to win every time," he said, which words seemed to take the fight right out of her. Though she squeaked in token protest, she let her head fall to his shoulder, sighed as if with resignation, and said nothing more.

When Ash got Lark back to his dressing room, the hearth had been cleaned out, dry wood and kindling set, and the fire flaming to life. This time Lark let him undo her shirt buttons—his shirt buttons—then she climbed into the tub of her own accord. "Give me the soap," she said, grabbing it from his hand with as much force as she'd previously used to fight him.

Ash reared back. "Is this a trick?"

"I had forgotten how good it feels to be clean," she said. "You should put some dry clothes on."

"Right, and leave you alone? Since I'm daft, of course I will do exactly as you suggest."

"You'll catch your death."

"You wish." He knelt and grasped her shoulder to try and wash her face, only to have her knock him off his feet, not for the first time that night, and wash her face herself.

As he righted himself, he saw emerge from beneath the grime, skin of lucent cream porcelain and eyes so deep and clear, they showed all the facets of a mystery and all the hope of a bright new dawn. Damn.

Her exposed innocence so tied his tongue, he did fetch dry things, but remembered the danger, grabbed them fast, and came right back, only to find she hadn't moved. She was washing her hair, and the more she lathered, the more appeared a rich mass of cropped honey, gilded in firelight by licks of ivory and strands of pure gold.

Ash had been right; she had not stopped fighting. The minute he dropped his trousers, she stood screaming again, this time as if he were about to commit bloody murder.

Ash clamped a hand over her mouth. "I'm changing into dry clothes, nothing more, and I'm doing it here, so I can keep a close watch on you. Do you understand me?"

Larkin nodded, her eyes wide and fearful.

"I'm only changing, as you suggested. Sit back down and finish washing your hair. Just turn your head if you do not wish to see anything more of your new husband than that for which you are prepared. I will be dressed in a minute."

As Ash took his hand away, his bride regarded him as if he might eat her alive, then she released a breath, turned her gaze, and lowered herself again to the water to finish washing her hair.

Ash wondered what prompted her fear and nearly laughed. Her father had all but sold her to a stranger, and he, the stranger in question, had stripped her naked, and scrubbed her porcelain skin as if it were tree bark.

From her perspective, his actions did appear frightening, but what had she said about knowing men and knowing them well? It made no sense, though it did remind him to send for the doctor the minute he left her, so he could be certain, before he attempted to sow his seed, that the seed of no other had previously taken root.

"The bedchamber through that door," Ash said, now clothed in his inexpressibles, shirttails hanging out, "is my wife's. You will sleep there, of course. My bedchamber is through the door opposite. 'Tis the chamber we came through when we arrived."

After a silent minute, Larkin nodded and returned her attention to her bath.

"Grimsley is bringing you another pot of tea," Ash said. "And since you've decided to behave yourself, I shall send a maid up to help you finish and show you to your room. No tricks, mind. I stationed guards at all the doors."

Chapter 5

Pouring himself yet another brandy, Ash sat in the butter-soft leather chair beside his bed and thought that perhaps he should not have drunk quite so much while waiting for Doctor Buckston to examine his bride.

Though curious as to why the medical man had raised a brow as he pronounced Larkin "untouched," Ash dismissed the quandary as of no consequence. "May as well put an end to that right now," he said to the empty room.

He placed his half full glass of brandy on the table beside him. "Arky." Ash scoffed and reminded himself that all he had to do was mount her and close his eyes, as Myles suggested, and plant his seed. After all, he'd been practicing for years for this event. How hard could it be?

He looked down at his flaccid self and sighed. "Not hard enough, by damn, to pull this one off," he said, laying hands on the key player in this farce. "Liven up there, soldier, and give us a salute," he said, closing his eyes as he tried to work himself into a semblance of arousal.

Ash imagined his bride as he'd last seen her—cropped hair, clean and honey gold, sparking cat's-eyes intense, full creamy breasts, heavy·in his hands, dusky nipples pouting, as if for his mouth.

He moved a hand along his length through his breeches, as he imagined the taste of her on his tongue, the feel of her gloving him. . . .

No more than a minute later, he groaned, opened his eyes, and stopped short of spilling his seed. Well pleased with his hard accomplishment, he rose.

When he entered his wife's bedchamber—his bravado borne of drink and a great deal of sexual experience—Ash was certain his bride would enjoy his attentions, if she cooperated for once, so he might keep his arousal long enough to do the deed.

'Twas the least she could do. He'd done her the favor, after all, of taking the irritating brat in boys' clothes, turning her into a wife—a lady, no less—and removing her from a life of ale-stink drudgery.

But when he beheld her, the clean and sweet-smelling seductress who sat in his bride's bed bore no resemblance to the hoyden in filthy clothes he'd rescued, and every likeness to the fantasy siren who'd hardened him to granite not five minutes before.

All sleeping sensuality and burgeoning promise, Larkin Rose sat in wait, her ripe breasts damned near spilling from his ebony brocade dressing gown, a profusion of milk and honey curls tumbling toward shoulders of rare porcelain.

"This is not me," she said, halting him.

"Not you?" Ash cocked a brow. "Well, whoever you are, I find myself amazingly pleased to find you awaiting my pleasure."

"I await no man's pleasure."

Ash wished he could focus on her better, wished he'd not drunk more during his wait, for she spoke so softly, he was not certain she was the same woman to whom he had pledged his troth at pistol-point.

A sultry seductress had replaced the she-cat who'd throttled him through the bath from hell. "Your hair is the color of the wheat, on the stained glass in the chapel, when the sun shines through," he said, surprised and gratified.

"It's clean, you drunken dolt."

"Larkin?" He moved her way again, trying to keep his balance as the walls and floor shifted.

"Come one step closer and die, you whelp of Satan!"

"Ah." Ash grinned. "The Lady Arky, I presume?" He bowed but raised himself quickly, for he'd damned near cast up his accounts.

His red-faced bride raised the blanket with a trembling hand to cover her breasts. "Get out."

Ash saw the worry in her look and wondered if she were trying the kind of trick any tavern wench worth her supper might, by employing a pretense of coy innocence, though had not the doctor confirmed her virtue?

"A bit late to act the prude," Ash said, "given your cheating sire, our forced marriage, and your salty selection of sailor's curses. While I suppose your profanity should not be a surprise, I would like to commend you on the intact state of your maidenhead, so the good doctor swears."

Larkin licked her lips, panic replacing innocence, until she slyly slipped her hand beneath the covers, as if for something with which she might titillate him.

Ash's manhood gave a hard willing salute at the prospect, as Lark rose to her knees, increasing his appetite, his imagination, and his lust.

He stepped closer, her blanket fell away, and the dressing gown she wore parted down the center, revealing a perfect sliver of naked womanhood.

His body roared to raging life, until she cocked the pistol that appeared as if by magic in her steady hand. "A man will swear to anything," said she, "with a pistol to his ballocks, and the good doctor is no exception."

His bride now pointed said weapon Ash's way and lowered her aim as if to make it true. "Get out."

Ash continued his slow approach, certain, in the back of his muzzy mind, that like her father's henchmen, her pistol was as empty as her threat, and that for his part, sobriety *might* be preferable at this point. Nevertheless, though he heard running footsteps, he stood so near his goal, he continued boldly forth.

"She has a pistol!" came a shout.

Ash made to reach for her even as he turned toward the sound . . . and a shot rang out.

Before he opened his eyes, Ash registered the fact that he hurt everywhere. His head pained and pounded like a military tattoo, as did his eyes, his limbs, and especially his left butt cheek, as if some unknown force kept stabbing a knife into it.

Finding himself flat on his belly, a position he detested, would indicate that he had been left abandoned on some battlefield far from England's shores.

Odd, for he'd dreamed the war was over.

"My lord," he heard, barely above a whisper. "My lord, are you awake?"

"Where am I, Grim?" Ash asked, his eyes too sore to open.

"In your bed, sir."

"What country? What year?"

"The master bedchamber at Blackburne Chase. In the year of our Lord, eighteen hundred and eighteen."

"The war is over, then? Good. I thought I'd gone for dead in battle."

"Well . . . nearly. Do you not remember your wedding?"

"My bride jilted me before the wedding, man, do *you* not remember? Found someone with more blunt, Ellenora did."

"I mean your second bride, my lord."

"The actress? What *was* her name?" Ash managed to peel back an eyelid. "Bloody hell. What the blazes fell on me? Why does every part of me hurt?"

Grimsley held a cup of tea to Ash's lips, for which Ash was supremely grateful. "You have two black eyes," Grim said. "And assorted cuts."

Ash nodded imperceptibly and swallowed dutifully. "I don't remember how it came about."

"I see." Grimsley appeared pained, portending some disagreeable duty. "You also have cracked ribs, according to Buckston, various scrapes and bruises, a minor gunshot wound in your er, backside, and oh yes . . . a wife."

Ash raised his head, groaned, and lay it down again. "Oh God, it's coming back."

"I was afraid it would, sir."

"She shot me? She actually pulled the trigger on a loaded pistol and shot me? Did she threaten the doctor, as she told me she did, so he would give me a false report? Was she telling the truth about that?"

Grimsley nodded with regret. "If Buckston had tried to examine her, he would not have been allowed to keep all his manly parts, he swears, and hopes you understand his predicament."

"I shall beat her, as soon as I am able to raise my head."

"She wishes to see you."

"Not bloody likely."

Grimsley stood his disapproving ground.

"Bloody hell," Ash said. "Send her in then, but on *your* head be it."

"Yes, my lord. She is understandably afraid, my lord."

"And well she should be. She shot me, man. And stop my lording me."

"Yes, my lord."

Lark came in wearing a jonquil muslin morning dress ten years out of date, and three sizes too big, two silk rosettes hanging by threads upon her skirt. She still wore the mismatched pair of shoes in which she came to him, not quite dry after their bath.

Since Ash was forced to remain on his stomach, given the location of the wound she had inflicted, he saw her shoes best but decided to forget for the moment, what still needed improving. "Where did you get the dress?" he asked, looking all the way up at her, shocked anew by her beauty without the soot.

"It was either your mother's or your grandmother's." She smoothed her skirts in an erratic, uncharacteristic movement, and dislodged another of the rose ribbon florets. "I believe Mim found this and another in the attic."

Ash nodded with a clearer head than the night before, and realized, as he should have then, that perhaps his bride would need a bit of wooing before he tried to bed her again. On the other hand, would he survive another attempt? "Did you hear?" he said, testing her. "Some thief broke into the house during the night and shot me."

"I shot you."

"Hah! I did not think you would own up to it."

"I own up to everything . . ." *Eventually.* Lark made a promise to herself in that moment that she *would* tell him about cheating him into marriage, but not today. Not until Micah arrived, at the soonest, or in a letter, after her death perhaps, at the latest.

"You do not appear so menacing in women's clothes," her surprised bridegroom said.

Which is why I wear men's clothes, she thought. "I will remember that you are of the opinion the next time I wish to menace you."

"I have created a fiend," Ash said to himself. "But now that I see you clean with your honey curls tamed, I find that I can no longer, in good conscience, call you Arky. It smacks of an expression for casting up one's accounts. As if I might say, 'He's had so much to drink he's arking all over the place,' which I still feel like doing, by the way."

"You drink too much, which is why you feel the roiling need." Lark knelt, all skittering nerves, beside his bed, at amazingly close eye level with the man about whom she had dreamed for years. She had forgot the beauty in his pale gray eyes, the way his mahogany hair flowed as if from that one remarkable point upon his brow. She wished she dared move that lazy lock from his eyes.

"Why Arky?" he asked. " 'Tis a terrible nickname."

She agreed with half a nod. "When I was a babe, the word Larkin emerged from my small mouth as Arky. It stuck."

His teeth were perfect, his smile deadly. "Unfortunate," he said.

"So is your drinking and gambling. Is that why no woman would have you?"

"What?"

"Why were you jilted? Your friends made the task of finding a bride for you sound impossible."

"Because society women are aware of my situation."

"And should this situation concern *me?*"

"No, for it is better, by far, than the one I took you from."

"Most situations would be, but I did fear you would hurt me last night."

"So you hurt me, first?"

Lark regarded her hands and fisted them to hide her broken nails. "It is the only way I know. You were deep in your cups, you must own, and not in your right mind."

He granted as much with a grimace. "Perhaps we should become better acquainted for the nonce, while I recover, without drink, so that we may form a more prudent opinion of each other for the future."

"I bathed again this morning," she said, surprising him, by the look of him.

"I am prodigiously pleased to hear it. You will not be required to chase pigs here, by the way. We leave that to others. But I would be delighted if you bathed regularly."

"Now that I am here, what will I be required to do, besides bathing, I mean?"

"Be my wife . . . and all that entails."

Lark remembered the way he looked, and she felt, after he gave her his shirt in the maids' room, her cheek against his naked chest with that mat of hair that appeared coarse but felt the way silk must. She shivered. "I do not understand the meaning of 'all that entails.'"

"We will address it in time, and when I am no longer indisposed with a gunshot wound, we shall try again."

The skittering inside her trebled. "Try what?"

"Becoming better acquainted, to begin with. Fair enough?"

Lark hesitated. "Fair, I suppose, to begin with."

They learned more about each other as they played cards through the first week of his recovery, because Ash liked to gamble and Lark appreciated every opportunity to test her skill without cheating.

She usually only cheated people who deserved it, of course, the same with picking their pockets, and she usually never shot anyone. Ashford was an exception in every way.

Marrying him had been another exception, with something greater than integrity in the balance. In her eyes, Micah's future made Ash—the best man she knew, when not in his cups—fair game, or foul, however you regarded the issue. Besides, he had admitted to being desperate for a wife, so she had done him a favor, had she not?

"I cannot believe I am admitting this," he said, at the end of the second week, "but I am sick unto death of gambling."

Lark stopped shuffling her cards. "The stakes are likely not high enough," she said.

"I had Grim bring some books. Perhaps you would read to me?"

"I, er, have a scratchy throat," she said in panic. "Perhaps, you could read to me?"

* * *

At the beginning of what Lark expected to be his third week of recovery, she found him in his chamber, dressed and champing at the bit, handsome as ever, and attempting to walk with a cane. "I must escape this room," he said. "Have you toured the house yet?" He offered his free arm.

Lark took it and felt the heat of his nearness to the pit of her belly. "I wandered a bit, but the house is so large, I feared becoming lost. "I have noticed, however, that there are several paintings missing. Did you realize?"

"What makes you think so?"

"The squares of bright wallpaper here and there."

Ash winced. "I had not thought them so obvious. The large library painting paid my father's gambling debts. The one from my study satisfied his tailor. The three in the south parlor replaced five cottage roofs. The one over my bed shall be shortly sold to pay my voucher to your father."

Lark nodded. "Good, then you have *not* been robbed."

"Only by my father and my own stupidity."

Lark grimaced inwardly, certain his regret *must* extend beyond losing the painting to being stuck with her. "I have spent some time outdoors," she said to steer him from the conclusion. "Yesterday, after you took your medicine and slept, I stumbled upon a field of wild lavender, in blues and purples, just coming into flower, a breathtaking sight."

Ash nodded. "One of my mother's favorite spots, mine as well. She used to dry the flowers and place them in vases about the house."

"Would she mind if I did so?"

"Not at all. I miss the scent about the place. Let us start our tour with the house, however, shall we, for I do not think I can walk quite as far as the lavender field today. I'd like to take you to the attic, so as to find you more dresses. You may think two will do, but until I can arrange to have a new wardrobe made for you, I would like to see you with more."

Ash could barely raise the leg on his wounded side the height of a step, so Lark hooked his cane on her wrist and placed an arm about him. He gave her a side-long glance as he leaned upon her and they started up. Did he doubt her sincerity? After that night, who could blame him?

"Thank you," he said, releasing his breath, several steps later.

"'Tis the least I can do."

He raised a speaking brow. "The very least."

Amid a musty disharmony of discarded furniture, beside grime-glazed windows, spider-webbed corners, with the faded scent of lavender about them, Ash absorbed Larkin's delight as she rummaged through a score of life-scarred old trunks.

To her, every unearthed buckle and feather appeared new and unequaled. Seeing the world through her guileless eyes gave Ash a glimpse into her true nature—not a dyed-in-the-wool gutter rat so much as a stalwart mouse, raised in the gutter, open to better . . . desperate for better.

Nothing jaded about his bride, not when it came to female fripperies. Every striped ribbon and scrap of lace a treat, her face alight, she stepped audaciously away from real life for a time as if to play at dress up.

She found two cambric night shifts with sleep jackets and nightcaps from the last century and fell in love with them. He thought they must be his great-grandmother's, but little did Larkin Rose care. She adored them. She found a threadbare chemise next and claimed that too.

The corset she wrapped about herself over her clothes made her groan as if in pain and roll her eyes, so she tossed that back like an undersized fish into a lake.

Ash sighed for losing the corset, as he tossed the nightcaps after it. "I prefer your hair unadorned," said he, certain that his appreciation of her tresses would not be welcome at this early stage.

When he found a cream high-waisted afternoon dress with burgundy overskirt that he liked, she sighed as if to humor him and stepped behind an old Chinese screen to try it on.

"Must be one of my mother's more recent purchases," he said as she emerged wearing it. "It fits you well."

Lark shrugged, returned behind the screen and came back folding it. Though damned near fashionable compared to the rest, the dress got placed in the trunk, rather than with the treasures she wished to keep. "I am not ready to meet your mother," she said, her gaze trained guardedly upon it.

"You will tell me when you are?"

She sighed with relief, until Ash claimed the dress and slipped it beneath his arm. "I like it on you," he said.

"I like these better." She indicated her choices and turned away, as if dismissing the subject, or him, or both, only to unearth a trunk filled with nothing but slippers. Dozens of matched pairs in every hue and fabric. With a squeal, she knelt like a child over a new box of toys.

Ash sat careful and offside on a previously plundered trunk, so as to observe her, a new and simple pleasure.

"I am in heaven," said she as she placed her two shod feet before him, to show off a pair of blue-satin heeled slippers with silver buckles. "I have seen none so fine."

Oddly pleased to be included in her enjoyment, Ash rifled through the trunk as well, found an embroidered pair in jonquil to match the dress she wore most often, and she let him slip them on her. A minute later, they each held one of the same pair, which amused her no end. Ash realized then that he had never really "seen" his unlikely bride. With the least attention and happiness, she, like a butterfly, emerged, a specimen of rare beauty.

She found five pairs of matching slippers that fit, no less in her glory at finding them than at the notion of wearing them.

Ash added his mother's dress to her hoard. "We will send a maid for these later, for you will need both arms to help me down the stairs." He thought she might remove the dress he liked from her stack, but when she saw that he watched, she shrugged and made to precede him out the door.

A papered polygon hatbox tied with tasseled red ribbon stopped her. She pointed it out. "What is that?" she asked with the excited curiosity of a child, so much so, that Ash was pleased to take it down.

"Untie it and look inside," he said.

Larkin's anticipation told him he'd made the right decision. She removed the lid, sounding as though she savored a sweetmeat deep in her throat and tore through the treasure. "Look, brocade bells, ribbons, silver stars, bows, and rosettes." Her face softened. "Fine-cut snowflakes made of parchment, almost as perfect as the real thing." She regarded him as she stroked the snowflake in her palm. "Did you ever look at a real one? It's a work of art." She regarded him quizzically. "What do rich people do with such beautiful things?"

"They're Christmas decorations. We place them about the house for the holiday," he said, "at least we used to when my mother was—"

"I never saw Christmas."

"What, never?"

She shook her head. "Same day as any other at the pub. I would not have known it was Christmas but for the rogues who stopped for a pint with holly in their buttonholes. That's how I first knew *you* were a rogue."

"So you knew, did you?"

"How does holly make a man a rogue, Ash?"

"'Tis not the wearing of the holly makes him one," Ash said with a wink. "'Tis what he does with the sprig later that counts."

Chapter 6

"What *does* a rogue do with the holly in his button-hole?"

Ash dropped a handful of parchment snowflakes over his naïve bride's head, which made her lips twitch and her eyes twinkle. If he didn't know better he'd think that Larkin Rose sometimes hid a giggle beneath the surface. "At Christmas, I will be pleased to show you," he said. "If you will allow me."

"Promise?"

"I certainly do."

Lark collected the scattered snowflakes, from her hair, her shoulders, and even the floor, nowhere near as interested in his roguish nature as Ash would wish. "We can make more snowflakes," he said. "They're only paper."

"I do want to learn how to make them," she said, "and I will have you show me, but I'd like to keep these as well."

"We will have to give you a rousing good Christmas this year to make up for the ones you've missed. I shall roll out all the old traditions."

Her eyes widened. "What kinds of traditions?"

Ash told her about evergreens and kissing boughs with bells and ribbons in them, and the big cedar their old German estate manager, Bud St. Nick, who still lived in the dower house, had brought right into the picture gallery the year before he went to fight Boney. They had decorated the tree with nuts and pinecones, and ribbon rosettes that Bud's wife Olga had made.

That had turned out to be his mother's last real Christmas.

"I want a tree too," Lark said, "a big one, and a yule log, but may I take some of these decorations downstairs now, just to look at?"

"You may take anything you want. This is *your* home now too," he said, catching the glimpse of wonder his statement brought to her expression.

Ash spent the rest of the day in his office going over estate issues, problems, and expenses. He found so much work, after his weeks of recovery, that he failed to see his bride for the next two days as well, though he looked in on her every night as she slept.

He watched her throughout dinner at the end of that week, thinking he might have missed her, and saw that she took in everything he did, from the way he used his fork, as if she'd rarely seen one before, to the way he spooned his soup. He almost wished they weren't economizing so that she could entertain him with her self-effacing eagerness to learn through several more dinner courses.

She'd changed into a simple green-satin evening dress, not quite as new, or well-fitting, as the cream and burgundy afternoon dress he preferred, but not bad all the same, though it did already have a new tear at the shoulder, and it matched a pair of the slippers they'd found. Ash caught her every so often—whether in the dining room, the drawing room, or even walking outside—raising a foot and pointing her toes, so as to admire her slippers.

For a consolation prize of a bride, this new wife of his had potential. Ash cut a piece of beef and wondered how she'd react when he climbed into her bed later that night.

He toyed with the notion of preparing her for his nuptial invasion, by warning her in advance, but he feared she'd simply bolt if he did, so he kept his own counsel. "You might have noticed," he said, "that we are running the house with a quarter the normal staff."

Lark shrugged. "You might have noticed," she returned, "that where I come from nobody runs the house but me, so I wouldn't know a normal staff to save me life."

Ash nodded, stifling his grin, and giving her half an apology for his careless statement. "Likely then you will not fall into a fit of the vapors at my news, but I find myself very nearly without funds."

"Your pawned paintings tell that tale," she said with a dollop of sarcasm. "You gamble too much."

"That too." He sighed. "As my new wife, you should keep me otherwise occupied," he teased, "and I'll never have the desire to venture forth and gamble again." But Ash could see from her blank expression that Larkin did not understand the nature of his insinuation.

"At any rate," he added. "Cook is also the housekeeper of sorts. There are two maids, Mim and Nan, and Grimsley is my valet who also acts as butler. Brinks is not only the coachman but the stable boy. I am not only the master but my own man of affairs and estate manager."

"Everyone works very hard," Lark said. "Especially you. I had noticed that."

"My father kept the outside of the house in good repair—I must give him that much credit—but as for the inside, I hate these telltale signs of a depleted fortune, up to and including a short staff, but I will do what I must to keep the Chase. As for running it, old Bud still lives in the dower house with his wife, Olga, and acts as my adviser. They are a hard-working lot, my staff. I'm glad you've noticed. I want them to know and respect you as well. I'll present you formally tomorrow."

"Good, because I can help."

"You know how to run a staff, then?"

"I know how to scrub a floor and change a bed and I could dig a ditch too, come to that."

Ash winced. "Which my bride will most assuredly not do."

Lark rose at his tone. "Then what the bloody blazes *will* your bride do?"

Ash rose to meet her ire. "She will keep her husband happy in the bedroom," he ordered, throwing down his napkin, "beginning tonight."

"Hah! She bloody well will not!" Lark left the dining room and ran up the stairs to her bedchamber. There, she tried to lock her door against him, but the lock had gone missing. Then she went for her pistol, but the dresser drawer where she had left it came up empty.

She stood on a chair, feeling along the high shelf in the wardrobe, thinking the maid must have moved it to a safer spot, when her bedroom door opened and Ash came in, closing it firmly behind him. He threw his dressing gown on the bed like a gauntlet, his lips firm. "You won't find it," he said.

"Find what?"

"The pistol. No, nor anything sharp or capable of drawing blood, for you do mean to beat me off, again, do you not?"

Lark watched alarmed, as her husband began to unbutton his frock coat, with more determination than she liked. "What are you doing?" she asked, afraid the weapon in his trousers might be deadlier than her missing pistol.

Ash removed his coat with a look that said it should be obvious, appearing, for all the world, as if he were baiting her, she thought.

"I am undressing as you can plainly see. We are, after all, husband and wife." His eyes held a spark of wicked intent, a roguish look that Lark had liked a great deal too much in her growing up years.

She raised her chin, so as not to show her fear. "If you do not leave, I will scream down the house."

"I thought you might. As to that, the staff knows we're married and want to keep their jobs. None will interfere. They will ignore any and all outbursts from this bedchamber and will probably cheer, if they do hear."

The thought of Ashford Blackburne, the Earl of Blackburne, the man of her dreams, sleeping in her bed, wearing exactly what, she wondered, turned Lark's knees to jelly. At first, she thought the weakness must be caused by fear, but if not, what did this inner trembling signify? 'Twas a traitorous reaction, no doubt, and Lark found herself furious with Ash for causing it.

"I dare not leave you after our dinner-table disagreement," Ash said. "As I would not put it past you to bolt."

Larkin jumped from the chair she'd climbed upon, so as to pace. She'd never come up against anyone who made her feel so much anger, so much . . . warmth, so . . . alive. She regarded her husband now, standing there watching her, strong hands on pleasing hips, shirt unbuttoned to reveal his thatch of dark satin chest hair, his inexpressibles hugging a bounty of hard-hewn muscle. God help her, she liked the magnificence he presented.

Before she anticipated him, he stepped forward and pulled her into his arms. She used her hands to hold him at bay, startled anew by the feel of the hair on his chest, wishing she could test it by curling her fingers into it. Heat scorched her face at the notion and she tried to push herself away.

Despite her best efforts, Ash pulled her closer, crushed her breasts against him, and even through the fabric of her dress, she felt the burn.

With his arms around her, he unfastened the buttons down her back, breathed warmth against her temple, grazed her brow with his lips. On purpose? Or by mistake?

Lark brought her face the merest breadth closer to test him, and he did it again, lips against her brow, there but not, a whisper of affection—so much more than she had ever experienced—tears filled her eyes. Emotion rose in her, righteous and painful.

She wanted more—she wanted none of it. She raised her foot, and he quick-stepped from harm's way before she could crush him under her heel, but he did not let her go.

Ash raised her chin with a finger, held it steady, against her will, and gazed into her eyes. She was afraid he saw too much, especially the moisture gathering there.

In his own eyes, she read speculation, need. Did she really see so much? Did he "need" as much as she? She would feel better if he did.

She tried to gather her wits, but suddenly his lips met hers, soft at first, his cool and sculpted, hers never before touched by the lips of another. The satin of his moved gently across hers, once, twice, thrice, drawing awareness from the deepest recesses of her being.

Parched, she felt, for the taste of him, greedy for more. Her first kiss. Sweet. Almost too sweet to bear.

Despite her defiance, Lark responded to his silent plea, allowed herself to be swept into the kiss with abandon.

The touch of his tongue against her own, and the resultant budding of her breasts woke Lark to a fear that flowered into hot heaving waves of trepidation.

She tried to escape, but he held her tight. She thought to kick him, but as if he read her, he positioned her legs between his and pinned her there. Even his hand held her head in place.

Nowhere to go, save one. She sank her teeth into his lower lip.

Ash cursed, pulled back, and with raw shock in his expression, he raised a hand to assess the damage. His fingers came away bloody. Blood filled his eyes as well.

Instead of moving from harm's way when he let her go, Lark raised a knee to make her point.

Ash anticipated her move a mere second too late to completely eliminate himself as her target and received the brunt of her blow off-center. He gasped nonetheless and caught his breath. "You wretch," he said, but his words held an edge of new-dawning respect.

Lark nodded in satisfaction. "My sister taught me that. Never thought I'd get to use it so much, though I always wanted to." She laughed and threw herself on the bed.

Ash raised a brow. "I do not find your resistance in the least amusing."

"I refuse to undress," she said, "until you quit my bedchamber."

"Then you may damned well sleep in your dress, because I am sleeping beside you. I own this bedchamber." Ash grabbed the towel beside the basin to wipe the blood from his lip, though he moved as if he might be bruised in that mysterious place.

"Taming you is going to be a painful process for one of us," he said as he sat on the edge of the bed and removed his shoes, "but I do not intend for it to be me." He crawled beneath the covers, still wearing his trousers, and said nothing more, for which Larkin was grateful.

After the fire died in the hearth and the bedchamber became dark and chilled, and Ash's breathing evened to a snuffling snore, Lark rose to change into her night rail before crawling back into her bed beside him.

Her husband. Ash. Her Ash was sleeping beside her. Imagine that.

Lark drifted in and out of consciousness after that. One minute she dreamed Ash was kissing her, the next he was carrying her to the bath and getting in with her, touching her, doing the delightful things she had dreamed of him doing, no pain or blood involved.

Then, he was riding away in his carriage without

her. "Come back Ash, don't go. If you go to war, you'll die and never come back. Don't go."

She dreamed Ash brought her close, whispered words of comfort, his breath warm on her face. "Do not cry, Lark. Everything will be all right. I will not go away again."

Lark moaned and sought his mouth, warm, soothing, as she'd always imagined. Threads of fire assaulted her in strange places, a new depth to the dream. She moved closer to him, seeking to cool the fire, tame the flames.

Ash stroked her hip, her breast, butterfly touches with strange threads linking each sensation to every other, to parts of her body she could not name. Whirlpools of passion built to a frenzy held her captive. Lark whimpered against his lips and her mind registered the sound.

Her eyes flew open. No dream this, but a flesh and blood man . . . in *her* bed. Lark pushed him hard away, and sent him flying.

Rising to her knees she looked down and saw Ash on the floor, bare-chested, at the least, and if not for the tangled bedclothes—well she simply did not want to know. He must have undressed while she slept. "I . . . I didn't realize it was you," she said.

"Who the bloody devil did you think it was?"

"A man."

"I am a man."

"There's always a drawback, have you noticed that?"

Ash worked the first part of the following week on estate business, but he gave Lark a tour of the property on Friday, and a thorough tour they took. From buttery to dovecote, from empty wine cellar to the near-empty carriage shed and similarly barren stables.

Then he lined up all five servants and presented her as his wife. Funny thing, he thought, Lark already knew their names, even their children's names in two cases, as well as spouses and a sick sister.

"I never know what to make of you," he said as they walked away. "Who are you Larkin Rose Blackburne?"

"I'm a clumsy girl who knows only how to be a boy and who doesn't know how to dress or act in company, and I'll tell you another thing, you got no bargain, because I can't read neither."

"Or speak properly, half the time, *either,* all of which we can fix—we *will* fix. I had concluded that you could not read when I was forced to read to you and saw how amazing you found the experience. I am determined to begin teaching you myself at this very moment." He led her to the library, sat her on the settee, chose a book, and sat beside her.

Ten minutes into the impossible lesson, Lark rose in a huff and bolted.

Ash went looking for the spoiled termagant to give her some lessons in proper deportment as well, not certain if he'd brought the book to teach her or beat her. If she had not chosen to wear that god-awful red dress of his great-great aunt Harriet's today, he might never have noticed her nestled in a thick low fork of the flowering horse chestnut at the far reaches of the spinney.

When he got there, Ash said nothing, but climbed up to scoot himself into the same spot and wrestle her onto his lap. Except for the small bite she gave his hand, he succeeded admirably, and ended up holding her in place with all the strength and frustration that had been gathering momentum over the past weeks. Not that she stopped trying to free herself, she fought him, calling him all manner of low creature, including ruddy-necked lecher and gaoler of women.

Larkin stopped struggling when she realized her husband had her pinned, good and tight, with one of his big blasted hands spread in the center of her . . . or rather, at the bottom of her . . . front.

As if that were not bad enough, some kind of pressure was building there, beneath his hand, a sizzling pressure she did not like one bit.

He seemed almost to be working the heel of his hand against her with a lethargic rhythm. Despite her dislike of such treatment, there came from her body a strange answering pulse, as if she wanted what he was doing to continue, even perhaps beneath her clothes against her very warm skin, like an itch that wanted scratching.

When she shifted her legs, Ash's hand moved the slightest bit lower, and she bit her lip so as not to release her rising moan. What was he doing to her? Should she ask? Tell him to stop? Did she want him to stop? Sitting in a tree had never seemed so amazing.

When he stopped, she waited, and when he failed to continue, she regarded him, and he opened his lips over hers.

With a bright new yearning, she welcomed his kiss with a treacherous sound deep in her throat, but the pulsing of his body beneath her made her realize that something was happening that could make a man dangerous. She pulled from the kiss with a start. "I don't like this."

"I can tell," he said, and for the life of her, she could not pull from his gaze.

"No more reading today," she said.

"One sentence," he said. "Read this note I wrote for you to memorize. I'll point to the words and say them and you may repeat them after me."

"I," Ash said as he pointed to a letter.

"I," Lark repeated.

"Am," he said for her to repeat. "A," he said, and she repeated, and then, "troublesome," then, "brat."

Lark continued up to and including troublesome, because she had turned to look into his mesmerizing gray eyes again, and did not for the life of her know what she was saying, until the word brat touched her lips.

She tried to break free of the spell his hand at her core still wove, with a screech of outrage.

Ash didn't think twice but took advantage of Lark's open mouth to open his own over it. Still in full control of the small but dangerously writhing woman on his lap, he kissed his wife the way he'd been dreaming of doing, when he slept and had no control over his mind. And his body reacted as if it were taking over the fantasy.

Larkin's attempts to escape slowed as their kiss became mutual and seeking. She moved her bottom in such a way as to stoke his desire, almost as if she knew in her unconscious mind that she was bringing his arousal to dangerous proportions, though her kiss told a story of innocence and unmet passion.

Ash became so aroused he cupped her breast, and that fast, he was sitting on his arse at the base of the tree.

Lark landed beside him, both feet planted firmly on

the ground, both hands as firm on her shapely hips. "I am not a troublesome brat, but you are the greatest rogue I have ever encountered."

"Why thank you, Lark."

Chapter 7

A few nights later, before dinner, Ash took Lark for a romantic stroll through the avenue his mother used to call her "ghost walk." It was a shadowy quarter-mile arch of trained hemlock, a gothic cathedral formed by nature, from which they emerged upon the orchard, a breathtaking sight at dusk with blossoms lacing row after row of trees.

He'd left his cane at the house so he could use the excuse of needing her arm on uneven ground, and wondered what justification he could give in a week's time, two weeks? Perhaps he'd pretend she hurt him more than she thought with that pistol shot.

Then again, his agility would surely show in bed—providing he ever managed more than sleeping with her—and the pretense would be over.

He'd decided to get her a little drunk that night, because he was damned well going to consummate this bloody marriage. A good stiff drink, or three, just might help her to relax, maybe enough for him to tell her the whole sordid story of his grandfather's ultimatum.

Christmas was only eight months away, after all, and though he need only *get* her with child by then, Ash knew that the process sometimes took more than one try. He intended on trying often, of course, but damnation, he needed to begin as he meant to go on, did he not?

After their walk, he gave her claret before dinner, champagne with dinner, and port afterwards. Later, he poured her a brandy in the library over a game of cards; then they retired to opposite chairs before the fire. He refilled her glass twice more before she relaxed enough to initiate a conversation.

"I was glad you survived the war," she said out of nowhere. "I prayed you would."

Ash sat forward, a little muzzy from the drink. "You did not know me before the war, did you?"

She laughed. "We met when I was eleven."

"Refresh my memory."

"I was running, fell, and you picked me up, there at the Pickled Barrel. You wiped my tears; dabbed at the blood on my skinned knuckles; and kissed them, all three. Then you said I was a brave little lady."

Ash was certain he'd picked up any number of fallen children over the years, calling them either brave ladies or soldiers. "I must have been all of twenty-one, and that was you?" he said, as if he did remember. He wished he did. She must not have dressed like a boy then, if he'd recognized her as female. "You've been at the Pickled Barrel all these years?"

Lark nodded, head high, tears filling her eyes. "I was born there."

Did she weep because she realized he didn't remember, Ash wondered, or had life been that insupportable at the pub?

"I always thought you were different, better, more honest," she said in a sleepy voice, her words unguarded and dangerously earnest, Ash thought.

"Honest, I might agree, for I pride myself on it, and

I have the utmost respect for honesty in others, but better? I think not. I know not. Better than who?"

"The other men who came to the pub."

"I am not, believe me."

"You are better in every way. Better than one most of all."

"Which one?"

"The one who hurt my sister and gave her a babe."

Good grief. How hurt? Had her sister been brutalized by some man? "What happened to her?"

"I saw naught but blood, then before a few months passed, she was fat with a baby. My father threw her out, but I found a family in the country for her to live with."

Bloody hell, no wonder she had been afraid when he approached her on their wedding night, no wonder when she awoke with a "man" in her bed. "How old were you at the time."

"Fifteen; my sister was sixteen."

Worse and worse, and then he understood. "Was that when you stopped dressing like a girl?"

"My sister said if I looked like a boy, most of Da's customers would leave me alone."

Most, but not all. "And did they?"

She placed her brandy on the table, rose, wavered, and lost her balance. Ash lunged and caught her before she hit the floor and pulled her onto his lap.

She curled right into him as if he would keep her safe.

Ash had never been more shocked or awakened by anything. His body took to trembling, accepting her presence with all the enthusiasm called for in a husband. No question of holding up his responsibility, if consummation were called for at this moment, except that it most assuredly was not.

He had realized some time ago, of course, that he could perform with her. And tonight, well, if she were curling into him that meant he'd got her too drunk for a gentleman to take advantage. Damnation.

No matter, her story would have stopped him dead anyway. Then again, she might not have told it without the drink. He was a cad. She needed time. This new wife of his was skittish as a purebred filly and with good reason.

Her sweet-smelling hair and delicate features only made her appear the more fragile. Did she understand the significance of his fast-beating heart beneath her hand? It mattered not, for she needed comforting for her sister's agony, and for her own resulting anguish, perhaps for the first time.

Ash closed his arms about her, slow and easy, to give her an opportunity to escape if she chose, and held her like a frightened child.

The other night, before she bruised his ballocks, he had kissed her and lost his head to passion. He would not make that mistake again. He would be patient and consoling, show her that she need not fear him in any circumstance.

She sighed and closed her eyes, knowing full well where she found herself.

Ash closed his own and wondered where her sister had ended, but he dare not ask. She had not mentioned her or the babe further. He must draw his own sad conclusions.

"Are you tired?" he asked, some fifteen minutes later, when she readjusted their positions and got close enough to bruising his ballocks once again to make him sweat.

"It's the drink. Makes me sleepy."

"I take it you're not afraid of me anymore?"

"Not so much, and you look sleepy too, I can tell. I do not like the way drinking makes me feel."

"I do not think I will ever drink again," he said, meaning it. She'd just frightened the urge right out of him. "I believe I'd rather keep my wits about me from now on. No wonder you pulled that trigger and shot me."

"I'm just glad I only pulled it once."

Ash barely stopped trembling over her answer when a snuffling sound made him realize his bride had fallen asleep in his arms. If not for the drink, she would never have let her guard down this much. He knew her at least that well.

Ash rose and carried her up the stairs and toward her bed—his wife's bed—the bed of the woman with whom he was supposed to sleep, he thought, with a bit more and less regret today than yesterday for his hasty marriage. And 'twasn't regret so much for the marriage now as for the way in which he married her, because damn it, he was beginning to like her, and she deserved better than a husband who'd brawled with her on her wedding day and scared the life out of her on her wedding night.

When Ash lit the candle, he saw stars, silver stars of all sizes, the ones she'd brought from the Christmas decorations, hanging by uneven lengths of sewing thread from her curtain tops to dangle in the windows and catch the sun by day or the candlelight by night, as if she were keeping Christmas in her heart.

He placed her atop the covers and brought them

over her, then he looked down at her. No consummation with his Christmas-in-April bride tonight, he thought, his eager body disagreeing with the pronouncement. But how could he leave her and go back to his own bed when he had set the rule that he would stay?

He needed to follow through and sleep with her every night from now on, or she would realize that a sad story, and a sleepy bride, could turn him away. "No," he affirmed aloud. He must keep to his strategy, as Wellington would say, and sleep with her.

As Ash unwrapped her, she curled into a ball, for the bedchamber had gone cold. He wrapped her warm again, stirred the embers to flame, and placed another log on the fire. He undressed himself as the chamber warmed. When it was toasty, he rolled Lark onto her back to undo the buttons down the front of her gown.

"What are you doing?" she asked, too sleepy to open her eyes or care.

"Getting you ready for bed," he said, taking her arms from the sleeves of the cream and burgundy gown he'd encouraged her to take. "I shouldn't have given you so much to drink," he said as if to himself.

"I know." Lark sighed, rolled to her side, and raised a knee, which made getting her gown over her hips and down her legs a little more difficult, but he managed.

He found her wearing her threadbare chemise, with no corset, of course, or stockings—oh God—and proceeded to strip that from her as well. Then he fetched his great-grandmother's night rail, the one she'd chosen from the trunks upstairs, looked it over, and decided against it.

Throwing back the covers, Ash placed his wife

naked beneath them. "I do the work to undress you, I make the choices," he whispered, as he kissed her brow. "You're a fine figure of a woman Larkin Rose Blackburne."

Then he went around the bed, removed his dressing gown, and slid beneath the covers in the same naked state as his oblivious bride. Ash slid to the center of the bed, took Larkin into his arms, and she burrowed into him—for body warmth, at least—a fine state of affairs, until she went back to sleep.

His body had no intention of resting; it had other pursuits in mind. Hard pursuits that would take a great deal of throbbing attention, and if he moved her just right in his arms, like so, he could at least snuggle that aching part of him there, at the warm moist apex of her, where he and she would be the most comfortable.

She arched when he did, not taking him in, quite, but nestling him more snugly, so that his man part did a small dance, joy and enthusiasm in one tightly wound package, a great deal of energy with no place to go.

Ash cursed and ignored the pointless pulsing thrust, and took to savoring the feel of his bride's skin beneath his hand, like silk or satin, unblemished and perfect. He skimmed the cleft of her spine starting at her shoulders, learned the breadth of her hips with his palm, the better to embrace and stroke. Her shoulders were wide, her waist trim. Her breasts crushed against his chest, he had yet to explore, other than in the bath, oh, and in the tree, which had nearly got him killed.

Nevertheless, he wanted a breast in his mouth. Now.

His body agreed.

He moved her again, found himself a handful, and tweaked the nipple with his thumb.

"Ash," Lark whispered, giving him greater access.

"Lark?" he said. "Do you like this?"

She found his mouth, no doubts there, she'd initiated the kiss. As he kissed her back, he continued to tease her nipple, budding it and torturing it, and her hips came for his, not once, but twice, then a third rhythmic time.

"Lark, do you want this?"

She surged again, her hips begging for his, her breast pouting for more attention, her mouth open and greedy. Lord, she could be sensuous, but he wished she were awake.

He tried to tuck her face into his neck, pull her back into his arms, to settle and sleep. "Not tonight," he said, for both their sakes.

When the day came that he finally took her, he wanted her to know what he was doing to her, no matter how much she seemed to appreciate sexual byplay in her sleep—her drink induced sleep, he must remember.

But she would have none of it. She whimpered and threw a leg over him, tossed her head back and her breast forward so that there was nothing he could do but take it into his mouth. A man would have to be mad to refuse such a gift.

Larkin whimpered and moaned as he suckled her, begged him to continue, if only she knew it, with each thrust of her hips. He was near to spilling his seed, but he'd only given her half his attention, and it did not seem fair.

"Lark," he said to wake her. "Lark, love, wake up enough to know what you want."

"Ash?" she questioned and he knew he'd gotten through.

"Lark, do you want me to touch you?"

He moved his hips to indicate his meaning. "I'll only touch you if you want me to."

She looked frightened for a minute, half asleep then half scared to death in two beats, but he took her hand and guided it between them, closed her palm around him. "There is nothing to fear. I am only made of flesh, see?"

Her hand on him felt divine. He could spill in a blink if he let himself. In the shaft of moonlight crossing the bed, he saw her fear recede, saw her beauty trebled the same way. His wife, he thought, almost breathless. His wife was truly beautiful.

She moved her hand along his length, tentative at first, then with a surer knowledge. She saw when she'd moved him, acknowledged the change in his breathing with a feline smile.

"Do you know what you're doing to me?" he asked.

"Perhaps," she said. "Is it good? Am I doing good?"

"It's very good." A beginning, he thought, and slid his hand slowly up her leg, waiting for her to stop him, though she never did. He stroked near her center, caught a throat-squeak of appreciation, stroked closer. She gasped, inviting him with a single hissed breath.

He found her nether lips, stroked them, all the while she worked him, slow and easy enough to make him burst. He turned his attention her way, knew by her reaction when he found her perfect center, worked her with the same easy rhythm she worked him, until she indicated she wanted more and faster.

Again she initiated a kiss, open-mouthed and hungry, and her tongue met his for the first time. She reached the stars then, like a cataclysm, with a scream and a gasp of shock; then she whimpered and rolled into him, as if she had done something terrible. He soothed her and called her his own, and asked her to let him do it again, which made her regard him with wonder.

"Let me," he said. "You liked it."

She nodded and he touched her again, tried to go slow, but they'd started from a higher plane and she reached her peak fast; then he lowered her and called her beautiful and gave her release two more incredible times.

"No more," she finally said. "No more. I cannot anymore, er, no more. It'll kill me." She rolled to her side, away from him, likely embarrassed of a sudden by her hearty reaction.

Ash chuckled and curled up behind her to hold her close, him throbbing so hard 'twas a wonder he hadn't spilled all over her.

She looked back, likely distracted by his urgency, by his . . . knocking at her door, so to speak, because she looked him full in the face and furrowed her brow. "Ash, is there something more to this? I could swear that your manhood is prodding me to action."

Chapter 8

Ash felt his face warm for the first time in twenty years. Not since a randy fourteen-year-old, invited to the hayloft by a world-wise maid, had he felt so uncomfortably embarrassed over the evidence of his arousal. " 'Tis only me, that ugly man part of me, that's all, wanting attention too. Ignore it, it'll go away."

"Did I not give it enough attention? What more does it want?" she asked even as she slipped a hand between them to pet his excited man part as if 'twere a docile kitten. And before Ash could answer, she took him in her hand again, as she had been doing while focused on her own pleasure, and she began to focus on his.

Ash groaned at the amazing amount of gratification her inexperienced hands wrought, more than he had ever experienced at the hands of even the most practiced of women. Then again, this was Larkin Rose, his own guttersnipe bride, pleasuring him. At the notion, his ecstasy increased and multiplied. Praise be, she was awake now and knew what she was about, more or less. At least she now freely gave the rapture consuming him, which made her touch the more spectacular.

"Teach me what to do," she said, leaning over him,

her breasts there for his eyes to feast upon, her nipples budding and waiting for his tongue, her offer nearly enough to bring him to culmination. Ash groaned, amazed, so grateful for her determination to gratify his sexual needs that he took her up on her offer and showed his bride how to pleasure him.

When his brilliant pupil exceeded his expectations, Ash took that budding breast into his mouth, and placed his hand at the junction of her thighs to stroke her essence in an effort to raise her with him, and so he did—so they both did—to unimagined heights. And when his bride shuddered and cried his name, Ash spilled his seed in a culmination that rocked his world.

A damned good beginning, and then some, he thought, which boded well for a consummation and marriage that might prove better than he dreamed. Sated and hopeful, Ash drifted to sleep, entwined with the innkeeper's talented daughter, the scent of sex all around them.

His grandfather could make enough noise to rouse the dead, Ash thought, wondering how his grandmother had stood the overbearing old rattle so many years, until he realized that his grandfather's booming voice must mean he was here at Blackburne.

Larkin sat up as well, obviously awakened by the same burly commotion. "What is it?"

"Blast it," Ash said. "My grandfather's on his way up. Kiss me please and no arguing. I'll explain later."

Ash had no sooner taken her into his arms, and opened his lips over hers to swallow her predictable objection—for she could be contrary—when she gave him her cooperation, shocking him to his marrow, as his grandfather burst in on them.

"Well, is she with child yet or not?" said the prattling old patriarch.

Ash swore and Lark squeaked and slid beneath the bedcovers.

Annoyed to have been interrupted, when Lark had rare cooperation in mind, Ash nevertheless thanked the saints that he woke in time to present the picture of marital bliss. Judging by his wife's thunderous expression, however, he might not have wholly managed it.

Was it the kiss—which spoke of mutual participation—the memory of the night before, or his grandfather's crude query, that brought the heat of battle to his reluctant bride's tiger eyes?

"Grandfather," Ash said pulling the covers over his wife's creamy shoulders. "That is scarcely a civilized question in mixed company." To punctuate his pronouncement, Ash added a reproachful sound.

Nevertheless, rather than regard his grandfather as if he were daft, his bride awarded *him* that silent appellation with all the censure in her gaze.

A rare grin cracked the old man's stony expression, then, as he looked from a one of them to the other. "How many weeks married?" he wanted to know, his wink blatant.

"Four," Ash and Lark said together.

"Christmas is coming," the aging meddler warned with a vile cackle, a more civil admonition than Ash expected, actually, and favorably vague, praise be.

Now, Ash thought, planning his next move, if he could move the old reprobate from their bedchamber before Lark gained a precipitous knowledge of the final stipulation contingent upon his becoming heir, he and his grandsire might both escape with their skins intact.

"Yes," Ash said. "Christmas is coming, so why not go down to the dining room and get Grimsley to serve you a celebratory breakfast? I'll be down directly to join you and discuss the situation." He turned to Lark. "Man talk, darling. Business. You wouldn't care to—"

"Yes I would," Lark said.

"Yes she would," his grandfather echoed, and just like that, the thorns in his side appeared to unite against him.

His grandfather requested kippers for breakfast and ate mounds of them, with toast and strawberry jam, of all things, and tea and Scotch eggs too, by God. He seemed pleased as Midas that Lark preferred toast, and Ash cringed at the reason he must suspect, while the wily old codger regarded his only grandson as if he doubted Ash's ability to perform that blasted duty.

"Christmas," the old coot said again, pointing a chiding fork his way, in answer to which Ash simply shook his head. "No need for her to be suckling it or any such thing," the old man added. "Just get it in the oven, will you, before the day, and you'll be the wealthier for it."

Caught and gutted, Ash thought, hanging his head in defeat.

Lark raised hers. "Excuse me?"

"That's my terms. Got to follow them or forfeit the blunt," the old man said. "Your choice, m'dear. Do not take up the gauntlet then lie down on the job." His grandfather cackled, this time at his questionable wit, and Ash asked Grimsley for something to strengthen his tea.

Lark shook her head, reminding him of his promise the night before to drink less, and Ash sighed and shook his head after all when Grim approached. Need to be up on all counts for this at any rate, he thought.

Lark laced her hands together on the table linen and regarded his grandfather and then him, in turn. "Grandfather," she said. "Please explain the terms of your will to me as if I had never heard them before. You know how forgetful Ashford can be when it comes to details."

His grandfather shook his head sadly and Ash wanted to strangle her for falling in with reprobate's age-old "remiss grandson" tirade.

"Well, as you must be aware," his grandfather said, forking another piece of kipper, "after Ash's mother— my dear daughter . . . faded away, Ash's no-good father gambled away the family fortune, which had actually been brought to the marriage by my daughter."

"Right," Lark said, as if she had known.

"And Ash, being of the same unfortunate blood as his sire, has the same regrettable tendencies, I am sorry to admit."

Lark shook her head with regret, much as his grandfather was wont to do, Ash thought, regarding his cunning bride with daggers in his eyes. At least he *hoped* she could see the daggers he shot her way.

"Besides gambling too much, Ash drinks to excess as well," she added.

"Aye, that he does, and I'm that hopeful *you* can break him of his filthy habits."

"God knows I'm trying."

His grandfather patted his wife's hand, while Ash watched, dumbfound, as she covered those gnarled old penny-pinching fingers with her own. "Poor Grandfather. Such a trial Ashford must be. And to help him overcome his failings, you set some rules, did you not? As I said, give me the details again, if you please, in the event the unfortunate boy forgot to impart them all."

"Damnation!" Ash said as he rose, but the two at the table ignored him, more or less.

His grandfather pointed to Ash's chair with his fork, and Ash looked to the heavens for guidance and sat, determined to stand—or sit—his ground.

"I did it to grow him up, mind," his grandfather said. "He needs a great deal of growing up."

"And so he does," Lark agreed.

"As you know, the matter is a simple one," Ash's grandsire told his hellcat bride. "All Ashford needs to become my heir—with your cooperation, of course, my dear, now that he has found a bride of good sense—is to get you with child before Christmas."

To give Lark her due, Ash thought, though she paled somewhat, and appeared as if her breakfast were about to make a return appearance—which foolishly pleased his grandfather—she did not tell the old man that her husband had withheld that last appalling stipulation. Instead, she took a breath and nodded for him to go on.

"I'd give you a hefty enough allowance right off," the pleased old meddler said, as if he were offering a boon, "starting the first of the year, to keep you from losing the estate before my hopefully timely demise." He patted the inner pocket of his frock coat. "Got it right here in the will, an allowance right off. First of the year."

"Thank you, Grandfather," Ash said, tongue in cheek, and judging by the brow raised his way, it seemed as if Lark had been the only one to hear the wit in his caustic tone.

"Nonsense, my boy. The least I could do. The Chase has been in the Blackburne family for centuries, after all. Too bad to lose it now." The old man turned back to Lark. "Ash's blighted father—the Black Blackguard many called him—inherited it with debt, added more debt in his life, and predicted with certainty that Ash would be the one to lose it, you see, which is why our boy is so stubbornly determined he will not."

"Grandfather, please," Ash said, for the old charlatan had revealed so much more than Ash wished Lark to learn as yet. Besides, in addition to revenge against his father, Ash wanted to save the place for his mother. 'Twas the least he could do for all but stealing her life.

"Nonsense, boy. Lark's a member of the family now. She needs to know what a scurvy sot you come from." The old man returned his attention to Lark, and Ash prayed he might be struck mute before Lark learned the disgraceful truth about what he'd done to his mother.

"Because of the reprehensible way Ash's father treated my dearest daughter, neither Ash nor I can bear to let the blighter win even in death."

"Grandfather," Ash said, "I do believe Lark has learned enough of our tedious family history for one day. She does not appear at all well for what she has already learned."

His grandfather regarded Lark with a keen eye and patted her hand. "Go and rest, my dear. We will continue at another time."

Lark thanked him, excused herself, and left the dining room, her last fleeting look at her husband boding him ill.

"How did you know," Ash asked his grandfather, "that I married at all, given the fact that the ceremony was a hasty one?"

"I keep my ears open. Knew you'd paid a trollop to wed you, didn't I? Knew if she took money to do the deed, she'd take more not to."

"You paid the trollop, er, I mean the actress not to wed me?"

"Tripled her earnings and sent her to France."

"You pernicious old meddler. I should be furious." Unfortunately, Ash could only contemplate the horror of having a trollop rather than a guttersnipe for wife. Then again, he shuddered to think of the ramifications. "This could all have gone tragically wrong."

"But it did not, did it? You deserved better than the trollop. Looks like you found better, and sooner than I expected, I am forced to concede. Good job, boy."

"Hah! Now I wish I had introduced you to Lark on our wedding night," Ash said with due disgust, though his grandfather's foul means had garnered a surprisingly optimistic result . . . perhaps. "You like her then?"

"She is a bit rough around the edges, I'll grant you."

"If only you knew."

"Whatever the problem, I'd warrant she can be fixed."

"Perhaps. Only time will tell."

"We do not have time. At Christmas, your bride must be heavy with child. You have barely enough time to ensure that happens. And you will make it happen, come fire or flood, if you know what you owe your mother."

"Right." There it was, glaringly loud, however unspoken, between them, a reminder of his insidious sin, his greatest failure, a failure for which his mother had paid. "I will not run from my responsibilities again," Ash said.

His grandsire was almost as talented a schemer as his father, Ash thought, and he, himself, nearly as bad as both of them. But he had one worthy bone in his body, revenge, and one bit of himself to give—repentance—to what was left of his mother, to his tenants, and to Larkin and the children they might have, despite the fact that he'd had to sell his soul to his grandfather to do it.

When the old man was set to take his leave, Lark returned to stand beside Ash at the top of the Chase steps. She embraced and kissed his grandfather as if he were her own, affectionate and loving, and she smiled as they waved him off. And when the old man's carriage cleared the gates, she rounded on her unsurprised husband. "You have to get me with child before Christmas?"

"Those are his terms for me to inherit."

She whipped a small packet from the folds of her skirts and shoved it at him. "Read this to me."

Ash hesitated before he took the packet. "What is it?"

"His will," she said. "Go ahead. Read it, and you had better not omit anything important."

"Where did you get it?"

"I found it."

"Where? In my grandfather's pocket?"

Lark shrugged and dragged him, awestruck, and certain his suspicions were correct, into the drawing room to sit. "Read it," she said.

Ash shook his head and read the bloody will, because frankly, he had always wanted to be certain he would face no surprises after the old scoundrel stuck his spoon in the wall.

For fully ten minutes after, Lark sat in amazed and uncharacteristic silence.

"Speak to me," Ash said. "Would you like a glass of water?"

"You should have told me the final stipulation. I once thought you the most forthright of men."

"You were wrong." Ash knew, if his bride did not, that he was everything his father said—a good for nothing, a rogue, a scoundrel, who'd as good as killed his own mother with selfishness.

"Your grandfather is difficult to read," Lark said. "I cannot decide whether he is proud or ashamed of you."

"And I cannot decide if you are a lady or a pickpocket." Lark tilted her head, as if deciding whether to answer, but she remained silent.

"As to whether my grandfather is proud of me, he is not. We dislike each other tremendously, always have."

"That, I did not realize. You put on a good show."

"He disowned my mother when she married my father, and when I was born he disowned me by association. We had no contact for years and have one thing, and one alone, in common. We both detested my father and everything he stood for. Ours is a pact of vengeance, pure and simple."

"But your father is dead. And what about your mother? Where is she? Both you and your grandfather spoke so little of her, it made me wonder."

His mother was all but dead as well, Ash thought, swallowing regret. "May I reserve the right to tell you my mother's story at another time?" he asked.

His wife regarded him curiously then, and he saw

recognition in her gaze, of sorrow perhaps, with a spark of understanding as well, and she nodded.

"My mother loved Blackburne Chase almost as much as she loved me. I intend to save it for her, and for her grandchildren, by God, even if that means making a pact with the devil, which is where my grandfather came in."

"So you and your grandfather created a hell into which I stumbled?"

"Into which your father pushed us both, make no mistake, not that either of us is wholly without blame."

"Right," Lark said. "You have me there."

Chapter 9

Ash stood staring into the fire in the drawing room, aware he must convince Lark that it would be in her best interests to aid him in his determination to become his grandfather's heir. She had intelligence and a ready wit, and must understand the importance of his need. Besides, there was no getting around the old codger's determination any more than his own.

"When were you going to tell me of this final stipulation? That was the last, was it not? You did read to me every word on that will? I am not to bear six babies in six years or any such wild requirement am I?"

"A babe in my bride's belly by Christmas was the final condition. To be truthful, I did consider telling you last evening, after I got you drunk."

Lark raised a brow. "I knew you were up to something."

"But you let me hold you in my lap, a clear indication you understood nothing of my intent."

"I had told you my sister's story and frightened us both. I felt safe enough and sleepy enough not to worry. Foolish probably, but I survived. We both did."

Barely, Ash thought, remembering the hard night's sleep he'd had later, the worse for having spilled his seed in her hand, and for the erotic dreams he'd weaved as a result. " 'Twas a true story, then?"

"Unfortunately."

"Since, for the most part, all is laid bare between us what do you say to helping me?"

Lark started. "Help you do . . . what?"

"Save Blackburne Chase by bearing my child?"

"That is an excessively large and . . . personal request."

"I swore to take revenge upon my father in my mother's name. You would take revenge upon your sister's tormenter, if you could, would you not? I would help you vilify *your* own sire, if you wished it. He deserves taking down, that one. I detest the way he treated you."

That brought her head up. "May I call upon that offer at some future date, perhaps?"

"I will be at your service, and will you be at mine? Is having children not what married people do, after all?"

"People who are married in the conventional way do, without stipulations. But since we were not married without conditions . . . on *your* part. . . ."

Ash prepared for battle. "I feel an additional requirement coming on."

"My sister's babe . . ."

"It lived, then?"

"It did. She did not. It is—he is— Micah. His name is Micah. He lives still in the country, and because I pay them to care for him, they treat him almost as a member of the family, but that is not the same as a family of one's own, do you not agree?"

Lark rose as well, forestalling his response. I will go along with your grandfather's requirements, if you bring Micah here and raise and educate him as you would your own son, and—"

"And?" Ash said, encouraging the thought she had abandoned.

"When you inherit, you put ten thousand pounds in each of our names, mine and Micah's, as security against an uncertain future."

"That's robbery."

"Equal to the deceitful trick you were planning that might have broken my heart."

Ash scoffed. "Is a guttersnipe's heart so delicate, then?"

Lark paled, "*You* will never know," she said, raising her chin. "For my heart will never be open to your view. But if you wish to get me with child, I'd as soon know the reason why beforehand and not lay it at the door of a foolish notion like forever or any such rubbish."

Ash hated himself for the angry insult. "Speaking of rubbish, what do you mean by demeaning such a cherished notion? Many a lady has lived on the hope of forever."

"Many a lady has also perished from such an ill-fated aspiration, besides I am no lady, as *you* just pointed out."

"I have been known to be wrong-headed as well as fork-tongued. Remember that you are *my* lady. You will accept my apology."

"I will accept ten thousand pounds for each of us," she said, stubborn as ever.

"For what uncertain future? You are my wife, until death us do part. No uncertainty exists in those words."

"Unless you leave this earthly plane and another of

your relatives with more money than brains writes a will with the power to send me packing. Besides, 'tis for your own good as well as ours."

Ash gave her a sardonic smile. "Explain."

"After your grandfather passes—if either you or I, or both of us, chooses—we will be free to go our separate ways. You would be due your freedom, if you wished it, after the way . . . my father tricked you."

"And you, what would you be due?"

"Recompense, for my suffering."

"What suffering?"

"You must realize that I am . . . fearful of being hurt by the act necessary to creation. I am not partial to the idea of all that blood and pain just for a babe, though I do love Micah, and I am certain I could love a child of yours."

"If you tried very hard," Ash said, aware of the bite in his rejoinder. Yet, about his wife there suddenly existed a broken doll quality that he had certainly not glimpsed at the pub, or later when he brought her home. The fragility seemed to emerge as he peeled away each hardened layer of her hopes and dreams, layers of a past that might break a lesser being.

Ash saw the defenselessness in her, because he had experienced it on rare occasions in his own lifetime— and not just as a child. As a man, he considered himself a failure when he experienced dejection, because the male of the species were not supposed to feel, much less acknowledge the susceptibility toward vulnerability.

Nevertheless, in Lark, the frailty called to him, as if some invisible thread connected them, a sturdy thread he wished he might cut, for in many ways he ached where it tugged at him. He disliked understanding her pain, seeing her helpless. He abhorred her mirroring his powerlessness, even more than he detested the weakness in himself.

"One more problem," she said. "I do not know precisely what to do to get with child, so you will have to teach me."

"I would have thought that living at a pub with transient 'guests' . . ."

"Exactly." Again her chin came up. "While I suspect that I know what to do to *keep* from getting with child—as the result of an incident I have tried to put from my mind—'tis the brutality of conception that seems to have slipped utterly through the fabric of my education."

There, he saw it now. Through Larkin's pain-filled eyes that broken-doll vulnerability regarded him.

"I would rather a minimum of pain and blood," she said, "if you please." She went to gaze out the window, too pensive by half, her spine and shoulders bent with the ugly weight of the single brutal conception she remembered, however distorted.

Dear God, if she wept, in the way his mother had been wont to do, to get her own way, he could be done for. Then again, he did not intend to become bitter over the effort to touch his wife, as some men did. One way or another, easy or difficult, theirs would become a true marriage. He could be patient.

To his great relief, she turned to him, her shoulders firm, her tense tiger eyes becoming as inflexible as the stone itself, calming him, for the fissure in her broken-doll porcelain seemed to be healing of its own accord. "And when I am with child," she said, punctuating her words as if he should heed them, "you will stop coming to my bed."

A strike to the solar plexus. A loss of breath. Her final condition hit him hard. Ash rubbed the back of his neck, scrubbed his coarse-stubbled chin. Now he knew, by God. Larkin Rose Blackburne could outfox him in a trice while remaining even more coldhearted and unemotional than he. Good God, what had he gotten himself into?

Whatever the depth of his predicament, he must remain strong, for this woman could break him. He knew it in his bones. "Fine," Ash said, firming his spine, for his immediate goal sat more heavily on his shoulders than his absurd wish for an enduring physical relationship with his wife, though he'd not relinquish the notion. "We start now."

"Now?" The sudden lack of color in his wife's cheeks softened her and reassured him that she was not totally lacking in sensitivity. "But this is the middle of the day!" she all but wailed.

"You think what we did last night cannot be done in the middle of the day?"

That fast, scarlet washed her flour-paste skin. "What we did last night can hardly make a babe," she said. "There was not a drop of blood anywhere."

"No, but there were drops of that which really counts."

She colored and turned back to the window. "I do not know what you are talking about."

"Fine. Then get you up the stairs and strip to the dress God gave you, because I am about to teach you."

"Just like that, so cold and . . . brutal?"

"You are the one who requires no emotion. A hard cold bargain you offer and a hard cold bargain I accept."

"Well, there is no emotion between us, is there?

Ours is not, by any stretch of the imagination, a love match."

"Perhaps not, but what happened between us last night seemed rather intimate to me. I thought at the time that it might make for a good beginning."

"A beginning to what?" His wife's face flamed. "What did we do last night? Do you not understand that I have no name for what happened between us? I do not even know. I did think I'd surely die and go to hell for whatever it was, for it seemed supremely wicked to my mind, and I was honestly surprised I woke this morning . . . alive."

'Twas not her innocence that made Ash laugh, but his own at doubting her, and the harder he laughed, the angrier his wife became, until she ran from the room and out the front door.

"Here we go again," Ash said, chasing her as far as the spinney at the far edge of his estate.

She was weeping when he caught up with her and that seemed to make her madder, but she was out of breath, almost as winded as he, and so she remained by the stream, sitting on a rock. He sat beside her, took her into his arms, and let her weep against his shoulder. "About time you had somebody to lean on," he said. "Life's not been easy on you, has it, Larkin?"

"It's not been terrible bad," she said. "Except for never knowing my mother, and losing my sister, and wanting to make a better life for Micah."

"Micah will come to us, as soon as may be arranged," Ash said, concerned over his ability to become a proper father to the boy, considering his own mischievous childhood . . . and adulthood, come to that. "I shall send for him today if you wish."

Lark wiped her eyes. "You would take him on, before I am with child?"

"He has a home with us, if you never get with child."

"Could that happen?"

Most assuredly, Ash thought, with the haste they were taking on this baby-making business. "We will have to try frequently to be certain it does not."

Lark looked at him suspiciously.

"I suspect you experienced pleasure last night, did you not?"

Lark's face flamed and she hid against his frock coat, though to give her credit, she nodded honestly.

"Good, and so did I, but the pleasure could have been greater, sharper, if we were, ah, hmm, how to explain this. You must have seen animals mating at one time or another?"

"Of course. Horses, dogs."

"Like other animals, a man becomes hard when aroused so he can 'mate' with a woman. You touched me there, remember? You also helped me spill my seed."

"So that's what that was?"

"Only we wasted it."

Lark's face turned pink. "All over the place."

"Hmm." Ash grinned for the wicked candor in her comment, a frankness that would make a woman of society swoon. "So you understand that I would have to insert that hardened part of me inside of you to plant my seed."

Like a shot, Lark flew from his arms and off their perch, then she was running once more, Ash chasing behind.

Finally, he stopped, gave up the chase, and watched

her disappear from sight. He shook his head as he bent and rubbed his legs. "I am going to die young from pursuing my bride about the countryside." He dropped into the grass to await her return and reclined to watch the clouds.

Before ten minutes passed, she stood over him, arms crossed, foot tapping. "It will *never* fit."

"It will."

"That's what made my sister bleed. He split her in half. I'm convinced of it."

"He forced her. There's the difference."

"What?"

"Come down here and let me explain."

Lark lay beside him in the grass and Ash rolled over to cup her center through the skirts of her dress. She gasped in surprise, moved her legs as if to dislodge him, but he didn't take his hand away, and she didn't make a point of asking him to. Ultimately, she seemed to relax.

After a time of staring into each other eyes, his hand firm, there at her center, he felt her begin to throb. "The difference," he said, "is a simple one. The other night, you wanted my hand on you, here, as you want it now, as you did in the tree."

"I do not. I did not."

"You did. You do. I can tell."

She harrumphed and looked away from him. "So?" she said, turning back after a minute.

"Two people wanting to mate with each other makes the difference. Even now, you're readying yourself to receive me, with a moist pulsing that will ease my way inside of you here." He stroked her. "You feel almost as good as you did last night before you let me touch you, and you would feel better if I did touch you, beneath your clothes, and altogether better, again, once I slipped inside you."

"I am not certain I can believe you."

"Because I am a man."

"How did you know?"

He placed her hand upon the swelling in his trousers, pressed her palm against him, felt the jolt of pleasure. "I have proof."

She smiled at his jest but stroked his turgid length as if measuring him with her thumb, and he took to stroking her in return and drifting into pleasure.

"I think we have a problem," she said, shattering pleasure and returning him to earth with a rude rush.

"*I* certainly have a problem," he said, tongue in cheek. "I am set to explode."

"*That* is entirely too big to fit where you say it must go. You feel about the size of a stallion, and believe me, I am no mare in heat."

Ash groaned at the analogy, and to make matters worse, he found himself inconveniently and uncomfortably stimulated by it. "You overrate my size, Lark, and if you do not rein in your imagination, I fear you will be sorely disappointed when presented with the sight of me."

"I will only be disappointed if you are larger than a thimble."

"Then you are right. We have a problem. I am larger than a thimble, thank the gods, but I am smaller than a stallion as well."

"A parsnip? A carrot?"

"Are you comparing my manhood to a vegetable? Parsnips and carrots come in all sizes, as you very well know. Besides you held me in your hand last night."

"But I could not *see* in the dark. It felt inordinately huge." Lark rose and took his hand to drag him up.

"Neither were you of a mind for looking," Ash said. "And thank you for the compliment. Where are we going?"

"The root cellar. You're going to show me a root vegetable that precisely matches your manly size."

"Surely you jest."

"I most certainly do not. This is a serious business and I must be properly prepared, unless you want another beating like the one I gave you at the pub before we married."

Ash pulled up short. "Excuse me, but as I remember it, 'twas I who won that battle."

Lark laughed, a sound that cheered him even as it annoyed him. "With my knee at your knockers, I think not. One good shot and you would have been at my mercy, much as you were the other morning when I threw you from my bed in that precise way."

Ash remembered that occasion well enough. He hurt for remembering it. But had she bested him on their wedding night at the pub? He thought not. Well, possibly, though not as well as with the pistol later, of course.

"At least have the decency to call my man parts by their proper names, if you please. 'Knockers' are what rogues call women's breasts, 'ballocks' are the proper word for a man's . . . resources."

She threw open the door to the root cellar and proceeded down the steps. "Fine, then I had you by the ballocks. Feel better now?"

Chapter 10

In the chill, dank underground storage beneath the scullery, Ash watched with no little amusement as his bold-as-brass bride rooted through a bin of carrots, then one of parsnips, to see if she could find a vegetable that matched the size of his not inconsiderable manhood at its saluting best. She began by holding up a parsnip the size of a pizzle on a two-year-old.

Ash shook his head in denial with regret for her sake and relief for his own.

"This one then?"

"Too thick on the bottom, too pointed at the top."

"But the length?"

"Too short."

"Bloody hell," said the Lady Blackburne, falling into her guttersnipe vocabulary as she went back to searching for a root to match his own.

She chose one, looked it over, swore like a pub drunk, and made to put it back, but after a bit of hesitation, she raised the biggest parsnip Ash had ever seen in his life and watched for his reaction as if with baited breath.

Ash considered it for a moment, to make his bride squirm, saw her eyes grow wide, and her face go pale. He lost the fight. "Too big."

"Thank the bloody gods," she said and then she beamed, a sincerely beautiful sight, until she frowned. "You frightened me intentionally, did you not?"

Ash failed to answer, but he hid his smile and lowered himself to a wooden crate. He crossed his arms to watch, beside himself enchanted by the sight of her. Perhaps they had not quite come to a stage of comfort between them while discussing the sexual act, but this must surely be a first step toward marital intimacy, however skewed her approach.

He considered searching with her, for just the right sized representation of his manhood, but he preferred to feast his eyes on the child-woman before him. Even in a dress, stained and tattered though it had become in the hour she'd worn it, she moved like a boy, likely from long practice, and he could clearly see that skirts hampered her progress in a way that annoyed the devil out of her. Another notion that charmed him.

Yet there was a vulnerable womanliness to her as well that called to him; there was something in her that needed nurturing, or healing, he was not certain which. He knew only that she seemed more broken than he, and he wanted suddenly to be the man to heal her.

She raised another parsnip, and another, and Ash continued shaking his head, keeping his amusement at bay.

Even at rest, he was, unfortunately for her peace, but providential for her pleasure, rather well endowed, judging by many—though not all—of the comrades he'd seen in the buff during their frequent river-baths in the army.

"Ashford Blackburne," said his bride, "you are

alarming the devil out of me. I wish you would come and help before I run screaming into the wilderness."

"Surely the Larkin McAdams who bested me on our wedding night is not admitting fear," Ash said as he rose and approached her.

"Certainly not." She straightened her spine. "Only that the prelude to fear is beginning to . . . sneak upon me with snapping teeth, and if you do not put period to my torture, the mere anticipation of alarm will get the better of me."

"I see," Ash said, searching, for all the world, through a season's worth of parsnips for one the exact same size as his ponderous pride.

Finally, he came upon a fearfully large parsnip, too large actually, and held it forth for her perusal.

Lark made to swoon as if in a comedy on the stage, delighting him with her antics. But when he caught her sobering gaze, he snapped an inch off its top, which went a great distance toward relieving the true anxiety she tried valiantly to hide.

"For my lady wife," said Ash, presenting it with a bow and a flourish like a handful of posies, "for your delectable and insatiable pleasure."

Larkin took the respectable parsnip, regarded it with silent assessment, then she gripped it as she had gripped his lance, testing its length, ran her hand up and down, down and up—growing him, if she but knew it, as if 'twere his root she stroked.

Then sighing in loud resignation, she placed the prototypical parsnip in her pocket and led her silent way up the steep granite steps of the dank root cellar and out into the spring sunshine.

They walked the perimeter of the house after that, she rather forlorn, for longer than he'd like. "You still haven't given me a full tour inside the house," she said, making an effort at turning her mind, he thought, as she regarded the front of his bay-windowed, brick-faced home with curiosity. "What rooms occupy the matching towers at either end?"

"The tower rooms are all circular," he said. The east tower boasts a library on the main floor, and above it my study, down the hall from the master bedchamber suite, and below it, on the first floor, a small receiving room. The west tower rooms are used for . . . storage . . . mainly."

Lark nodded and turned unexpectedly toward the spinney, but she passed it and continued on toward the horse chestnut tree beyond, where she had hidden the day of her reading lesson. She climbed back into the crook she preferred, tearing a ruffle from her bodice in the process and patted the limb beside her.

Ash climbed up, oddly honored to be invited, wondering if she wanted more than to rest. The last time he'd joined her, she had ended by tossing him to the ground, a rather significant parody, actually, of their courtship to date, now that he thought of it.

"What is it called?" she asked, her hand in her parsnip pocket. "This making of a babe?"

Before answering, Ash settled himself with his arms around her, glad she let him, because he believed that embracing her whenever he could might help her become less fearful of his touch.

"The most respectable term is, 'making love.'"

"But we do not love each other."

"Right. We do not even know each other very well, do we, which will change in time, but I like you, Lark. I like you better than either of the two brides who jilted me."

"How fortunate for me."

"No, the fortune is mine. I never knew I could like a woman, much less the one I married. You are quite the revelation. We will make you into a fine lady. You shall see. I will hire a score of tutors, but for now, what I need most from you is for us to make a babe."

"It does not seem right," she said.

"What doesn't?"

"Making a baby to save an estate."

Ash sighed and smoothed his hand away from her dress, where he'd been about to place it close to her breast. After her words, touching her did not seem right of a sudden. "I had not thought of it in quite those terms."

"Let us make it some promises and write them down."

"It?"

"The baby we're going to have. Do you know how to write?" she asked.

"Yes, and I shall have someone teach you that too. Wait. What good will promises do if we decide later to go our separate ways? Your suggestion, you will remember."

"For my part, I would evoke that condition only in extreme circumstances. In my own way, I am a woman of honor, as I know you to be a man of integrity; therefore, I feel justified in making promises that I am confident we will both keep."

Ash did not feel justified in vouching for his *own* integrity, which made him wonder why he felt comfortable depending upon hers. Nevertheless, her words presented him with a modicum of relief in the face of her earlier inflexibility. He nodded. "What kind of promises shall we make it then?"

"We promise it we will . . . feed it whenever it's hungry, change its bottom, keep it warm with clothes, and give it a snug home to live in. We will promise to embrace it and let it cry on our shoulders when it must. That's important, I discovered today." She regarded him. "What would you have liked your parents to do for you that they neglected?"

"Tell me they liked me, even though I was not normally a well-behaved nor even a good son. Teach me to be responsible."

"Oh yes." She sat straighter. "We will definitely like our baby, though we might not always like what he or she does, and we shall tell it so. We will also teach it to be responsible." She touched his arm. "We have to stop calling our future baby, 'it,' you know. We shall write two letters, one to a boy and one to a girl, so we may present the right letter when the time comes. What shall we name them?"

"Them?"

"A boy and a girl. We shall choose a name for each."

"Ah, I see." Ash was enchanted.

"And Christmas," she added. "We have to promise that in the letter; we'll give them Christmas every year, because my father did not, though I heard of it and yearned for it."

"Christmas," Ash said. "Splendid idea. And their names are? Let us pick them now," he said. If she knew more about her children, he wondered, would she be ready to let him start begetting them? He certainly hoped so. "Are there any names in particular that you like?"

She did not have to think for long. "Isobel is the loveliest girl's name I ever heard. It sounded like music the first time I heard it. Can we have a daughter named Isobel?"

That sobered him. A daughter named Isobel—it felt so real, frighteningly real. "Any special reason you picked that name?"

"It was my mother's and she deserved the kind of life we're giving our own Isobel."

Our own Isobel. "Fine," Ash said, feeling his cravat tighten. "Isobel, it is, and for a boy?"

"I'd like a son named Zachary. Perhaps we should have one of each."

Ash crushed his bride in his arms, without thought, and gave in to the sort of inner merriment that reminded him of children rolling down grassy hills in sunshine. Then he stilled and sat back and regarded her curiously, as if seeing "inside" Larkin Rose for the very first time.

He placed a finger beneath her chin and lifted it until their eyes met and held; then he touched his lips to hers, a teasing flutter at first, cool silk grazing warm, until within the kiss, almost without conscious thought, he passed the fullness of his feelings, whatever they might be, over to her without words.

She nodded, the movement of her head so slight he might have missed it, and he thought she might be as pleasantly confused by the exchange. "Thank you for liking me," she said her throat working. "I do not believe anyone has before, other than my sister. Why do you?"

"Why do I like you? For . . . naming our children before you let me beget them, for that parsnip in your pocket, even for siding with my grandfather, though I should put you over my knee for that."

"Yeek!" Lark jumped from the tree and ran.

Ash jumped as well to chase after her, as ever, and he could have sworn that when she found an idyllic spot, she let him catch her.

They fell to the ground and kissed in the lavender field beneath the warm spring sun. Rolling in tall grass, and beside fragrant azure blossoms, they explored each other's mouths, with lips and tongues, as if that kiss had been the first and she wanted more. They slipped curious hands into each other's clothes, undid a few buttons, and gave into an afternoon of unexpected laughter and erotic exploration.

Tonight, Ash thought. Tonight they would begin trying to make a baby. Isobel and Zachary. *Or* Zachary. Good God, having given his possible children names, he had begun to think of them as real, *both* of them. What daft notion ailed him now? And letters to be written to unborn children, by God.

Whatever his mad fancy, Ash knew that for the first time in years, Christmas suddenly seemed an event to look forward to, rather than dread. If all went well, he would have a family of his own with whom to share it.

He sent Larkin upstairs before him that night, to prepare herself to receive him, relieved to learn, shortly after, that she had ordered herself a bath and that she could not possibly find a new way to fight him on this.

They had struck a bargain, and Ash felt reasonably certain that Lark would not bite, kick, poke, knee, or shoot him tonight, no, nor find any other excuse to stop him.

Then again, she had long equated the sexual act with a painful, bloody brutality. He must approach her as he would a high-spirited filly, with gentle words and pleasure-filled touches. Soft kisses and caresses. Tease her mind with images of pleasure, mating images, horses perhaps—no that would frighten her. As would he, for his body had already taken to rising to the occasion, even as he told himself to approach his bride with slow and easy caution.

Would his aroused state frighten her, or had her parsnip done the trick? Ash grinned despite his apprehension. Perhaps he would wear his inexpressibles at first, until she was ready for more of him, keeping himself under a measure of containment.

For more than an hour, Ash paced, regarding the brandy container several yearning times, but he continued to deny himself. Gad, but with Lark's help, he was getting good at this self-denial business, both with his drink and his sexual gratification.

Finally he shook his head, checked his watch, and made his way up the stairs, though for some reason he felt as if he were on his way to his own hanging. Perhaps because he knew she was frightened. God knew, he would take her pain to himself, if he could.

What the devil ailed him? He was not going to hurt her—well, not beyond the first barrier—if there were a barrier. "Damn it!" Should he explain that to her as well? Yes, he thought, and in great blathering detail. The notion of it made him sweat. He stopped in the stairs to take out his handkerchief and mop his brow. Then, rather than enter her bedchamber direct, he went to his own first, to give her a minute more.

Then he went through the dressing room, because he hated dithering, stopped short when he saw the results of her bath—a good sign. Then he saw a smear of blood on a damp towel and worry began to ride him.

He stopped short of throwing open her door, but entered as if he belonged there, which he damned well did. Had she cut herself, done herself a harm . . . to escape the marriage act?

No, his bride had more strength of character than that. But her bedchamber sat empty. Her bed had been turned down, and a dresser drawer stood open, boys' clothes spilling out. Atop her dresser, an empty inkwell had been employed, as if in the guise of a candleholder, to hold an erect . . . parsnip.

Blast and damnation! She'd bolted.

Ash found Grimsley reading beside the front door, where he'd stationed the man every night since he brought his bolting bride home.

"Sorry sir, but she did not pass this way. Brinks is bunking at the kitchen door, I suggest you check there."

Lark hadn't left, both men assured him. They'd been keeping guard since before she said good night in the drawing room earlier.

Ash began a methodical sweeping search of the house, until he remembered her questions about the towers. Rather than the tower rooms in use, he went, with a sinking heart, toward the ones he told her they used primarily for storage.

He found her there, in the west tower, as he suspected, on the family bedchamber floor, in the room he least wished her to find.

Wearing her trousers once again, his bride stood with tears in her eyes, staring down into the face of his mother, who stared blankly back, looking like a skeleton, swallowed by the huge bed in which she lay.

Nan stood to the side, horrified.

Chapter 11

"Who is she?" Lark asked when she saw Ash enter the beautiful round bedchamber. "She does not speak and Nan will tell me nothing."

Nan curtsied as if in apology.

"Go and have a cup of tea, Nan," Ash said. "Then you may return directly."

Ash placed his arm around Larkin's trembling shoulders and together they stepped closer to the bed. "She is my mother, or what is left of her."

"Why did you not tell me or bring me to meet her? Because you are ashamed of me?" She looked straight at him and lowered her voice. "Or because you are ashamed of her?"

Ash winced but did not deign to lower his voice. "Because I am ashamed of me, and because you said you were not ready to meet her, if you will remember, and were to tell me when you were. Besides, I did not wish you to be frightened here at Blackburne. She is like a ghost, you see, almost alive, not quite dead."

"What happened to her?" Lark asked. "And why should *you* feel shame?"

"She suffered an apoplectic seizure when I went to war and never recovered. This is the result. Before his death, my father accused me of running off to war to escape my responsibilities, and in the running, of killing my mother. I am beginning to believe he was right."

"She may yet recover."

"It has been five years, Lark. Nevertheless, in that unlikely event, I am trying to keep from losing the estate. She loves this place, you see. It is her home. I would not want to move her from it, in any state. I think she would know somehow, mourn the loss, and die after all."

"You should have told me."

"What good?"

"I may be wrong, but was there not something in our marriage vows about good times and bad, sickness and health?"

"As I remember, you spoke also the words, obey, serve, and honor him. Should we now take our vows to heart, and begin again? Neither of us stands blameless in this unruly marriage of ours."

Lark nodded, conceding his point. "I would like to begin again."

That surprised him, but with no time to examine his feelings, he evaded the issue. "If it is any consolation, I did plan to bring you here at some point soon. That is the best I can offer in my own defense, though perhaps I did not feel hurried to reveal my greatest sin to you."

"I see no sin, only sorrow."

Ash looked away as Nan returned. He thanked her and made to leave.

"Will you not take your mother's hand?" Lark said. "Speak to her or kiss her cheek? She will be hurt for the slight."

Ash started as if struck. "Nonsense. She is aware of nothing."

"And suppose you are wrong? You seem to like being touched. Why would she not?"

"Larkin, stop it," Ash said, taking his wife's arm and shutting his mother's door behind them. He disliked her scold as much as he had disliked her underserved absolution.

Forgiveness he found to be as difficult in receiving as in giving. As for the reprimand of neglect, especially as pertained to his mother, he detested it, no matter the giver.

"What may I ask were you doing wandering the house at half past bloody midnight, and wearing your boys' clothes besides?"

Lark stopped, pulling him up short. "You said this was my house now as well."

"And so it is." Ash urged her along.

"If you must know, I want to turn one of the tower rooms into a sitting room. I never had a room of my own."

To Ash's surprise, Lark was not walking with her usual manly stride but with short, careful steps; her head bowed, more yielding than he imagined possible. "The circular room above my mother's current bedchamber was her own sitting room," he said, watching Lark closely. "She would be pleased for you to return it to its former glory."

"Thank you," Lark whispered, all humility. "I am sorry for what she is going through, and for the guilt that must be your companion after your sire's unjust accusation. I believe I am beginning to dislike your father every bit as much as you and your grandfather do." She slowed. "Did your grandfather not visit his daughter when he was here? I do not remember that he took the opportunity."

"He rarely does. I think he becomes upset, even ill, when he sees her like that, though he is too hard-headed to admit as much."

"Hmph. And what do you think of so shoddy an excuse for neglect?"

Ash respected her anger on his mother's behalf. "As I told you at the time, my grandfather and I dislike each other, and always have. His neglect does not surprise me."

"You are a better man than he is, Ash."

"I appreciate your vote of confidence," Ash said, "and believe that you are a better woman than I had surmised upon first meeting. One who keeps her word . . . speaking of which, did we not have a bargain set to begin this night?"

Lark's pallor negated the possibility of forgetfulness on her part. "No, but we cannot begin tonight after all."

"Because of what you have just seen? It has given you a disgust of me?" Which he would comprehend, truth to tell.

They stepped into her bedchamber, and he saw that her face shown again like pomegranates.

"I understand," he said, "but I must remind you that however distressing my mother's situation, you need to be with child by Christmas, or I may lose what she values most."

"I would think that she would value you most."

"Was a time she did," he said, then he chose to move from the maudlin past to the living present. "Why are you wearing trousers again?"

"Christmas is a long way off."

"You are correct," he said, "but these things take time, Lark, and since we do not know how much time, once you have recovered from the shock of this evening, we must begin as soon as possible."

"You are right, of course." She nodded as if she meant it, "but I am not suffering from shock. That is not the problem."

"So we may begin tonight after all?" Ash reached to unbutton the flap on her trousers before she changed her mind.

She slapped her hand over his. "What are you doing?"

"Getting you out of those trousers."

"You cannot!"

"We can hardly make a baby with you wearing them. Or have you changed your mind again?"

"Oh please no, not tonight . . . or tomorrow night. Next Tuesday would do. How about next Tuesday? Perhaps even Monday."

"Lark, this is not about my mother, is it?" he asked, hoping to God it wasn't and that she would be willing to take him into herself and obliterate his own memories.

"No, it is not."

"Then remove your trousers, if you please."

"I do not please. I cannot!" she wailed as tears filled her eyes.

Now this caught Ash off guard, gave him pause and a worry of no inconsequential magnitude. Larkin McAdams had beat him to a bloody pulp previous to their wedding, and though he had not fought back, precisely, he had kept himself from being injured to the point that she must have become at least half as bruised, and she'd shed not a tear.

Her father had swatted her that night as well, which made him furious to remember, and no tears had come to her eye at those times either. And now she swore that seeing his mother had not given her a disgust of him, so why the tears?

"Lark," Ash said. "Please tell me what is wrong."

"I must wear my trousers or something terrible will happen."

Ash was startled by the melodramatic tone of her statement and tried not to smile.

She turned away. "I cannot tell you, because it is too terrible to say."

"Show me then."

"No!" she said with a gasp. "Good God no."

"Lark, I am your husband. Whatever is the matter, you must tell me, for husbands and wives should face the terrors of life together. Sickness and health, good and bad, remember?"

"You will know that you made a very bad bargain, if I tell you, and it will give you a disgust of me as well, then you will not want to make a baby with me. Better you should not know."

Ash was intrigued no small bit and looked her over very closely for some clue as to her passionate concern. Her honeyed hair, he saw still hung damp from her bath, the only sign she'd taken one, except for the towel with . . . a smear of blood.

Was it possible she did not understand the natural way of things?

With a father like hers? Entirely possible.

Ash sat Lark on the edge of her bed and knelt before her. "Do you have your monthlies, Larkin?"

She seemed relieved he'd changed the subject. "What are they?"

"They," he said, talking to himself, wondering how to go on. "You do know that every woman of an age to bear children goes through a monthly bloody flux."

Pomegranate cheeks, she wore once more, to match her dawning recognition.

"You do not remember your mother's bleeding every month?" he asked.

"She died when I was born," Lark wailed, her embarrassment flying at full mast.

"Your sister?"

"I thought that was because of what *he* did to her."

"The bleeding is normal Lark, every month. It's happening to you now, is it not? You never realized that it happens around the same time every month?"

"I do not read dates, so how would I?"

"What did you think the blood signified then?"

"I suppose I thought that someday I would . . . bleed to death. Sometimes I wondered when, or if I would have time to help Micah before it was too late."

"So you basically thought you were dying for years?"

Lark raised her chin, pride in every line of her high cheekbones. "After a while, when I didn't die, I . . . put up with it and worried less."

Ash knew he'd been right; his Lark shed no tears for the possibility of dying, or even the reprieve thereof. Only extreme embarrassment brought tears to the eyes of Larkin Rose. That, and the suffering of another— her sister, her nephew, his mother.

"It occurs to me, Lark," Ash said, "that your sister's bleeding might have been natural at the time you found her. She might not have been forced but simply gave herself in the midst of her flux."

Lark looked horrified.

Ash stroked the hair from her brow. "Do not fret; I will not importune you at this time. Not for your first experience, though I would hope, there might come a time when you would offer yourself, whatever your state."

His bride looked as if she doubted his sanity, while he faced the happy realization that her virginity, or lack thereof, made no mind. He now had physical proof that she carried no child of another, though her innocence had long since implied as much.

"Whatever you think," he went on, "a man and woman may come together then and 'twill be messy. Just know that you might have misunderstood the blood, and your sister might not have been hurt after all. Did she complain of pain? Did she weep afterward, for instance?"

"She wept always when he was done with her. She loved him you see, but he would not have her for wife, not even when she got herself with child and begged him to take her."

"But no bruises afterward, no mention of pain?"

"No," Lark said, her brows furrowed in thought.

"Your fears, I believe, have been magnified," Ash said, "by an unfounded assumption made by a young girl who did not know better."

"And your conclusions," his bride snapped, "have been drawn by a man looking for a means to his own end."

Ash grinned despite himself in appreciation of her strange blend of cleverness and naïveté. "We shall see then, for only time can prove me correct." He reached for her trousers once more, but once more she stopped him.

"Larkin, I have undressed you previous to this, so

why not let me take your trousers off you now? Or I will leave, if you would be more comfortable, so you may don your night rail and climb into bed to await me."

"The trousers hold everything up . . . It's ugly, Ash."

"It's not, it's natural."

"The folded cloth gets ugly. How do women in fancy dresses hold them up without trousers, anyway?"

"I . . . have no idea, but I'll go fetch Cook, shall I, and get her to show you?" He rose.

Lark caught his hand. "No, please. Let me just wear my trousers for a few days and then I will wear dresses."

"You would wear trousers to sleep as well?"

She nodded, and he raised a finger to her lips as she made to respond.

"I intend to continue sleeping with you," he warned, "in whatever state you find yourself, but I would like to see you sleep comfortably."

Lark threw herself back on the bed with a sigh, her legs hanging off the edge. "I cannot believe I am having this conversation with a man."

"With your husband," Ash corrected as he made to leave the bedchamber, "and do not forget it. Do not move from that spot. I will return shortly."

Ashford Blackburne. Her husband. Teaching her about the bloody ailment that had been scaring the bejesus out of her for half her life. The bleeding between her legs, where he would put himself, if he were to be believed, and she believed everything he had to say, for as he himself had affirmed, he was an honest rogue and respected honesty a great deal in others.

Lark sighed for her own shortcomings, for the blasted dishonesty he would never forgive, that set her in his path, in his life, his bed, at his mercy, even into this most embarrassing situation. She supposed she deserved whatever he doled out, blast him.

Lark sighed, rolled to her side, raised her legs against her belly, and closed her eyes while she waited for her honest, gentle, tyrannical husband to return, with whatever new torture he could concoct for her.

By the time he woke her, Lark thought she'd been sleeping for some time, and could barely rouse herself. Besides, she was too embarrassed to open her eyes, as he slipped her trousers off her legs. Then she refused to open them as he slid the bloody rag from between her legs, washed her with a warm cloth, and replaced the soiled rag with something soft and tender. Then he slipped something akin to trousers, but not, up her legs and fastened a binding of a sort around her waist to keep the padded rag against her.

She should not become attached to him, Lark thought, as he went so far as to slip one of her new attic night shifts over her head and place her beneath the covers. She would be foolish to become fond of him, which was why she set the condition that he stop coming to her bed when she found herself with child.

In the moment she made the stipulation, she had been afraid that she was already in danger of liking him too much. That was another reason why she had told him they could part, if he wished, after he received his inheritance, because she owed him that much at least, for cheating him into marriage.

And though she owed him a babe, she already

wanted his child as much as he did, perhaps more. She must remember that however much he wanted a child and a wife before Christmas, she could be left in the literal cold after Christmas, if she were not cautious.

Yes, they had talked about a babe as if they would raise it together, but you never knew what the rich might do. Simply regard his grandfather's machinations. No, she would be wise to be strong-willed where her bridegroom was concerned and not become overly sentimental or dependent.

"We will try making a babe in a few days," he said now as he climbed into the bed with her, almost as if he had read her thoughts. "As soon as your flux is finished, so you may as well rest while you can."

Lark hated that his "threat" to get her with child felt of a sudden like a hoped-for promise, an unsettling reaction that centered physically, there, where she bled, where his hand had made magic inside her, and where his manly parsnip would later invade her.

Lark hid her face against the shoulder of the very man she should be running from. When he tucked her head neatly beneath his chin, she placed her hand against his softly rising chest. "Tell me how people celebrate Christmas," she said, and her husband covered her hand with his and did.

The following morning Lark woke alone, but before she dressed, she took the time to examine the "sling" he had dressed her in and discovered that it must be nothing more than a pair of his own underlinen. Nevertheless, with trouser-type legs and a tie-fastened, three-button front, the short drawers did a fine job of holding up the folded rag she used for her "monthlies," and she marveled at his resourceful kindness.

Her fist thought was to thank him for his personal garment, but she decided that in the light of day, no such comment could be made. Husbands and wives must speak only in the bedchamber of such things, though now that she thought on it, they had become quite outrageous in their whispers in the orchard the other day, not to mention her search in the root cellar.

Her "feminine sling," as Ash dubbed his gift at breakfast—speaking about such things outside the bedroom obviously did not embarrass *him*—worked marvelously well beneath her dress and made Lark feel, for perhaps the first time in her life, like a real woman. A woman not expected to die young. Fancy that.

When she learned that he would be attending to estate matters all day, and that she would not see him until dinner, Larkin visited his mother, and gave Nan an hour free. She told her mother-in-law about their marriage, every foolish detail, omitting their baby bargain and what went on in their bedchamber, of course. When Nan returned, Lark promised Ash's mother that she would visit on the morrow.

Afterward, Lark turned to cleaning out the sitting room that would be her own. Cook and Mim came to help. "On the earl's orders," Cook said.

Lark chose several beautiful old pieces of furniture from the attic for her sitting room—everything she needed for a place where she might go to rest, or dream, or read, if she learned. A place where she might sew clothes for the babe, when she learned to sew, and when she expected a babe. A place where she might draw or paint on parchment sheets, like a fancy lady in a fancy dress.

She had always liked to draw. Her sister had taught her to burn corks. She'd sketched with their charred edges on any surface she could find. Her favorite had been the smooth limestone wall out by the pigsty.

Chapter 12

Ash stood waiting for Lark that evening in the drawing room and offered her his arm to escort her into the dining room. They sat in silence while Grimsley served.

Beside Ash's plate there sat a missive that he opened after Grim finished. "I received this note today from Gideon St. Goddard, duke of Stanthorpe, another rogue of the club, and I thought you might enjoy hearing it. Would you?"

Lark nodded, honestly interested:

Dearest Ash,

Though Myles and Hunter still suffer the aftereffects of your decline into depravity on the day of your last jilt, they have finally confessed that your own consequences will be of some longer duration.

If you expect to be congratulated, my friend, on your nuptials, you could at least tell a fellow rogue that you have stepped into Parson's mousetrap. Sabrina and I were never so shocked. Had we not been in mourning, we would surely have been at the church to witness your "echoing" disgrace. And I mean that in the broadest of terms.

Sorry old boy, but it is somewhat amusing, a rogue of your caliber being so oft jilted. At any rate, Myles and Hunter feel that you "won" yourself a bride that wants taming. I am ordered to tell you, on Sabrina's behalf, to be gentle and kind to her.

For my own part, I will confess—providing you promise never to reveal as much to Sabrina—that I never did succeed in taming my own bride, and I was never more glad of anything in my life. Congratulations and best wishes.

Yours, G. St.G.

"I like Sabrina already," Lark said. "I want to meet her . . . and the duke too, I suppose, for he is funny in teasing you, though the notion of meeting him frightens me witless."

"You will, eventually, meet all the rogues and their wives, but first we will have to teach you how to entertain in society."

"I suppose pig riding is out of the question, then?"

Ash raised a brow, not finding her statement the least amusing. "My grandfather sent a note 'round this morning to remind me that you will need lessons in walking, talking, and acting the lady."

"Lessons?" Lark laughed. "I could not act the lady if you trussed me up and shoved an apple in my mouth."

Ash looked to the heavens and stabbed a piece of boiled potato with his fork. "To act the lady, I would truss you up and shove a fan in your hand."

"Same nonsense. I refuse to simper and gossip."

"I will hire tutors and you will learn to be a lady,

by God. I will also hire a dressmaker, because you really cannot go into society wearing those clothes."

"What is wrong with these clothes?"

"They do not fit, to begin with, plus they're years out of date."

"Why do I need clothes that fit? Why would you want to pay dressmakers and tutors when you are trying to economize by doing your own estate work? You can teach me, yourself, what you believe I need to know, even if *I* do not believe I need it. And I am perfectly happy wearing the clothes I already have." Larkin smoothed her bodice lovingly. "These dresses are a hundred times better than anything I've ever owned before."

"Which is not saying much. Look, you have already torn the sleeve at the wrist, precisely why you must learn to act the lady."

Lark found the tear, winced, and firmed her jaw.

Ash placed his fork against his plate. "I apologize, Lark, but your current wardrobe is simply not fit for society, though the dresses that were my mother's might do for a start, while you learn, and if you do not tatter them too badly."

He shook his head. "Though how I will keep the locals from calling for much longer, I cannot imagine. Not that this is a big village—it is particularly small, as a matter of record—but the gossips *will* want to examine you."

"I was going to ask why you must keep them from visiting, but if they are to come only to inspect me, I'd rather they remained at home, thank you very much. But why have they not come sooner?"

"They are respecting our honey month."

"Which is?"

"The month after marriage when a newly married couple normally *try* to make a baby."

Her face warmed. "Oh, then they will come soon."

"Unless I can think of a way to stop them."

"You may tell them I am contagious."

"What manner of disease should you have?" Ash asked, the light in his eyes making him look rather more handsome than a man had the right, Lark thought.

"I heard of a disease that sounds so exotic, I think I might like to have it. Have you ever heard of the French pox?"

Ash spit his tea across the dinner table and took to coughing so hard, Grimsley came running to smack his back while Larkin offered water.

"I cannot do it," Ash said when he recovered his breath. "I cannot teach you myself. You need tutors of every kind, yesterday, if not sooner."

"Tutors perhaps," Lark conceded. "But can I not keep the clothes I have?"

"Why must you always choose clothes that do not fit?"

Lark turned from his gaze. "You know why."

"So men will not treat you in the same detestable way that some fiend treated your sister, which simply means that you want respect. What if men and women, both, were to respect you and treat you as an equal? Would you not prefer as much?"

"I do not need respect. Safety will do."

"But you would like to be respected, would you not? Be honest."

Lark folded her arms and set her mouth.

"If you wore the proper clothes, learned to talk properly, had table manners, and could dance, we might attend some fine and fancy dress ball where even the regent might partner you."

"Hah!" Lark slammed down her fork. "The day the regent dances with *me* is the day I tell you my deepest secret."

"You have those lessons, and I will take you to the Regent's Ball in three months' time."

"But no dressmaker, not yet. Let me wear what I have for the nonce, please?"

"Fine for now, but you will have a dancing master and a tutor for a start."

"What will the tutor teach me?"

"Reading and writing to begin with."

"You can teach me those things."

"That did not work, if you will remember."

Lark pouted for half a beat. "Fine, but I would rather *you* taught me manners and how to act. You would know better than a snuffy-smelling tutor."

"You want *me* to teach you manners and how to act the lady? Excellent. We shall begin this instant. You will please remove your elbows from the table and stop eating your peas with a knife. Now."

Lark sat back and laughed, then she chose a pea pod from her plate, split it with her thumb, bent it like a bow, and pelted him across the table.

"Dear God, I have my work cut out for me."

Ash's lectures on deportment began the very next day, while Lark tried not to listen. He lectured her as he drove her to the dower house to meet his father's former estate manager and his wife.

Norbert "Bud" St. Nicholas, Ash's father's retired estate manager, and his wife, Olga, epitomized Lark's every interpretation of what grandparents should be. Both with kindly eyes and white hair, Olga's tied in a bun at her nape, and Bud's cropped and waving, they welcomed her with surprise and graciousness, after she embraced them and realized, from Ash's stern look, that as the lady of the manor, she had erred.

Olga, kind and generous to a fault, fed Lark tea with plenty of milk and asked her plans for the house. Lark told her about her sitting room and how she wanted to learn to sew and draw like a lady, and Olga offered to give her sewing lessons.

"Eventually, we will hire you a drawing master," Ash said. "But I will order drawing supplies tomorrow."

Bud stroked his long white beard thoughtfully, then he said with a twinkle in his eye that he would build her an easel for painting. He liked to work with wood, so she talked him into building a Christmas stable and carving the figures for a nativity scene.

Lark thought that if she were to judge by her new neighbors, and by Ash's explanation of the spirit of the holiday, that Christmas had surely come early this year.

Over the course of the following week, her husband continued to lecture her in ladylike behavior between visits to his tenants, one thatched roof cottage after another, while she did her utmost to ignore his words.

All the village men seemed to work the Blackburne Chase Estate, all except for the "curmudgeon" of a doctor, Phinias Buckston—Ash called him Buckstubborn behind his back—who also served as apothecary.

Lark was glad the doctor was not in when they stopped, for she wondered how she would face him again after threatening to shoot him in the ballocks if he examined her on her wedding night.

"Basically," she said, during an evening's drive

home, "the village of Gorhambury consists mainly of the Blackburne Estate and its tenants."

Ash looked about him, at his property as far as the eye could see. "Ours is like an old feudal estate that never grew beyond. We have to drive all the way to St. Albans proper, fifteen miles away, to purchase anything of significance that we cannot raise, grow, weave, thatch, or make ourselves." He urged the old farm horses to move faster while the rickety estate wagon bumped them along the rutted dirt road like pebbles in a bouncing pot.

"The original Chase burned down in the sixteen hundreds," Ash said, "and didn't get rebuilt until seventeen-fifty, but the village kept going, barely, until my great-grandfather's family returned to rebuild."

"It must be wonderful to know your family history."

Ash mocked himself with a laugh. "I come from a long line of liars and cheats, men who put themselves first, right down to my father. My mother cautioned me from the cradle that I had a responsibility to turn the tides and not let the villagers flounder again. My father, on the other hand, did not give a flying leap whether the tenants, or my mother, lived or died. And that's the unforgivable truth."

"Will you never forgive him, then?"

"I do not forgive my own failings when I am sincerely sorry for them; why would I forgive my father's, when he was not the least repentant?"

"So you might be described as unforgiving but not suspicious."

"I suppose that is correct, for if I were a suspicious sort," he said with a wink, "I would have approached you with more caution on our wedding night."

Lord, would her sordid past never set her free? And

yet, free she felt, especially when she saw the Chase come into view, as if she were coming to a safe haven, a new and amazing experience when once her only haven had been a loft cot where, for the most part, she escaped her father's drunken customers. But was she safe now? Was she home? Would her unforgiving husband let her stay when he learned how she forced his hand in the card game that united them?

"I have a surprise waiting for you," Ash said as he threw the wagon's reigns to Brinks at the stable. "Actually, 'tis more in the nature of a double surprise."

He covered her eyes with his hands at the base of the curved main stairs. They took a clumsy climb, and turned, not right, but left, at the top. She knew then that he was taking her to her "sitting room," and she hoped he hadn't taken it upon himself to purchase "better" furniture than the rickety old attic pieces she'd fallen in love with and that Bud promised to fix.

But when Ash took his hands away and Lark looked about, she saw in a glance that every piece she wanted had been fixed, polished, and buffed. Even the old curtains she loved had been brought to life and hung from her windows, but none of it, not an inch of her beautiful new sitting room mattered as much as the shy little boy sitting in the needle-worked chair she'd chosen as her own.

"Micah!" she screamed, rushing him, but she was no faster than him as he ran from her, as if he'd sat pinned like a butterfly on wax one minute, and came to life the next.

He seemed too small for a seven-year-old, Lark thought offhandedly as he flew from her reaching arms to huddle in a corner, and too bony by far. We're going to fatten you up, she thought, ignoring the tears spilling from her eyes as she began carefully to approach him. "I am so happy you are come," she said. "Micah, do you remember me?" Though his clothes were clean, as was he, they were old, and as tattered as her own had been.

He was like a small wounded bird and did not seem to know her, but why would he? It had been a year or more since she'd been able to visit him, though she'd paid for his keep regularly, and was shocked to find him in this deplorable malnourished state.

She'd met a number of seven-year-olds among the tenants recently, all better fed and clothed, and when she realized it, she looked at her husband through new eyes and with a new dawning respect as well.

Ash did his own estate management to economize for his tenants' sakes, tenants who ate well and lived in warm, well-kept cottages. So much for his roguish ways, she thought. Perhaps Ashford Blackburne was as much of a fraud to the better, as the family to whom she'd sent money for Micah's board were, to the worse.

"Ash," she said, stopping before Micah when he began to tremble. "This is my nephew, Micah Micah, you may not yet remember me, but I am your Aunt Larkin and his lordship, here, the earl of Blackburne, is my husband. We will see that you are cared for now and neglected no more."

Micah looked at her with surprise, then as silent and wide of eye toward Ash.

Ash rested on his haunches before the boy. "I am pleased to make your acquaintance, Micah, and glad you will be living with us."

Micah said nothing but slid down the wall and closed his arms around his knees, narrowing his small shoulders, as if he could become invisible.

"You will now be living in a very special village," Ash said. "Did you know that Gorhambury is famous?"

Though Micah made no move to show he'd heard, Ash continued. "Father Christmas lives here," he said, hoping the name might evoke some life in a child. "Many of the villagers have actually seen him." Ash regarded Lark. "Does he not know Christmas either?"

"Look at him and tell me why he should." She wiped the tears from her cheeks with her hands.

Ash sighed and rose. "Then it will be up to us to teach him."

"We had best start by showing him that he will eat regularly," Lark said.

They each took Micah by a hand and brought him up to the old nursery that housed more toys than most children would see in a lifetime, more certainly than Micah had ever seen, if he had seen any, Lark thought.

There, Lark was surprised to find Mim waiting as if she knew they were coming.

"Mim has brothers and sisters," Ash said, "and she is willing to sleep in the bedchamber adjacent to Micah's and help you with him whenever needs be."

"Thank you, Mim," Lark said, grateful her nephew would not be alone at night in a strange place, but more so for the look on Micah's face as he fingered one of a regiment of tin soldiers.

"That was my regiment," Ash said, "The Life Guards, the regiment I joined to fight Bonaparte under Wellington's command."

Micah regarded her husband with wide eyes, but not as wide as the look he gave the tray of food that arrived shortly thereafter, which he denuded like locusts in a wheat field.

Lark took several of the tin soldiers and dropped them before Micah in the corner, then she returned to stand beside Ash to watch her nephew.

"When he used to speak, he called me Aunt-eee, as if I were someone special to him," she said.

"How long has it been since he's spoken?"

"As long as a year, perhaps longer. I could not visit all that often. It took me months to gather enough money to make the journey."

"Gather?"

"Da's customers . . . sometimes . . . when I served drinks?"

Ash nodded and Lark breathed easy again.

"At least we know that he *can* talk," Ash said, "though I would feel we made progress, if he did not look so frightened in our presence."

"I agree. Perhaps he needs to understand that he has a home for good. Perhaps when we write that letter to our babies, we should write one for Micah. Could we? I know it would be asking a great deal of you?"

"Asking a great deal? To write a letter?"

"No, not to write the letter, but to abide by the promises in it . . . until Micah is grown."

Chapter 13

Ash regarded the boy he had promised to raise—sleeping now, curled in the corner he had chosen for himself—and determined to ease his life, not because he was a good man, but because Lark had asked him to do so.

He knew his weaknesses well. He was a rogue, pure and simple, quick to place a bet, bed a wench—until he married. He was always quick to spend a guinea. In fact, he was so quick he'd spent the few he had before responsibility came to him. He used to think his lust for drink, women, money, and a good time had saved him after his first jilt. He was certainly looking for all of those distractions when he went to the pub after his second jilt, but he got Larkin Rose instead.

Amazingly, now that he had her, he was beginning to think his consolation prize of a bride might prove to be his salvation, in more ways than the obvious, and frankly, the notion made him skittish. He did not know if he wanted to be saved, but he did not think he could avoid it if he wanted to.

Lark never took for granted what another woman would surely demand. She appreciated every kindness, no matter how paltry or late in coming. Somehow, she served as a mirror and made him see good in his own reflection.

"I will abide by our letter in regards to your nephew," he said to her now, meaning it, as he took the sleeping boy and placed him on the small nursery bed in the next room. He bid Mim keep watch and took his wife's hand to lead toward their own rooms. "I will raise him until he is grown."

Lark stopped walking and stepped into his arms for the first time ever of her own accord, encircled his neck with a freely given embrace, and toyed with the hair at his nape as she offered her lips for his kiss.

Ash accepted her unspoken offer.

"You deserve better than me for wife," she said when he came up for air, "better than a guttersnipe with her sister's misbegotten child in tow—"

"Do not!" Ash snapped. "Do not speak in that way about my family."

Lark followed her husband toward her room. She understood. Ash had his pride. Fine. None would hear the brazen truth from her lips again, but she would still know in her heart, what she was, what Micah was, and she would be sorry until the end of her days for the way she had cheated and trapped Ash into taking them both on . . . well, into taking her on, anyway. Getting him to take Micah had turned into the good that came of her own wicked ways, and for that she would never be sorry.

More than ever, after the gentle way he'd treated Micah, she wanted to tell Ash the truth. More than ever, now that Micah was safe and in Ash's protection at last, she dare not take the chance.

The truth never helped anybody, so her Da often said, and so life had often proved.

"Ash," she said, as she stood by her bed, her stomach quivering at the notion of fulfilling her bargain, of pleasuring her husband, of him pleasuring her, "my monthlies have stopped. We can begin making that baby now if you wish."

"*If?*" Ash's body stood at ready attention. Her words alone had accomplished the deed, though he doubted his sanity in hearing them. Then again, Lark was a prideful woman, a woman true to her word. They had made a bargain—Micah for a babe in her belly, and now she had Micah, 'twas her turn to pay.

Ash almost wished she wanted him as much as he wanted her, another turn that did not fit any previous philosophy in his roguish life. He must be going soft with all this talk of babes, and welcoming little boys with big eyes who needed knowing they had a home . . . and with broken-doll brides who needed knowing they were cherished.

He looked into those doll's eyes now, with every shade of green and gold imaginable, changing from facet to facet, revealing her as vulnerable and intense, giving and wanting.

Did she want him as much as he wanted her?

Ash called himself a fool as he turned her to undo the thousand buttons that must march down the back of her dress. Little bone buttons stuck into littler fabric loops, one by blasted one, Ash undid them, until he was harder than the proverbial rock and as randy as a strutting cock.

"If the act isn't called making love, which ours would not be," Lark said, "what other way can you describe what we are about to do? You never told me."

That fizzled his cock. "You mean, you want to know how to refer to it?"

Lark nodded.

How could he find an expression that would not turn her from baby making forever? "Nothing I tell you can be spoken in company, only when we're alone, do you understand? This act is never, ever discussed other than between a husband and his wife."

"Not even between a man and his mistress, or a trollop and her customer, because we had a few of those at the Pickled Barrel, and now that I think back on it—"

"Forget the inn! I'm talking about now—from now on, all right?"

Lark nodded, looking a little surprised at the tone of his voice. "As you wish."

"Thank you," he said. "You may refer to the act as 'doing the matrimonial.' Now that isn't too shocking, is it?"

"What else?"

Ash wanted to smack his head against the wall. "You would want more. How about we're 'taking a tumble,' or I once heard a Scot refer to it as 'playing the blanket hornpipe,' and then there's plain old 'ballocking.' Your choice m'lady."

"Can't we just call it making a babe?"

Ash barked a laugh and pulled Larkin into his arms. "Making a babe, it is. Let us begin, shall we?"

"I do not know how, precisely, and the only references I have are animals, but I don't like the way dogs and horses do it."

"Can we not simply enjoy getting there," Ash said, "and stop talking about it?"

Lark crossed her stubborn arms as if to protect herself. "If I am worried about something, I need to talk about it."

"All right." Ash clamped a hand to the back of his

neck. "All right. I can see that you do. Fine. Not like dogs or horses. Fine. There are plenty of other ways."

"What are they?"

Ash cursed and apologized. He harrumphed and sighed. "You can lie on your back and I can hover over you."

"No!" she said, with rising panic. "No, I don't want you hovering over me."

"We could do it standing up."

"That would work," she said. "Then we would be equal and you would not be looming over me as if to attack. I could not bear that." She looked around the room. "Where can we stand? Here?" She went to stand against the wall, fully clothed, and closed her eyes, as if she were waiting to be shot, or run through. Er, fine, a near-enough description. Perhaps he understood.

His bride opened her eyes and huffed as if he had been dawdling too long. "Come along, then," she said. "Let's get it done."

"This is so exciting," Ash said, tongue in cheek as he went to stand before her. "It might help if you took off your clothes."

"But this is wrong, that part of you meets my chicken peck."

"Your what?"

"She pointed toward her middle. A chicken pecked me here and gave me a scar."

"Who told you that?"

"My sister, when she was ten."

"Then how do you account for the fact that I have one too?"

Lark shrugged.

Ash sighed. "Can we talk about the chicken peck another time? That's not what it is by the way."

"Fine," she said, and her eyes twinkled.

"You've been trying to distract me," he accused.

"I succeeded, did I not?"

"You little—"

"Is there something I can stand on?" She went to grab a footstool and drag it over. A turtle could have carried it faster on its back. Leaning his palms against the wall, above where his procrastinating bride had just stood, Ash shook his head.

She placed the footstool before him, ducked beneath his arms, and climbed atop it. "There, we'll meet at just the right place now." But when she stepped close enough to make contact, the stool wobbled, and she toppled into his arms. "Not so good," she said as he lifted her higher against him.

"Not so exciting, either," Ash said. "Please, let us get into bed and frolic, as we did in the lavender field the other day, and work our pleasant way into baby-making as we go?"

"Oh, that sounds lovely."

"Lovely," Ash repeated, feeling the knot in his stomach ease. "I believe you have it right."

"You seem tense, Ash. Should we start afresh tomorrow, instead?"

"No, my darling Larkin, we will begin tonight." He stood her on her feet. "Let us start by sliding that dress off your shoulders."

For the past few nights Ash had taken to dreaming about making fast impatient love to Lark one minute and slow patient love to her the next, of exploring her to his heart's content, every delicious milky inch of her, if only she would welcome him.

He'd imagined making her touch the stars in ecstasy,

while he watched her eyes close in pleasure and open in shock to renewed arousal.

As her dress slipped to the floor and puddled at her feet, and she stood before him in her shift and stockings, the intensity in her gaze was enough for him to take her hand and lead her to the bed.

"I am afraid," she said.

"I know, but you need not be." He urged her into the bed, still half dressed, because he was certain that rushing her into nakedness was unwise. "I promise to be a patient teacher," he said.

While she settled herself and watched wide-eyed, he removed his waistcoat and shirt studs, shirt, shoes, and stockings, but nothing more, exactly as he'd planned, and Lark sighed with what he could only imagine was relief.

Lark stopped holding her breath when Ash climbed in beside her and wrapped his arms around her to bring her wonderfully, incredibly, close. She closed her eyes and remembered her dreams of him, years of dreams, where he did exactly this, with no fear on her part, and she let herself slip into the old fantasy. This was Ash. Her Ash.

Her hero. Her husband.

"Now, my wife," he said, in counterpoint to her dream, as he nibbled her earlobe, which she liked very much. "It is time for a gentle teacher and an eager pupil. These are lessons I have never needed to teach before, you understand. No innocent has ever been allowed to climb into my bed. I am a jaded rogue, a cad, a scoundrel, you see, just so you know, but if you tell me what you want, I will try to comply. And if I go too fast or forget your fear, you must promise to remind me. Will you?"

Lark nodded as he came for her mouth with his, his kiss deep and achingly slow. Gentle. Her heartbeat quickened in a surprising response, sending shafts of soft pleasure to every hidden spot within her.

He touched his bottom lip to her upper, urging her mouth to open against his, his breath warm and teasing. In the same coaxing way, he touched his upper lip to her bottom one, and then back again, as if their lips should not meet precisely, which made her ache for them to do just that. All the while he teased her, spirals of something distant and achy, foreign yet delicious, invaded Lark in odd tingling places.

Then he did something amazing: he pulled away from her, sighed, and threw back the covers to reveal his entire breathtaking torso to her view, the tight mound beneath his inexpressibles bringing all manner of imaginings to her mind.

Despite her fears, she could not ignore his manly beauty, even half dressed, like a peacock in his plumes on a silver platter.

"Have your wicked way with me, wife," he said, presenting her with every power and decision.

Wife. Lark's heart warmed as she rose over him, incredulous at his offer, grateful. She knelt and looked down upon his beauty. "Does this mean I can do whatever I please? I can touch you wherever I choose?"

Ash shifted and nodded. "I am yours to command. I will dance or lie still, touch you or not, whatever is your desire, with one exception. We will do the deed tonight, if at all possible. No more putting off to another day."

Lark smiled and placed her palm on his chest. "Tell me then, what is your pleasure?"

Ash groaned as if in anticipation. "I have many pleasures, but I am certain that I will like whichever you choose to administer first. If you would rather I guide you than experiment on your own, I shall, or you can explore at your leisure, every mountain and valley upon me, every muscle and furrow. It is entirely up to you. I am at your disposal . . . exclusively, unequivocally . . . yours."

His husky voice licked desire through Lark in warm gentling laps. She combed her fingers through the mahogany waves at his temple, again and again. She had never dared to touch him in so intimate a fashion.

Ash sighed and closed his eyes as if he liked her touch a great deal.

Emboldened by his reaction, she grazed his cheek, thumbed his chin. Then she smoothed her palm down his chest, scratching ever so slightly against the silken mat surrounding his nipple. She knew a sense of power when he shuddered. "I wanted to do that the first time you got into bed beside me," she confessed.

Ash's heated gaze held hers captive. "I would have let you."

"I wasn't ready."

"And now, Lark? Are you nearly ready to play the blanket hornpipe?"

Lark giggled at his choice of description and surprised herself with a laugh. "Soon," she said, shivering, as he took her hand and slid it down his chest and along his belly. She pulled away from his hold to dip her finger into his chicken peck, and giggled.

Then, when she'd distracted him sufficiently, his brow raised to regard her, she let him begin to guide her hand again, until he slid it toward the placket on his inexpressibles. There he placed it, palm down, to cup his sex.

Heat flowing through her, Lark turned toward the erect parsnip she had left on her dresser as a reminder of her duty. She looked back at his trousers, the parsnip, and shook her head at the disparity. Nevertheless, his sounds of appreciation urging her on, her fingertips skimming the fabric of his trousers, she examined, at her leisure, what seemed for all the world like a living, pulsing entity unto itself.

When Ash's gaze upon her became hot and intense, and when his appreciation turned guttural, and he became harder even than she expected, Lark slipped her hand beneath his trouser flap to cup him and learn his manly secrets.

Knowing full well that she must be prepared to gaze upon her husband's "hornpipe" for the first time, she hesitated even as she held it pulsing in her hand, as if clamoring to be free. With a sense of power, she kneaded it and brought it to larger life. "It is bigger than you led me to believe," she said, her accusation laced with wonder.

Ash chuckled. "I promise you, it is exactly the right size for our purpose."

Lark did not know if she believed him or not; she knew only that she could not for the life of her let him go. She unfastened his trouser flap one-handed, despite the barrage of fearful reservations warring with dreadful anticipation inside her, and lowered the flap to reveal . . . not his hornpipe, but his snowy underlinen, with a similar flap that she had breached.

With a sigh, as much relief as regret, she pulled the drawstring to free him into her waiting hands. As fast as a windup toy, he rose to the occasion and she squeaked in surprise.

Ash arched, groaned, and chuckled all at once, even as he made to reach for her, but Lark reared away from his greedy grasp. "Not yet," she said, and so he grabbed the bedclothes instead, as if he must hold on or fall off the edge of sanity.

"You *will* have your wicked way with me," he said, through clenched teeth, as if she were paining him as she pleasured him. "I spoke true and did not realize."

Lark raised her chin. "I will not be denied. I must have as much time as I require to become acquainted with the hornpipe."

Chapter 14

Ash barked an involuntary laugh. He gasped. He arched and groaned, caught in the wave of bliss Lark wrought with word and action. She cupped his ballocks in one hand—gently, praise be, fear and joy riding him—while she slid her thumb—he thought before closing his eyes and giving himself up to sensuality—upward along his shaft. As if that were not enough, she completed her first amazing foray with small wet titillating circles at his crown, about raising him off the bed.

"Not yet," Ash said, swollen to painful proportions, repeating her order as if to himself, bridling his lust and testing his sanity. And while he prayed her investigation would never end, he teetered so close to the sharp-edged brink of release he thought he'd go mad from the pleasure-laced torment.

"Was that a good groan or a bad groan?" she asked upon his involuntary emission of frustration.

"Better than good," he said.

His teasing bride tilted her head in consideration. "Better than good would be famous."

"Redoubtable."

"Is that bad?"

"Excellent. Please don't stop."

"Do you think that's about as big as it will get?" she

asked stroking him as if testing and considering him from every angle. "It's thicker than you led me to believe, you know."

Ash thought he would weep. "Let us not talk," he said, as tactfully as he could manage, given the nature of his duress. "Touch me again as you did before, Lark. I beg you. Please."

His wife pursed her lips, a sure sign of trouble, then she further unnerved him by raising a brow, and just when panic was about to set in, she jumped from the bed.

Ash cried out at her abandonment, rose on his elbows, aghast, and got a good look at the size and rigidity of his hornpipe. No wonder she'd run—

She was back so fast, he damned near wept with thankfulness.

She took him in her hand again and he fell back to the bed, more grateful than the boy that day in the hayloft.

"You lied to me," she said, and Ash opened his eyes, his appreciation waning.

She held her parsnip against his manhood, root to head, as if to compare them, and the parsnip came off looking enfeebled.

Ash regarded the foolish pair of unmistakably distinct rods, then he regarded his bloody daft bride. That's what you got with a consolation prize of a bride, he supposed—idiocy. Yet her hand closing around his shaft made him feel as if he'd won, not lost the game, as did the expression on her incredibly endearing face, half sad, half dismayed, with a slight tinge of excitement in the deepest depths of her wide burnished eyes.

"Ashford Blackburne, you're too long and too thick

for my peace of mind. What do you have to say for yourself?"

Ash shrugged and tried to look repentant inasmuch as he could, raised on an elbow, his naked hornpipe being played a lusty tune. "I gave you an approximation," he said in his own defense. "I was never called upon to measure it before, and never thought to be so."

One would think he'd wither at this turn of events, except that she had a talent with a circling thumb, did Larkin Rose, that could make a man her slave. And the angrier she got, the better she played him. "Unfair," she stated even as she shot pleasure through him in waves, increasing the very length and width of which she complained.

Ash bit down on a triumphant shout of pleasure and fought to hold his release at bay. "If you but knew it, Larkin, size has the advantage in this instance. If you would let me demonstrate—"

Lark gave him a withering glance, though he would never wither if she kept playing him in this way. That she did not stop sat splendid with him, until she raised a brow and took a loud, blatant, crunching bite off the end of her parsnip.

Discomfort replaced titillation. Ash felt himself go cold, felt the withering of his hornpipe begin. Insecurity replaced surety. "Is that supposed to be symbolic?" he asked, unable to bear the suspense, shriveling now, by God, at an amazing rate. "Because I have to admit that you are frightening me."

Of all the reactions he expected at this juncture— none of them good, given his bride's bloody bruising record for self-defense—he did not expect the secretive grin that transformed her as she tossed the parsnip over her shoulder, and reached for his hornpipe once more. With more enthusiasm than he'd heretofore seen in her expression, she took to playing him like a high-caliber instrumentalist with a love for her music.

Ash groaned and fell back to the bed—palpitating pleasure overcoming racking fear—sure in the knowledge that life with Larkin Rose would never be dull, and that he would forever walk a fine line between both.

Silken-smooth, thick and erect, pulsing power filled Lark, and yet she felt as if she were taming her scoundrel of a husband by the simple act of holding him in the palm of her hands. The slightest quiver of her fingers, the least stroke seemed to make him writhe and moan, curse her and bless her.

Heady, this command she held and wielded, enough to make a baby, she hoped, trying to believe what Ash had said about her sister, for it was consoling to think that Lise might not have suffered pain but rather love in the act. Lark pushed the old illusion of dark aside and looked toward a future bright with possibility as she concentrated on giving pleasure to the man she'd married.

She owed him this, and yes, she owed it to herself as well. She'd dreamed of him for years and now he was hers. "Ashford Blackburne," she said, "earl of Blackburne, you are at my mercy!"

"Be gentle," he said even as he lifted her to straddle him. On all fours she looked down at him, shocked, surprised, in control, as if she might be a threat to him, rather than the opposite, and she reveled in the arrangement.

He pulsed against her thigh, so she moved her leg to stroke him, make him want. . . .

"Take off your shift," he said.

"Take off your trousers," she retorted.

They shed the remainder of their clothing in a fever, barely changing position, her on top, him her captive. Nevertheless, somehow Ash managed to kiss and caress where each inch of her skin became exposed, and as he did, Lark rode a rushing tide of sensation. When her breasts grazed his chest, and when his arousal nestled against her warm and wet exposed center, she knew a moment of terror.

Ash saw, and hesitated, and she thought there couldn't be another on this earth who would stop and wait for a wife's alarm to recede.

"A minute," he said gentling her as she imagined he'd gentle a colt. "It will hurt for a minute, maybe two," he said. "I'm sorry. There may even be blood, as much as a cut finger, a thimbleful, perhaps less I'm told. Lark, you're my first virgin, so I cannot be certain. Will you trust me to take care of you?"

That she was his first anything made her rejoice as she sat towering over him, his eyes intense, alive, his body skimming hers. Skin to skin. Heart to heart?

She felt almost whole. "I have always believed that I could trust only me," she said. "But if I were forced to trust another, a man, you might be that man. It is the best I can give at the moment," she said. "Forgive me."

"Nothing to forgive, but you will understand if I say I have always felt the same about trusting, that I feel the same now, in reverse."

"I am humbled."

"As I." He watched her. "Are you comfortable now?" he asked, even as he began to stroke and ready her to receive him in the way he'd explained. She caressed him in return, readied him as well—not that he needed much preparation. Still, she would never tire of her newfound ability to move him to voice his pleasure.

He impaled her before she expected him to, so she screamed with surprise more than pain, and she tried to move from discomfort, but he held her still. "Shh, my love. It will not hurt for long I am told. I did not expect to hurt you so. I am sorry you must suffer such pain, more sorry than I can say. I would take it upon myself, if I could."

She believed he would. She loved that he stroked her at the base of her spine in tender circular motions, calmed her, and brought her close and kissed her brow, neck, and cheek. He kissed her eyes, wet with the tears she had not known she shed. He crooned to her and made her feel wanted, special, cherished, for the first time that she could recall.

More tears filled Lark's eyes. She blinked them away, angered by her show of emotion. "It . . . I no longer feel uncomfortable, as if I—you are stretching me. Can you feel it?"

"Indeed, I have felt every nuance of your virginity, from that first wild tear, to the amazing sensation of your stretching around me, and though the pleasure I have derived is nothing to any I have ever before known, I find myself humbled anew by your gift."

"Gift?" Lark sat up with surprise. "What gift?"

"Your maidenhood."

"You doubted me. That's why you sent the doctor in."

"I did not know you on our wedding night, Larkin. I had won you in a card game, you will recall, a drunken card game, where half your father's pot landed back in his lap. Do not fault me for prudence."

Lark sighed and raised her chin. "You should have said something, if you knew Da was cheating."

Ash shrugged. "Drunk is *not* prudent. Besides, for all that I was a horse's arse that night, look what I have for my trouble." He bounced her, as if to remind her where she sat. "More than I deserve, I'd warrant." He grinned and raised a hand to pebble a nipple. "Have I taken your mind sufficiently off your pain? We will take a minute more before we continue, shall we, so you may accommodate yourself to my size?"

Lark felt him pulsing inside her, the more for his words. She also felt an answering throb deep in her womb—especially when he touched her breast—as if she craved his seed, as if without her knowledge or co-operation, her body sought to . . . milk him, in an effort to steal it from him.

Lark understood the primitive impulse. She wanted to move, fought Ash's restraining arms, and succeeded in sliding against him. When he took to moving as well, finally, slow and easy, thrusting gently, as if he could not bear remaining still, pleasure came alive for her; it grew like stars awakening, scores at a time blazing to life. As she climbed toward a pinnacle, impossible to reach, she spiraled almost out of control, reaching, reaching. . . .

"Are we making a babe now?" she asked. "When will I know to stop? I feel as if I won't know, as if I never will, but I cannot bear to continue either. What is wrong with me? It is good and it is bad, this strange lethargy that borders on pleasure. Ash, tell me what to do."

He continued to work inside her, touching her in

ways and places that increased her pleasure. "No babe yet," he said, not time to stop ... . yet." His voice grew hoarse and breathless. "Soon—you will know soon when to stop."

"This is a splendid way to make a babe. I did not understand the vigor involved. I did not expect it to be so—"

"Brilliant." Ash moved with greater speed, greater determination. He held her hips and plunged deeper, took her higher, and they seemed to fly together toward the heavens on the back of a shooting star; then the earth fell as if from beneath them, and they toppled, lost themselves in darkness, and came to rest upon some distant alien shore.

In the aftermath, in moonlight, they kissed—sublime kisses made of dreams—her spread atop him like a wilting blanket, heavy of limb, light of heart. Him, slick with perspiration and all but purring. She adored the pleasure-filled sound he made deep in his chest. Contentment. Satisfaction. "Did we make a babe, then?"

Ash stroked the sweat-slick hair from her brow. "Only time will tell, my love."

Lark reared up to regard him but, that fast, her husband had dropped off to sleep. My love, he had called her. Did he mean it? Ashford Blackburne had called her—pub rat that she was—his love. Did he love her? Did she love him? How would she know? Would he teach her that as well?

Did loving mean trusting? Should she make what she had always considered would be the mistake of offering her trust to another, despite what she had told this new husband of hers? She had not given her full trust, praise be, even at a time when she had been more likely ever to give it.

She did not know the meaning of love. She had loved her sister and about died when she died, and she would give her life for Micah's—that was love. What about Ash? She would never be called upon to give her life for his, but she had dreamed of him for years. Was that love in itself? Was pulling him deep inside her a form of love? Or was love this heavy, tender, happy feeling in her chest because he was here? Lark did not know. How could she?

She knew only that when Ash went off on estate matters, she peeked outside every ten minutes hoping to catch sight of his returning. Did one who loved wait, as if for her next breath, for a lover to return? Lark wished she knew someone she could ask.

She awoke a short time later, for the candles were not much shorter, still blanketing him, and wondered if she were not crushing him. When she tried to move to his side, he urged her to remain.

"Lark," he said, closing his arms around her, holding her there. "Do not go. I like you here."

"Let us try for a babe again," she said. "I enjoyed the attempt."

"One way or another, you will be the death of me," Ash replied with a chuckle, kissing the top of her head.

"Did I hurt you?" she asked.

"I am most assuredly not hurt, but more sated than I thought possible. I am, however, no more than flesh and blood and must recover my strength so I may expend it once more."

"When then?"

"Soon," he said with a lazy chuckle before drifting back into sleep.

Lark remained where she was, a smile on her face. "I enjoyed my first lesson," she whispered into his sleep-warm neck, "and I am eager for another."

"Mmm," he said, mumbling something about his superiority to parsnips.

Lark smiled and memorized every chiseled feature of his face with her gaze, loving each angle, moon-kissed and handsome as sin, a rogue, yes, her very own. She guessed he had been since she was eleven.

As if he felt the intensity of her study, he took to nuzzling her neck, then her breast, then he suckled her greedily, which Lark could happily allow for days, until her hand found that his hungry hornpipe had surged back to life despite his earlier assurances that she had done him in.

"Time to try again," said she, mounting her favorite stallion.

Chapter 15

They woke at dawn to find Micah setting kindling in the hearth like the lowliest of servants. "Oh no," Lark said, which made the boy start and scurry into the corner.

When Ash slipped into his trousers and approached her nephew, Micah covered his head, as if Ash might strike him. "No, little one," he said. "I will not hurt you," and Lark thought she might find herself falling a little bit in love with her husband after all.

Unable to go to her nephew, for she lay naked beneath the bedcovers, Lark wept for seeing his fear. She became angry as well at the family who had kept him, especially after all the money she had put into his care, only to see that he'd not been kept at all well.

Ash lifted Micah in his arms and carried him to the window. He pointed out the ghost walk, the spinney, the orchard, the bridge over the lake, the lavender field—all the places on an estate a boy might like to explore.

"Lark," Ash said. "He is trembling in my arms. I will take him to my room while you wash and dress, but I think he needs a woman's touch."

Lark dressed and went for him in short order. Ash now wore a shirt as well as his trousers, and he held

Micah by the hand, as he showed him bauble after worldly bauble that had been purchased in his father's time.

Micah no more fought her, when she lifted him into her arms, than he had fought Ash, which made her fear that he had been beaten into submission over the years. Despite taking him to her heart and kissing him, her nephew remained stiff and unyielding. "I will take him back to the nursery," she told Ash, who regarded her as if he saw and understood her sadness.

Ash kissed her brow. "I must wash and dress, see to some estate matters, then I will find you up in the nursery."

"Go and see your mother," she said. "Take her hand, kiss her brow."

In response to her urging, Ash shook his head and turned toward the dressing room, giving her a wave without looking back.

Lark carried Micah up the nursery stairs. "You are not a servant in our house, Micah," she said. "You are family." She sang the lullaby she used to sing to him when he was a child, but though he looked straight into her eyes, he made no sign of recognition.

Mim bobbed Lark a curtsey when she arrived. "The boy slept well enough, my lady, but when he woke, he was afraid. I'm that sorry he got away after his breakfast and bath. I looked and looked, and couldn't find him anywhere, until I went to tell his lordship, who had him in his care."

Lark shook her head as much at a loss as the maid. "No need for apologies. I fear he is acting on years of training." Lark intended to take Micah on her lap in the nursery rocker, then she thought better of it and decided he should learn to play again. She took his hand.

"Come along, Micah," she said. "Do you remember when you were three and we climbed a tree at the Stewart's farm? And then we chased chickens around the barnyard?"

He walked silently by her side and Lark could see that he was listening.

"When you were five and I visited, we went for a walk and found a neighbor who had a good sturdy swing, a rope suspended from a tree with a wooden seat. Do you remember that I pushed you on it?"

Micah stopped and looked up at her, as if seeing her for the first time, and Lark nodded. "We once made a slide of hay. Another time, we rode a pokey old farm horse together, remember? I am sorry I was not able to visit at all last year."

Lark stopped at the top of the main stairs with its sweeping polished banister, the wood flat and wide, perfect for sliding, which she had noticed her first night.

Lark sat on it, and Micah took a fearful step back, before she pushed herself off. She gasped as she slid down its length, for she had forgot what she'd been about all night.

As she expected, the shape of the rail all but placed her gently on the foyer floor. "Go ahead, Micah. Your turn," she called. "Remember what I taught you? Never be afraid to try something new."

"A pity you did not remember that advice previous to last night," her husband said beside her, making her start and shriek.

Micah was on his way down before they realized it, as Grimsley walked by, dropped his tray at the sight, and nearly swooned from fright.

"It's all right Grim," Ash said. "There's no better

banister for sliding. I rode it often in my youth." Ash caught Micah at the bottom and whipped him into Grimsley's arms. "Grim, old man. You're taking young Micah, here, to visit Cook and have a glass of milk before his next slide."

Ash took Lark's arm, walked her into the green salon, and sat beside her on the sofa. "You have tears in your eyes," he said taking her hand. "Because Micah does not remember you?"

"No, not that." She shook her head. "I think he might be starting to remember some of the things I reminded him of. The tears are for—" She bit her lip.

"What?" Ash dabbed at the corner of her eye with his handkerchief.

Lark took it and blew her nose. "I cannot tell you."

"Do not play coy with me," Ash said. "You *will* tell me. After baby-making, and giving you a sling for your monthlies, I hardly think there is anything we cannot discuss."

Lark grimaced and plopped his used handkerchief into her husband's hand. "If you must know, I wish I had not slid down the banister on the morning after so much baby-making. It hurt. There."

Her husband could not contain his mirth, which Lark found annoying. "Thank you very much," she snapped. "Try sliding down the banister on your hornpipe and see how you feel!"

Ash was still chuckling over the last when Grimsley returned Micah to Lark's care.

"Micah needs new clothes," Ash said, touching a hand to the boy's shoulder. "What do you say to having Olga make him some?" Ash asked, as if hoping the boy would respond, but he remained silent and wide-eyed, looking from one adult to the other.

" 'Twould be the first time he's had clothes of his own," Lark said. "Can you thank . . ." She regarded her husband. "Uncle Ash?"

Ash nodded, but Micah simply stepped nearer to Lark.

"I shall stop and ask Olga on my rounds today," Ash said. "Micah," he added, "I need to take a ride about my estate this morning, and thought you might like to sit up before me on my horse and see your new home."

"I am afraid of horses," Lark said, as Micah's head came up and he looked straight and attentive toward Ash.

"I did not ask you to accompany me," Ash said with a wink for her, "I asked Micah."

"I am afraid for him to go with you."

"Are *you* afraid, Micah?" Ash asked.

The boy shook his head, stepped from behind Lark's skirts, and slipped his hand into Ash's.

"Lark," her husband said, "I suggest a nice, long soak in my slipper bath for, er, whatever ails you, and then I am afraid that, later in the morning, your dancing master is due to arrive. Forgive the poor timing." He winked and Lark chafed in annoyance. Nevertheless, she turned to leave the salon and head for the slipper bath, an excellent notion, actually.

Halfway there, she stopped to regard her amused husband. "I suppose if Micah likes to ride that I should like to have riding lessons as well."

"See Brinks, then, after your dancing lesson." He chuckled at his poor jest. "I will tell Brinks to expect you in, say, *three* days time, shall I?" Grinning, Ash squeezed Micah's hand and led him out and toward the stable.

Lark was not sorry that Micah had taken to Ash; she was only sorry that he had not as yet remembered her.

Her fop of a dancing master lasted two dreadful, horrible weeks of mincing lessons by day, but two glorious, unforgettable weeks of baby-making by night. Lark remembered it well, both the good and the bad.

"What do you mean, he broke his foot?" Ash shouted on the dancing master's fourteenth, and last, day, as the dance instructor was carried to a hired coach.

"It was an accident," Lark said in her own defense.

Ash scoffed. "How so?"

"I did not intend to hurt him."

"He said you stomped on his foot with your heel in a fit of rage."

"Well, I did stomp on his foot—in self defense—but I did not expect the bone to break. How was I to know that dandies had bones as soft as their hands?"

"Doctor Buckston said you broke several of the bones in his foot. He quit you know. Gave his notice and demanded his wages and passage to London as well."

"The doctor quit? Because I threatened to shoot him in the ballocks?"

"No, dearest, the dancing master quit, and I wonder you did not threaten *his* ballocks."

"Hah, I'd be surprised if the popinjay had any. Besides, you took my pistol, remember? I had no other weapon at my disposal. I hope you did not give in to his demands. He taught me nothing of value, except that damp hands leave stains on silk."

"And that foot bones are brittle, I'd wager. Now how do you expect to learn to dance?"

"You may teach me."

"I do not suppose I have a choice," Ash said. "If you are half as incomparable a dancer as Brinks says you are a rider, I expect you will do me proud enough."

"High praise." Lark sniffed, annoyed at the paltry compliment. "It upsets me that riding is so much a man's sport," she said. "Why do I excel at only manly sports? Why can I not dance a step or sew a stitch?"

"I could get Gentleman Jackson to teach you to box," Ash said, tongue in cheek. "Then again, who would you thrash, if you learned, but me? Overlook the suggestion, if you please. 'Twas a terrible notion."

"As my husband, you were supposed to say that you do not understand why I excel in manly sports since I am so soft and womanly."

Ash leaned close. "You are prodigiously soft and womanly when you are wearing the dress God gave you and riding your prized stallion—and I do not mean the one in the stable."

Lark felt heat on her face and turned away. "How many other women have you attempted to make a babe with?"

Ash barked a laugh. "Not a single one."

"You admitted that I was your first virgin, but you have done that before, have you not?"

"What, play the blanket hornpipe? Good God, of course I have."

"But you said 'twas to make a babe and you never tried to make one before."

"You can do the matrimonial without making a babe, Larkin."

Determined to tease her way back into her husband's good graces after her assault upon the dancing master, Lark shrugged. "Yes, I know, but why would anyone set out to do so?"

Ash gaped. "Have I read you wrong? Have you received no pleasure in making love? If you have not, I shall lay me down and die of shame."

Lark smacked him in the arm, though she did note that he referred to the act as making love, and held the knowledge close. "Doing the matrimonial *is* an agreeable pastime," she admitted, surprised he had not caught her jest.

"Just agreeable?"

"Delightful then?"

"It is splendid, you have said more than once, which is why people do it for sport."

"Sport, of course. That would account for Trixie at the Pickled Barrel."

"I beg you will *please* remove that pub from your memory."

"I lived in that pub for twenty-two years, Ash. It will never be gone from my memory, only distanced, and now that I think on it, I remember Da referring to a bit of 'ballocking' going on above stairs. Is ballocking also considered a man's sport?"

"Not my favorite term," Ash said, "and not entirely a man's sport, but for the most part, I'd wager it likely is."

"Drat! Another man's sport I like." Lark raised her hands in resignation as she walked away, leaving Ash to hope that since she liked it so much, she might rescind her rule that he quit her bed once he got her with child.

"What the devil?" Ash got shoved from behind and was forced to regain his balance, only to find that his bride had returned to accost him.

"I just realized what you had been doing with all

your women these many years. *That's* why they call you a rogue!"

Ash grinned, unable to hide his pride in the designation, despite his wife's ire.

"I do not approve," she said.

"I only do it with you now. There are no more women."

"I *am* a woman!"

"Thank the stars." Ash took his "woman" into his arms and kissed her. "I meant that I no longer play the blanket hornpipe with women *other* than you. I will keep me only unto you for as long as we both shall live."

"You will? Do you promise?"

"I did promise. So did you, by the way. If another man touches you, I shall break his arms."

"I might like that you would be jealously brutal on my behalf, except . . . how many women have you tumbled? I can break arms as well, you know."

Oh he knew. Ash raised his eyes to the heavens. "Forget numbers and think of my past as the practice that allows me to come so accomplished to your bed."

Lark was having none of it. "How many women, Ash?"

"I failed to count."

"Too many to count, you mean."

"If I gave you a number, Lark, it would matter naught, for you refuse to learn your numbers, except for the ones on a deck of cards."

She huffed. "I will begin my lessons tomorrow."

"You will begin when the tutor arrives. I will not teach you myself, for I will not have *my* foot broken, no, nor anything else, come to that. I will write and inform the schoolmaster that we are ready to retain his services. He will arrive as soon as may be, and you will not attempt to bolt, mind, nor will you break one bone in the poor man's body, or knee, or shoot him either."

Lark rolled her eyes. "He shall remain intact."

"And you will give your lessons due attention? No more bolting?"

"Why would I bolt when there is such baby-making to be had?"

"Wise girl." Ash tapped her nose. "Besides, I would miss you if you ran."

Lark stood on her toes and whispered her suggestion for a clandestine trip to the lavender field for an extra go at baby-making.

Ash rubbed her nose with his. "In the middle of the day? I am shocked," though he was tempted to say yes, until he saw Micah running their way.

Ash opened an arm to the boy, aware that during his weeks with them, Lark's nephew had taken more to his company than to Lark's, and how sad Lark appeared when Micah demonstrated the preference. While she must be glad Micah finally had a father figure in his life, she must hurt for the loss of kinship she had expected would grow between the two of them.

A hand upon Micah's shoulder and an arm about his wife's waist, Ash squeezed them both. "Shall we take the wagon and escape to the spinney for a lazy-day picnic? I am certain the tenants can dig the drainage ditches well enough without my interference for one afternoon."

As Lark looked set to agree, a bottle-green coach appeared, clattering up the drive, and stopped beneath the porticoed main entrance of the Chase. Ash released his grip upon his family to make his way toward the coach as the driver jumped from his perch and opened the door.

No sooner had he done so, than out flew a cursing wild-child, who ran past them as if running for his life.

"What is the meaning of this?" Ash demanded of the coachman who handed him a small, grimy fragment of parchment.

Ash read the note to himself, in the event it contained something upsetting. *Take her, Ash. Take our daughter and raise her*— There the parchment had been torn. Above the astonishing request was also written the better portion of his name, title, and address. Ash, fortunately, or unfortunately, recognized the handwriting.

The coachman then handed him a more formal note, of a high-quality, Bristol-type vellum, properly folded, of the excellence his father had been wont to use:

The termagant was found on the London streets carrying this piece of parchment. Since I am your family solicitor, the authorities brought her to me. I send her in the event you plan to honor the note-sender's anonymous request. If not, put her back in the coach and my driver is instructed to take her to the nearest workhouse.

Yours, MJC, Esq.

"She is Ellenora's daughter," Ash said. "My first jilt." He offered Lark both the parchment and the solicitor's note. "Unlike the solicitor who sent her to us, I recognized Ellenora's handwriting."

"Should we not send her back to Ellenora, then?" Lark said, accepting the notes.

"Ellenora died in France. I have known for . . .
nearly a year now."

"Why would someone send her to us then?"

Ash sighed. "Read the parchment," he said as he
urged the coachman toward the rose garden to confer
with him in private.

Ten minutes later, Ash dismissed the driver, rubbed
his neck, and looked out toward the spinney. He saw
Lark and Micah approach.

"The coachman carried no more than the notes and
the girl," Ash said. "The child owns naught but the
rags on her back."

"We must find her. She is frightened."

"Yes," Ash said, touching Lark's arm. "Yes."

"*Is* she yours, Ash?"

Chapter 16

Had Ellenora borne him a child? There was a question, one his wife wanted answered as much as he did, and who could blame her? "I must make inquiries," Ash said. "There are people in London, friends of Ellenora's, who might know, or a certificate of birth, perhaps, or parish registry to be unearthed."

Ash rubbed his neck. "I expect she married Ames to give the child a name, which would explain the speed of her jilt, at least. As to whether the child is mine . . ." Ash shook his head with regret. "I would not have thought it possible, and yet . . ." He shrugged. "I am sorry, Lark, but it *is* possible, though I would rather not foist upon you an unwanted—"

Lark crossed his lips with a gentle finger. "What did you say about the way I spoke of your family? That frightened little one could well be the newest member."

He should have known she would open her heart to a guttersnipe, to any child, he suspected.

"Do you know what became of Ellenora's husband?" she asked.

"Killed in a dual shortly after her death, in questionable circumstances, I heard. Seems she had taken a lover—nothing new for Ellenora—and her husband found out." Ash took Lark's arm. "Come, we must fetch the wagon." He reached for Micah's hand.

His gentle wife took her nephew's other hand to walk beside them to the stable. "Micah," she said. "You may no longer be the lone resident of the nursery. Will you like company?"

Micah shook his head vehemently, a sign that he heard and understood, Ash thought. Although it appeared that Lark was so pleased he did, she failed to take into account the significance of his negative response, which did not bode well for tranquility in the nursery.

Ash urged the aging pair of draft horses faster toward the spinney. "Any more unexpected arrivals of the infant variety and I will feel as if I am in competition with Reed and Chastity Gilbride St. Yves and their brood."

"Are the St. Yveses friends of yours? How many children do they have?"

"I fought with Reed under Wellington and was his groomsman when he married Chastity, but I'm sorry to say that I've lost count of their numbers, though I do know they're expecting their first any day."

"But you just said—"

"They take in abandoned children and make them their own, or Chastity did, and Reed had no choice but to join the ranks."

"Why did he have no choice?"

"Because he fell top over tail in love with the lot of them."

Ash and Lark regarded each other over Micah's head, saying everything and saying nothing. Lark kissed Micah's crown, and Ash followed suit, wondering if there weren't a bit of that kind of falling going on around Blackburne Chase. But he wasn't certain, not even of himself, though he clung to hope as much as he shunned it, and he surmised it likely, from Lark's speaking glance, that she hoped and feared for their future in the same bewildered way.

"Quite the interesting life I gambled us into, is it not?" Ash said.

"Interesting," Lark responded, tilting her head in tought, "but certainly not the worst situation I've ever found myself in. Not yet."

Ash looked up from driving the wagon, to her, and back, twice, not certain of her precise meaning, not certain he cared to know it yet at any rate. "Right."

The wild child was a disgrace, a she-wolf angry with the world, hair chopped as if self-cut with a dull blade, and she smelled worse than Lark on their wedding night. She fought them in the spinney for half an hour, Micah standing to the side, in total disgust.

Ash and Lark cornered and caught her halfway up a cherry tree. When they got her down, Lark tried to hold and calm her, but she bit Lark a good one, and to Ash's shock, Micah roared his disapproval, charged forward in Lark's defense, and shoved the she-wolf to her bottom in the dirt.

"Micah!" Ash and Lark shouted as one, but as they regarded each other, Ash could see the grin Lark suppressed, for her nephew had taken a first step toward speaking, not to mention the fact that he'd taken her side for the first time ever.

They got the girl back to the Chase under necessary

constraint in the wagon bed. Lark tried but could not keep the struggling brat in her arms, so she simply sat beside her, stroking her matted thatch of raven hair.

Micah sat up on the wagon seat beside Ash, as he had done on the way to fetch the termagant, and it seemed to Ash as if Micah retained his role as Lark's protector, for he kept looking over his shoulder as if he might jump to her rescue if needed.

Back at the Chase, Ash once again called for a bath, and Lark once again fought him on it. "No, get her up to the nursery. We will not frighten her witless on her first night," she said. "No telling how long she's been left on her own. If I lived like an animal with a father and a roof over my head, this one's like to be ready, after living on the London streets, to do injury in self-defense, or even for food. Mim, have Cook prepare her a meal, would you?" Lark asked, as Ash deposited the girl in her arms in the rocker.

Lark struggled to keep the child there while Ash stood before them, arms behind his back. "What shall we do with her?"

"Do with her? We will keep her, of course."

They turned as one to a crash and roar from Micah, no longer watching from the side but staring at his bleeding hand. Judging by the broken window and glass beside him, and the startled look on his face, he had surprised even himself by shoving his fist through the glass.

Ash ascertained that the cut was minor and turned the boy over to Mim for bandaging when she returned with the termagant's food; then he temporarily sealed the small broken pane of glass with a nursery book wedged into the spot.

However needless Micah's jealous drama, it actually

served to tame the wild child, Ash thought, for it had taken her attention from her fear, and she had settled against Lark to watch.

"How old do you think she is?" Ash asked as he completed his task at the window and moved the plate of food to the nursery table.

"Micah is seven and they are about the same size, though he is small for his age, so she might be five or six, perhaps. I should think you could better tell me."

His wife had raised a speaking brow, which managed to tighten Ash's cravat, and he warmed, despite himself. "If the note's claim is true, then she is likely about six years old."

As avariciously as the girl eyed the plate of steak and kidney pudding, she would not move from Lark's arms to come for it when Ash invited her. "I told Mim to bring meat," he said to Lark. "Is this all right?"

"I would likely have chosen something easier on her empty stomach like porridge or custard, but I'd wager she would prefer meat, if she were of a mind to say so."

"Do you think we should give her a name?" Ash asked. "It seems wrong to speak so rudely about her when she is sitting right here."

Lark smoothed the girl's tattered hair from her brow. "And she is likely understanding every word we say. You would not care to tell us your name, would you, dear?"

When no answer was forthcoming, Lark looked to him to provide a name, and again Ash felt himself flush. He was finding this newfound fatherhood business rather awkward in his bride's eyes.

Ash cleared his throat and raised his chin, determined to reclaim his dignity. "She is from France, so it is possible that she does not understand, though she must have learned some English on the London streets, depending upon the length of time she was there, I suppose. Let us call her 'Chere' for the nonce. It means 'dear' in French and it might be of some comfort to her. What do you say?"

"I thought you might name her for her mother," Lark said, not quite meeting his gaze, somewhat paler for the discovery of his possible daughter, if he did not miss his guess, and he was sorry for it. Hurting her had never been his intention.

That the very notion, and the possible reason, set his heart on end, disturbed Ash, for it likely meant he cared more than he should. If Lark felt unwarranted resentment toward his first jilt, because they might have produced a child, did that mean Lark cared too much as well?

Ash supposed some jealousy made sense, for Larkin herself had not as yet given him a child, and he should set her at ease over the matter, providing he discovered a means to accomplish it.

"Chere," she said, speaking softly to the girl, "are you hungry? Would you like something to eat?"

Micah took up the plate, as if to help, and the girl screeched like a banshee, so startling the boy that he nearly dropped it.

Ash caught it, setting Micah free to shoot a look of pure disgust the girl's way. When Ash offered her the plate, she shoveled the food into her mouth like one long-starved, and so fast that not a morsel was lost or left behind.

The revelation of her hunger brought Micah closer. It seemed even to soften his resentful stance.

"Should I fetch more?" Ash asked Lark, feeling the

same foreign paternal ache he had felt when he first sat Micah upon the horse before him.

"I fear that if she eats too much too fast, she will make herself ill," Lark said. "I believe I will just rock her for a few hours, before we feed her again, until she becomes comfortable in my presence."

"Hours?"

His stubborn bride raised her chin. "Or days. However long it takes for her to know she is safe and wanted."

Micah took several steps closer, until he stood expectantly before Lark.

Sensing her nephew's need, Lark took him on her other knee, but the girl stretched out before Micah could settle himself, as if there were no more room.

Micah pushed Chere aside.

Chere shoved Micah in return.

"Stop it, both of you," Lark said, "before I set you on the floor and abandon the battling pair of you." She appealed silently to her husband as the two in her lap continued their minor skirmish.

Ash raised his hands, as if they held no answers, the amusement in his eyes, at once annoying and charming. He turned and left the nursery, abandoning her with the scrabbling duo, while failing to stifle his chuckle on his way out, the rogue.

It took four days before the wild child let Mim take a turn holding her, and that only lasted long enough for Lark to see to her personal needs. Still dirty, the girl slept and ate in turn, always in Lark's lap. She knew how to use the chamber pot, but Lark had to remain with her or she would screech like an owl at midnight.

She disliked above all things, seeing closed doors,

using eating utensils, and sharing Lark's lap with Micah. It took two days before Lark realized the frightened child had slipped a butter knife into the sleeve of her tattered shirt.

Neither she nor Micah had as yet uttered a word, though the growls they tossed at each other seemed filled with significance.

By the fourth day, Lark feared she smelled as bad as the girl, and she didn't like the sensation one bit. As a matter of fact, she hated it and could not for the life of her remember how she had survived life in the pub for so many years without going mad.

That was the day Lark made up her mind that life in the nursery would change and fast. "Chere," she said, "One or both of us will be bathed before this day is done."

Lark made certain that Ash took Micah with him for the day, and then she ordered the slipper bath brought to the nursery.

"You may have your bath first, if you wish?" Lark told Chere, but she mulishly refused to respond or budge from Lark's lap.

"Well then I am having mine," Lark said rising from the rocker. She placed the girl in the chair, and began to disrobe before the steaming tub. Though the child watched Lark undress and climb into the bath, with no small amount of wistful interest, she refused to place even a finger into the water.

Lark closed her eyes and luxuriated vocally in her bath, expressing her enjoyment in a specific effort to persuade Chere of its benefits.

Finally, she heard a sound that made her think the girl had stood, and come closer.

"Where's the boy?"

Lark screamed at the shock of sound, opened her eyes, and sat up so fast that suds streamed from her hair and into her eyes. When she cleared them, the girl stood staring down at her, as if she had not just broken a four-day silence.

Chere remained so still that Lark could not credit what she had just heard. "What did you say?"

"Where's the boy?"

Progress, Lark thought, but she must proceed warily so as not to break the thin thread of trust her words revealed. "His name is Micah and he is with my husband, off on estate matters for the day. They left us to bathe in peace."

"I used to bathe."

"Then you remember how good it feels to be clean?"

"My mother used to rock and sing to me, like you do."

And what could she say to that? Lark wondered.

At her silence, the girl looked away, but not before Lark caught the sheen of tears in her eyes.

"Your mother sent you to us," Lark said. "Is that not correct?"

The girl regarded her then, allowing her tears to flow freely. "She was ill for a very long time."

"I am sorry to hear it. I miss my mother as well, though she died at my birth and I never knew her."

The girl sniffed, wiped her nose on a filthy sleeve, and gave a half smile, despite her tears. "I knew mine."

"Yes, and you are where she wanted you to be."

"Which is not so bad as I supposed."

Lark chuckled. "I will accept that as a compliment.

Are you feeling as itchy and uncomfortable as I was, and are you ready for a bath and clean hair again?"

The girl shrugged and played with the edge of the rug with the toe of a torn boot.

"Let me finish rinsing my hair," Lark said. "Then Mim can fetch some fresh hot water. Can you tell me your name?"

Chere raised her chin in a show of pride, and Lark was certain she would reject both the bath and the question, but she shrugged as if it made no matter. "Are you *really* going to keep me?"

"We don't know, yet, if we have the legal right, but we would like to."

"Could I have any name I wanted?"

Lark thought about that for a minute and knew the child's comfort in their home must be uppermost in their minds. "Yes, I suppose you could, though it would help us to know your true name, so we could attempt to arrange for you to remain with us."

"Though my real name is not the name I have been using, I was christened Ashley Briana."

Oh God, she had been named for Ash. Lark felt herself go cold, though she covered her shock for the child's sake. "A beautiful name," Lark said, seeking purchase in a careening world. "What name have you been using and what would you choose to be called now?"

"Brian."

"But that is a boy's—"

Snapping eyes, a raised chin. "I know."

Ah, Lark thought, and hadn't she herself remained disguised as a boy half her life for the sake of self-protection? Lark took the child's grimy hand in hers as they regarded each other, nothing hidden between them, and that's when Lark lost her heart. "You are safe here, Brian. We will keep you safe."

Brian retrieved her hand and looked away again, as if the promise were of no matter, but Lark knew how much she wanted to believe it, though she would not dare. Oh Lark knew. She cleared her throat. "And your last name?"

"Fairhaven, like the man my mother married, though I have been known on the streets only as Brian, which suited me."

Lark understood that her boy's name and clothing could well serve the same purpose Lark's had, especially in such horrid holes as homeless children tended to congregate in London. But why did she not even refer to the man her mother married as her father? It was all so confusing, yet the girl was too young to quiz on such a delicate matter.

Lark found herself nervous of a sudden over the responsibility of raising a girl. A girl in boys' clothes could be well-met and understood. But when the time came that Brian turned back into Ashley Briana—if the day ever arrived—how would Lark manage to mother a female child when she knew nothing of the ilk? Rat's whiskers, Ash new more about feminine fripperies than she ever would.

"We will need to have new clothes made for you, Brian, so you must tell me if you wish to have boys' clothes or girls'."

Brian sighed. "Boys' clothes, please."

Lark nodded, unsurprised, and made quick work of finishing so Brian could bathe.

The girl needed no help to undress, but tears filled her doe's-eyes as Lark scrubbed the grime off her bony little arms. "Am I hurting you?" Lark asked.

"No. It feels nice to be clean after so long."

"How long were you forced to survive on your own?"

"Forever," she said, as if wistfully looking back in time. "I do not know how long."

"Through this full spring just passed?" Lark asked. "Or only for part of it?"

"There was snow on the ground when the carriage Mama's servant sent me to London in went off the road and ended in a ditch, and a painted lady and rich gentleman found me walking and took me to London in their carriage."

Oh God. "Were you with them all this time?"

Brian shook her head and dutifully ducked to rinse her hair. "For a while, I had a corner by their kitchen fire to sleep, which was better than some, until the gentleman frightened me and I ran. Then I found children my own age and shared their cellar. If one of them had not knocked me into the path of the man chasing him, I would never have ended here."

"I hope you feel as if he did you a favor?"

The girl shrugged, reserving judgment, and Lark understood.

"This is where Mama wanted me to be," Brian said, as if accepting her fate.

The girl made no fuss when Mim brought out a clean pair of Micah's clothes for her to wear after her bath, and when she finished dressing, she herself tossed her filthy old rags on the fire.

"Tell me about your man," Brian said getting back into Lark's lap, sleepy after her bath. "My mother said there was a man who loved her and would love me. Is your man the one who loved my mama? My real name is like his, is it not?"

Lark stilled while her blood felt as if it left her body. "I . . . do not know if my husband is the man who loved your mama," she said, rocking again, "but your mama's note was addressed to him."

"Is he a good man?"

"Yes, Lark said. He is. Micah is my nephew, you see, but my husband takes very good care of him."

"The boy hates me."

"And you love the boy?"

Brian made a rude noise that made Lark laugh and bring her close.

"Are you going to keep the boy too?" Brian asked on a sleepy yawn. "What does he call you?"

Micah doesn't call me anything, anymore, Lark thought, because he hasn't yet spoken a word. "You may both call me Auntie," she suggested, or Mama, she dared not.

Chapter 17

Once Brian had begun talking, there was no stopping her. She not only spoke for herself, but for Micah as well, except that Micah did not always like what Brian said on his behalf, which made him angry and turned him into a handful of a normal little boy. Lark was as grateful, and entertained, as she was frustrated by her bickering children.

Ash taught them a great deal about the estate and often took one or both of them with him on his rounds.

Brinks taught them to ride.

Grimsley could most often be found teaching them manners.

Lark took them to visit Ash's mother for fifteen minutes every morning, holding her hand and speaking to her mother-in-law as if the frail old woman understood. Lark called her Mother and encouraged the children to call her Grandmother.

Lark took the children on playful adventures throughout the estate. In the spinney, they pretended to be explorers, lost in the trees and brush. They played hide-and-seek among the farm sheds, the buttery, the root cellar, and dovecote. They ran through the ghost walk as if chased by ghosts, played tag in the lavender field, and climbed trees in the orchard. On rainy days, they made lavender sachets, as Cook had taught them, played war with Ash's tin soldiers, or held banister races in the foyer.

Lark had Olga teach her how to sew Brian a rag doll and after she completed it, Brian took to playing house like a normal little girl, though Micah hated that game as much as any normal little boy.

Sometimes the resentment between them vanished, and Brian and Micah played like reasonably well-behaved children, but other times Brian would turn wild again. She cut a fence and stole a chicken from a tenant for no good reason, and only got caught when she let the squawking bird loose in the kitchen and politely asked Cook to roast it.

In early June, Bud St. Nick caught both children swimming naked in the lake. They had tied Mim to a nearby tree to get free. Brian admitted talking Micah into joining her in a cooling swim, while Micah admitted to ambushing Mim.

But nights were for her and Ash and baby-making.

"You would think that Micah would be a good influence on Brian, rather than her being a bad influence on him," Ash said one night as he turned Lark to undo the buttons down her dress.

"I do not even care," Lark said. "I am happy to see Micah play like a child, even a naughty one, for the first time in his life."

"Well, I'd be pleased if Brian didn't cause any more damage to my tenants' property."

"At least she doesn't scream the house down when I leave her to come to bed at night anymore." Brian had finally accepted that Mim was there for her at night and that Micah slept just across the nursery, and Lark was grateful that she and Ash had been able to resume their baby-making.

"Are you certain you still want to have a baby?" she asked as she climbed into bed with him, for she'd had a particularly difficult day with the children.

"Have you changed your mind then about how much you enjoy playing the blanket hornpipe?" he asked, as he touched her in such a way as to make her yearn.

She gave his body the same studied attention. "Not in the least, but I have discovered of late that children are a great deal of trouble, or haven't you noticed?"

"Oh, what kind of trouble?"

He was paying more attention to her body now than to her words. "They're both stubborn little tricksters, always into one scrape or another. If it isn't fighting like wildcats with each other, it's skinning knees or breaking something of value in the house, not to mention tearing their clothes and cussing like sailors."

Ash laughed and rose above her. "They are, both of them, exactly like *you*." He kissed her nose.

Lark gasped in outrage, and then she gave him a prideful grin. "Really?"

"Really," Ash said. "Let us make another."

Lark could do nothing, of course, but agree.

When the tutor finally arrived, Brian, Micah, and Lark, together, became his pupils. He was to teach them reading, writing, and numbers.

A prig of a miserable old schoolmaster, he looked down his nose at Brian's name, at Micah's silence, and at Lark's own advanced age. He chided her often and told her she was stupid compared to the children, which Lark could forgive, because it was true. She was his dunce, said he daily, and he made her wear a cone of a cap on several occasions just to prove it.

Micah was his brightest pupil. The man said Micah might have been his star pupil if he could only talk. Lark often wanted to use her knee on the prig where it counted most.

Brian was his constant interrupter, and when he called her on it, he sneered at what he called her "masculine" clothes. So what if the girl wasn't ready to wear dresses, yet? Lark could understand. Why not ignore the clothes on her back and get on with their lessons?

Unfortunately, Brian felt the schoolmaster's disdain, and when the man pointed out a word in her reading book that she'd read incorrectly—by tapping it with his ink-stained finger more times than was bearable, even to Lark—Brian swooped down, bit the offending digit, and promptly gagged.

He might have forgiven that transgression and forgotten the incident. But a few weeks later, when in the course of his incessant searching for his spectacles, the prig broke a bladder of ink someone had slipped into his claret frock coat pocket; he lost his temper, and when Brian giggled, he went for her in a rage with a strap.

Lark hit him with a chair to stop him from hurting Brian, and Ash dismissed the tetchy tutor without a reference. The following day, Ash himself began teaching them, but not before he gave them a talking to about their behavior during lessons.

He paced with as much pomp as the tutor, except that his inexpressibles fit him like a second skin, and Lark knew that his legs and shoulders were not padded. As a matter of fact, she knew what he looked like all over, and in the throes of passion as well, so she did not feel the least intimidated.

She and the children sat in silence at the nursery table, books open, waiting for their new tutor to finish his lecture.

Finally, he rounded on them. "One more thing," he said, looking from one of them to the other. "No more schoolroom pranks. Now, which of you put the bladder of ink into your former tutor's pocket?"

"Micah did it!" Brian charged, pointing the boy's way.

Micah rose to his feet and roared his outrage pointing back toward Brian.

"Lark," Ash said. "That leaves only you. Did you do it?"

Lark looked from one child to the other and raised her chin. "Yes," she said. "I did."

Ash made a noise of disgust. "You did not."

"You doubt that I could?"

"Not at all, but I do doubt that you would become a poor example for the children."

"I did it," Lark repeated.

"Fine then. You will stay late and do an extra assignment when we are finished."

"Oh, for Dirty Dan's Sake, I did it!" Brian said, sticking her tongue out at Micah.

Micah mirrored the action, while Lark refused to meet her husband's gaze, so he would not see her amusement.

"You lied," Ash said to Brian.

She hung her head. "Yes, sir."

Ash sighed. "I dislike dishonesty above all things, Brian. Do you understand?"

"Yes, sir."

"I would rather you told me when you were naughty, than lie about having done it."

"Yes, sir."

"Good. Now that's settled, let us open our reading books at page sixty-three. Brian, since you perpetrated the prank that lost us our tutor, you will begin. You will also have an extra assignment at the end of the lesson as punishment . . . for your lie, not your misdeed. By my account, the tutor got what he deserved."

Brian nodded. "My Mama *said* you would be strict but fair."

Ash started, as if he'd seen a ghost, then he glanced red-faced at Lark, before nodding for Brian to begin reading.

Lark had tried to forget what Brian said about Ash loving her mother. She had never asked him if he loved anyone before, only if he'd played the blanket hornpipe with anyone else, or made a babe with them, which he might have done with Brian's mother, as it turned out, and which bothered her more with each day that passed. It wasn't that she didn't love Brian; she did. But Ash was her husband and she felt a womanly ownership that she did not want to share. She wanted to know, damn it, if he had loved another woman.

She wanted to know if he loved *her*.

"Daydreaming during lessons, Lady Blackburne?" Ash said with a smile, and Lark turned her attention back to the book in front of her, her face warming.

The children were both bright. Micah helped Lark with her numbers, while Brian helped her with her reading, a sad and humiliating state of affairs.

After a particularly difficult lesson, Lark threw

down her pencil, rose, and went to the nursery window, where she sat on the window seat to look outside.

Ash followed. "Lark, is something bothering you?"

"I am not smart enough to be your wife, and I am not half good enough either. I do not know why you put up with me."

Ash's arms came around her, his cheek met hers, and she reveled in his silent support. "I do not know why, either," he said, his unexpected words cutting, despite his kiss on her neck. When he dared to chuckle, Lark rose and stomped on his foot with near as much force as she'd used on the dancing master, though to be fair, she was wearing less painful heels at this time.

When she saw her husband's pain, she placed her hand against her mouth, in shock at what she'd done, felt her eyes fill, and quit the room.

"Devil it! Why did you do that?" Ash called after her. He looked at the children. "Why did she do that? What the . . ." He sat and massaged his throbbing foot. "I never saw that woman cry for no reason."

Brian shook her head. "You were supposed to tell her you loved her, dolt."

"You are wiser than your years," Ash said, before he called for Mim to supervise in the nursery, so he could follow his bride to her bedchamber.

Did he love Lark? Ash wondered, finding the thought as frightening as ever. Would his mother have suffered so badly at his leaving for war, if she had not loved him?

To him, love had always seemed to cause more pain than joy.

True, he had discovered in Lark a wounded soul

mate and he could not resist the lure to heal her. He enjoyed spending time with her, talking to her, and joking with her—which is all he had been about this afternoon. She had never taken one of his jests so before.

He certainly took pleasure in having her in his bed. Lord, he could barely get enough of having her in there, or against the wall, or in whatever ridiculous position she wanted him, though he did not like getting his foot crushed under her heel, by God.

When he opened the door to her bedchamber, her emotions had vaulted from tears to ire, it was plain to see, so Ash sighed and advanced on her, giving her little choice but to wait him out, or run. "If we can get you quickly out of your gown, I believe it will be easier for you to forget what an idiot I am."

"Are you like to be making an apology, then?" she snapped, crossing her arms.

"I am no more versed at soliciting forgiveness than in granting it," he said kneeling before her, "though I pray you will . . . overlook . . . my earlier thoughtless comments."

Lark gasped as Ash lifted the hem of her gown to nuzzle her through her petticoat, there at her center.

"This is more than to make a babe," he said. "I want to be close to you. Now."

She knew she should stop him—it was the middle of the day, for pity's sake—but for the life of her, Lark could not raise a hand to put period to the pleasure her husband aroused. Her arms became heavy, as did her legs, except for their sudden need to buckle at the knees. What was wrong with her today?

Ash found the tapes at her waist and undid them so

her petticoat broke free and puddled on the floor at her feet.

She squeaked and raised her skirts, holding them against her bodice, so as to watch him undress her from the inside out.

He looked up at her, his eyes dancing, his hair endearingly askew, and she could swear that her heart did a small flip inside her chest before it lay itself at his feet. Was *this* love? she wondered.

Ash stroked her through her shift, rushing more warmth to her core, and he rested his cheek just there, raising her to new heights. But when he turned his head and opened his mouth against her center, whispering her name like a prayer, Larkin rose so near to release that she whimpered.

She closed her eyes and wove her fingers through his thick, silken hair, holding his head against her, for all the world as if she were begging for more of his magic.

Ash moved his talented hands upward along the backs of her legs, sliding them beneath the soft linen of her shift to cup her bottom, then he slid both hands forward to meet at her front, at the center of all feeling, and splayed his fingers to stroke and tease.

Touching could bring pleasure, Lark had learned, wild, amazing pleasure, when the man doing the touching was Ashford bloody-beautiful Blackburne.

She released the breath she had been holding with a shuddering sigh, and Ash rose like a ruthless, ravenous rogue and opened his mouth over hers. He swallowed her sighs, drew more, until his mouth became so much a part of her own, she might take to bleeding if he stopped.

When she thought she had reached a perfection of

sensation, nearly unbearable in its intensity, he moved to undo the buttons at her bodice, stroking her exposed skin as he moved down her torso. Heightened sensation, rising in promise.

He freed her arms from her sleeves without her help, for she was too ensnared in pleasure to think. Just as well, for she had no strength, either to help, or resist.

"That's my girl," he whispered as he slid her dress down along her sensitive quivering body, the palms of his hands skimming her, until he cleared her hips and her dress joined her petticoats on the floor.

Standing before him in nothing but her shift, stockings, and slippers, Lark wished she were a lady who wore fancy corsets of silk and lace just for her man. Her underpinnings were no more than serviceable cotton, plain, and well worn, yet her husband regarded her with an appreciation akin to awe.

He took her hand and she stepped over her clothes to face her lover, as if in the center of a bright cocoon, for the sun flowing through the curtains blessed as well as mocked them for this breach in the fabric of good manners.

"It is the middle of the day," Lark said, in a tardy effort to play the lady, but her rogue of a husband's wicked grin said he cared not a whit. She had daily evidence that the earl of Blackburne liked breaking rules as much as did his hoyden bride.

He slipped her shift up and over her head. Then he stepped back to regard her, like a connoisseur examining a work of art, assessing and delighting in the vision.

For the first time in her life, Lark felt . . . beautiful,

at least in the eyes of another, in the eyes of the rogue who mattered most.

She'd dreamed of him for years, tricked him into marrying her, yet she would not alter her life with him for anything, no matter his warranted anger when he learned the truth. And he would learn of it, for the more time that passed, the more she knew she must confess before they could be truly happy.

As if sensing her surrender, Ash began to remove her stockings with a renewed determination in his appreciative gaze, sliding the first slowly down her leg until Lark shivered in anticipation. Then he began again with the second, doubling her heartbeat.

Now she stood naked before the man she loved. Did she love him? Dear God, how foolish that would be, but she must. She adored every angle of his face, every twinkle in his eyes, his frowns, and curses. She treasured the way he encouraged Micah's studies and laughed at Brian's naughtiness.

More than anything, she appreciated that he respected her fears in the bedroom, allowing her outrageous requests in regards to position and timing, and that he pleasured her in whatever way she wished.

Did she love her handsome, stubborn rogue? If she did, and she told him so, would that not destroy his ability to be shed of her, if he wished it, upon his grandfather's death?

He stood and turned her, her back against his front, so he could cup her breasts from behind, as if weighing and measuring them. Lark leaned against him as he plumped each one, pebbled her nipples, and whispered his adoration of her body, his breath and nibbling lips warm along her neck, ears, shoulders.

Pleasure points coursed through her with an escalating force. Her contentment grew apace, her womanhood flowered.

Too soon, but not soon enough, her attentive husband turned her and lifted a breast to suckle her, while he reacquainted his hands with the shape of her bottom and the heat at her center, making her legs tremble.

As he rose up again and his smoldering eyes set her ablaze, she bent and disposed of his trousers in a thrumming heartbeat and got her first good look at his linen smallclothes.

"They look very different on you than they do on me," she said.

"Praise be, but I did give you a pair of the button variety."

She circled him and regarded him with the same hot gaze as he used on her, to play him and tease him, then she gave him back a bit of his own. Stroking the fabric ever so lightly across his front, she found the opening big enough and easy enough, without buttons, to accommodate her hand, silently applauding his choice of underlinen.

Ash gasped when she found him, his lance rigid and thick, his ballocks soft and supple . . . but her other hand ached for him as well, and so she knelt and slipped his linen down his legs and cupped his ballocks, even as she closed her other around his splendid manhood.

She reveled in the power to make him throw back his head and stifle a groan of roaring pleasure, a gratification that seemed as acute as pain.

She liked as well that she could make him beg, and buck, and plead for her to "stop," and "more," and "hurry," and "wait!"

Chapter 18

In a quick turnabout, Ash took control, lay her on their bed, kissed her ravenously, and came over her, opening his mouth over her own once more. He lay atop her for the first time ever; did he realize it? She did not stop him this time, for she found she liked the intimate weight of him. The position no longer seemed . . . threatening, as it used to do, but fulfilling and splendid. Right.

Hard to her soft, cool to her hot, Ash dipped where she curved, and arched where she plunged, all so deliciously and perfectly well. They fit together like two pieces of a hand-carved puzzle, making her wonder how even God had managed so perfect a match.

"Ash, you feel good. You're on top, did you realize? I like it. It feels better than—"

"Shut up, Lark, and kiss me."

She did. Tongues touching and dancing, mating. Hands, legs . . . mouths touching . . . everywhere.

As the sun shifted direction, Lark learned new variations on pleasure—a bliss she never imagined, a wondrous joy, as heart-stopping as fast-sliding down a snow-slick hill. It was a pleasure that grew to unimagined heights, burst within them both and set them free.

Like two spoons, they slept, until Lark sat up and realized the beauty of the man who lay beside her, and she took advantage of the opportunity to examine every texture of her husband's naked man-parts in the full light of day. She touched him, along and around, up and down, delighting in her ability to arouse him, painting his moist tip with a playful finger.

When she dared to kiss that silky tip, he woke with a moan and a start, saw what she was about, and as fast as that, she was on her back and he was deep inside her again.

In a frenzy, he brought her higher in three deep strokes than he had during any of their previous couplings.

So blessedly good, she felt, with his weight atop her, she wept for the joy of it.

They climbed and soared again, without rest this time; then like water cascading down a mountain—pure, bubbling, wild, and free—they floated as one, peaceful and at rest, for minutes, or hours.

Lark woke to find dusk had fallen, while Ash worked in her with slow purpose, making her beg for faster, then slower, then just plain more. She regarded him, looking down at her, incredibly handsome, too handsome for her.

"Come with me, Lark," he said. "Come with me to heaven. I'll wait. Come." Then, deepening each concentrated thrust, he dipped his head to suckle her, pulling hard shafts of leaping pleasure from so deep inside, she could have wept again.

He stopped suckling with a groan to move higher over her and increase his pace. She feared she might die of the frenzy before she shattered into a million star-bright pieces, hovered in the heavens, and became one with eternity.

A moment later, Ash shouted her name, gave her his seed, and she rushed to the firmament again, one last incredible time; then she let herself drift, safe, sated, and exhausted in her husband's arms.

After a time, he reversed their positions and settled her atop him like a blanket of lazy contentment, and urged her to sleep.

She closed her eyes without a word. She had never known such sublime contentment.

Ash woke with his answer, the one for which he had come searching. Brian had been right. He loved his wife, loved her as if she were his missing half; it was a frightening discovery, for had she not once implied they might go their own ways once grandfather's estate was settled?

She stirred in his arms, pushed her face deeper into his neck, moved, and moaned. Parts of her must be tender and sore. He would have to kiss each one just to make them better, and after that, perhaps he would let her out of bed.

Lark shifted and moaned again, and rubbed her nose, back and forth, hard, against the hair on his chest.

Ash laughed and his rogue's heart warmed. "Itchy nose means you're coming into money."

She smiled lazily and stretched her arms in that rod-stiffening way of hers, her silken limbs sinuously sliding against his own. "Don't need money. I have you."

"We both need money, remember? That's why we married."

Lark took her luscious bottom lip between her teeth,

making him want to bite it himself, or perhaps he should bite his own, come to think of it, because her sad eyes and sudden silence made him nervous of a sudden.

She rose quickly, placing certain parts of him in perilous danger of annihilation. Ash caught his breath, then expelled it in relief, and tried not to be distracted by her pert breasts and fine bottom. He watched her rummage and blush, until she covered herself to her thighs with his shirt.

He had to raise his knee to keep her from seeing how alluring he found her wearing it, or she'd find something else to wear. She seemed that annoyed, though he didn't know why.

"Brian called me a name for the way I treated you in the nursery," he said to make her smile, though he seemed rather to bring a more thunderous frown to her brow.

"Good," she said. "It means she has a true understanding of your personality."

Ouch. "I know," he said, rising, "that I acted like the hind end of a—" He caught her ludicrous expression. "What?"

She regarded his raging manhood with something akin to annoyed amazement. This time it was him who blushed. "Sorry. I forgot."

"You can forget something that big? You could trip on it, for pity's sake."

Ash stifled a chuckle. "I'm trying to get your attention here."

"You have succeeded, believe me." She sounded no less forgiving, despite the tease, while he did not understand for what he needed forgiving.

Too many silent minutes passed, the two of them

facing each other, her thighs beneath that shirt looking perfect and welcoming, his body ready to have them around him.

"Why the bloody blazes do you want my attention?" she snapped.

Ash started at her tone and knew that a confession of love at this juncture would seem insincere, especially as his old uncertainty over the emotion had risen, like a demon from the sea, in the past few minutes. "To tell you that I . . . missed you when you left the nursery yesterday."

Lark made a strangled sound deep in her throat, her cheeks strawberry-bright, her eyes filling again. "Will you please put on your clothes!" She grabbed them from the floor to toss his way.

"I'd rather you beat the devil out of me than cry," Ash said, ignoring his clothes, going for his dressing gown. "You never cry."

Lark sat on the bed, so forlorn, he sat beside her. "What is wrong, Larkin? You are not acting yourself."

"It is just that . . ." She accepted his handkerchief and wiped her eyes. "It is . . . everything of a sudden. Look, I've torn the pretty new dress Olga made for me." She pulled the dress off the floor and showed its torn overskirt.

"How can I teach Brian to act the lady if I act the ragamuffin? I cannot even read as well as she does, or do sums as well as Micah. Ash, my children have to help me learn my lessons. And you, you've ruined me by trying to make me into a lady. Now I do not even feel like beating you bloody, when you deserve a good throttling so very much."

"Why do I deserve it?"

"Rat's whiskers, Ash. If I knew, I might be able to work up the enthusiasm to do it."

Ash received a letter from Reed Gilbride St. Yves, which he read to Lark at breakfast the following morning:

Dear Ash,

You will forgive our tardy congratulations on your marriage. Our brood have kept us quite busy, and I now find myself pleased to inform you that we have increased our numbers by two. Yes two. Chastity, never happy with keeping things simple, gave birth to twins on the 18th of May.

Since I am also a twin, Chastity insists I accept at least half of the blame. Their names are Jillian and Meggie by the way; did I tell you they were both girls? Mark will never forgive us for giving him more sisters, though he agrees that they are the most beautiful babes imaginable.

Thank you again for your service on our wedding day. We think of you often.

Until the rogues gather once more, fare well.

> Your faithful friend,
> Reed Gilbride St. Yves.

"They sound like a wonderful family," Lark said, a bit envious, given her own lack of friends.

Ash nodded, accepted another cup of tea, and sipped it thoughtfully. "Any news of the rogues makes me miss the ruddy lot of them."

"I'd love to meet them," she said wistfully, then she

regarded her tattered dress and sighed. "We have not been 'at home' to visitors, I know, because I have not been willing to have the dressmaker in, but . . . perhaps we should."

"I thought you hated the notion."

Lark pushed a piece of egg around her plate. "Brian will need dresses, I think, judging by the way she fingered your mother's brooch the day I wore it, and once she asked about my petticoat, and I . . . would not want to shame you in front of your friends, Ash."

"You never could," he said standing and coming around the table to kiss her neck. "I will be happy to send for the dressmaker from St. Albans, if you wish, and as soon as your new clothes are ready, I shall invite Hawk and Alex to visit. They are our nearest neighbors among the rogues and you may practice your social skills on them before we are 'at home' to the locals."

"Where do the gossips come from, if the village is made of your tenants?"

"The gossips are the women of society who live in the larger houses between here and St. Albans. They have nothing better to do, you see, but report, and embellish, their neighbors' actions to each other."

"Sounds frightening."

"Alex will be an enormous help to you in preparing for their invasion, though Sabrina would be better since she did not begin as a lady, herself, though we aren't likely to see her and Gideon unless we go to London for the season.

Lark squeaked in pure terror. "Please do not say we will. I had hoped we'd missed the Regent's Ball."

"Oh we did, since you maimed your dancing master, but you will not escape society that easily, my dear. I hope to take you to an assembly in St. Albans at some point in the future."

"Damn," Lark said beneath her breath.

The dressmaker arrived in the middle of July, a tall, robust woman, mammoth of bosom, but tiny of waist and hips, which made Lark wonder why she did not fall on her face from the weight she carried up front.

Lark fidgeted as she stood on the dressmaker's platform, while the woman pinned and prodded, pricked and poked. "I am not certain that this is necessary," Lark said.

"Well, my lady, his lordship has hired me to do a job, and that means you must stand still and I must measure and pin. If you don't mind my saying so, many's the lady who'd be delirious getting fitted for so many beautiful new clothes. His lordship says you must have everything—corsets, petticoats, night shifts, ball gowns, morning dresses, carriage dresses, riding habits, skirts and bodices, gloves, redingotes, bonnets—"

"What do you find so amusing my dear?" Ash asked, coming in with Micah beside him and Brian trailing stubbornly behind.

"I have never worn a corset or bonnet in my life."

Lark ignored the dressmaker's gasp to regard the three people she most cared about. Ash, his brow raised, Micah and Brian, eyes twinkling with amusement. A family. *She* had a family.

"Make double the amount of dresses she orders," he told the dressmaker. "My wife is too thrifty by half."

"Morning, afternoon, and evening dresses, Ash? Carriage dresses? Rat's whiskers, was a time I wore the same clothes all day, and all night too . . . all week, come to that."

"I remember it well," Ash said, but Brian took to regarding Lark with a more interested gaze.

"I'll grant that I prefer bathing and changing clothes daily," she said for the girl's benefit, "but changing every hour seems to border on the ridiculous."

The fact remained, Lark knew, that if she refused the clothes Ash felt she needed, she would never become the "lady" wife *he* needed. She owed him that much at least and more for her trickery in bringing about their marriage.

The children depended upon her as well to make something of a life for them all. Besides, if she fussed, fidgeted, and complained too much, Brian would surely change her mind and refuse to be fitted for dresses of her own, and Lark would feel guiltier than ever.

"Bother," she said beneath her breath, a mild oath, considering how she felt about this fittings business. She had a good argument prepared too, one that involved the funds necessary to this extravagant endeavor; but with Brian awaiting her turn, as if prepared for her own hanging, there was nothing more to be said, and Ash knew it.

Ash sent the letter inviting Alex and Hawk to visit that very day, and within minutes of telling Lark so, he was pleased to find that she became aggressively interested in learning her lessons, all of them, but especially in ladylike deportment, and in becoming a gracious hostess.

It did help that Brian took "lady" lessons along with

Lark and that the girl often remembered, from her earlier years, how things should go on "in society." It also helped that Brian broke as many china teacups as Lark did, and that Brian's guttersnipe vocabulary emerged a bit more often than Lark's when things went wrong.

Ash made Micah his unofficial assistant estate manager, since the boy's proud head for sums became a helpful asset. Lark named Brian her unofficial assistant hostess, for strictly speaking, Brian had more experience than Lark.

Both children flourished under Lark's motherly care, and Ash could not help note that she showed no preference to her nephew. She scolded both children as needed, coddled both as needed, and loved both with a capacity for that emotion Ash envied.

He craved the ability to love as she did, as he craved her unconditional love for himself, and was shocked out of mind to discover it.

"I am proud of you," he told her one night after they'd made love.

"Because I have surpassed your expectations in baby-making?" she asked. "Not that we've succeeded in making a babe, I mean, but that I've excelled in learning the rudiments necessary to the attempt."

Ash grinned. "Because you have surpassed my expectations in your 'lady lessons,' as you irreverently call them."

Lark kissed his chin, the closest spot she could reach with her head on his shoulder. "No darling, if I were being irreverent, I would speak aloud the name I have given my lessons in my head."

"Which is?"

"*You* will never know, because I am too much the lady to say it."

Ash barked a laugh, brought her over him, and worked very hard to turn his lady into a quivering mass of begging pleasure.

Lark vomited, she was so nervous, on the morning the Duke of Hawksworth and his wife Alexandra were due to arrive for a visit.

Chapter 19

Lark was appalled that Ash held her hair back as she heaved into the chamber pot; then he insisted on seeing her climb back into bed for a longer sleep.

"I am going to have Mim come to clear this away and Cook come to see if there is something she can fix that might settle your stomach," he said, "and if you are not better by teatime, when my friends are due to arrive, you will receive Alexandra here. She will understand."

Lark moaned and needed the chamber pot again, and Ash became the more upset. "Have you eaten something that disagreed with you?" he asked sitting on the bed and taking her hand.

"I am about to receive my first visitors as Lady Blackburne, Ash. Do you not understand how frightened I am that I will make a horrible blunder or prove an abominable hostess and give your friends, and you, a disgust of me?"

"I had no idea you were this nervous about receiving them."

"It does not help that my new clothes did not arrive in time and that this must be the hottest summer in history. The heat alone is enough to sour one's stomach. Whatever will I wear?"

"The day is not that warm and you will wear the cream-and-burgundy day dress, which is my favorite."

"The morning feels excessively warm to me, and that dress will simply make me warmer."

Ash tested her brow. "Do you have fever? If you do, I will send a messenger with a note for them not to come. Alex is in no condition—"

"I do not have fever." Lark knocked her husband's annoying hand away. "I am nervous, and hot, and you are making me feel more of both. Leave me in peace and I shall be ready to receive them in due course."

"As you wish," Ash said, but Lark thought he was upset when he left her, and though that bothered her a great deal, she was surprised to awaken some three hours later feeling refreshed, astonishingly wonderful, and looking forward to her first visitors.

"The duke and duchess of Hawksworth, dear God," Lark said as the crested ebony coach stopped at the entrance of the Chase at two that afternoon. "I think I may need to vomit again."

Ash started and Lark chuckled. "A figure of speech, my dear," she assured him, amused by the look of horror on his face.

Hawksworth appeared aptly named, for he bore the look of a Hawk, Lark thought, enhanced as it was by the scars on his face. Yet she saw a magnificent beauty in his visage as well, especially when he looked upon his duchess as he helped her emerge from the carriage.

Lark gasped, for the duchess was so huge with child as to waddle a bit like a duck. "Oh my."

Lark accompanied her husband down the front steps to greet them, feeling every muscle in her belly tighten in apprehension. But she needn't have worried about formality because the duchess opened her arms and embraced her, and the child within the woman kicked so hard, Lark laughed, and relaxed and embraced the duchess in return. "Your grace," Lark said, with what she feared was a belated curtsy.

The duchess shook her head, raised Lark to her feet, and placed an arm about her waist. "Alexandra is my name and Alex you will call me. None of this toadying-to-titles business between friends. Have you met the rest of the rogues?"

"I have met none of the rogues," Lark said, dreading her imminent introduction to the man her husband called "Hawk."

The duchess—Alex—whirled them about as one, their arms still around each other. "Bryce, you will kiss Ash's frightened bride, if you please, and place her at her ease. You have frightened her witless, you see."

"Oh, oh no," Lark said, "you have not." She wanted to scold Alex for saying so, but she saw that in the teasing, something intimate passed between husband and wife, and the harsh planes about the duke's face relaxed. He smiled as he bent to kiss Lark's cheek. "How are you managing this old reprobate? I heard he won you in a card game, is that true?"

"Bryce!" Alex scolded.

"Yes," Ash replied.

"No," Lark countered.

They entered the drawing room amused over the confusion of answers. Lark called for tea right away; she was so nervous she would make an error as hostess, she wanted to get the formalities done with.

"Well," Hawk said to Ash as they sat. "Which is it? You won her or you did not?"

"He *lost* the card game," Lark said, wanting more than ever to confess her part in the deceit, "and I was his consolation."

Ash gave her a look of censure and Lark felt as if he were chiding her for telling the truth, which was so unlike her forthright husband she must ask what he meant by it later. But Alex and Hawk had fallen into peels of laughter and her husband relaxed.

"I should have known Myles and Hunter were too drunk to get your wedding story straight," Hawk said.

"Where is little Beatrix?" Ash asked. "I hoped you might bring her for Brian and Micah to play with."

"We would have," Alex said, "but she is spending the day with Claudia and the new baby. She will not be dragged from little Judson's side for long."

"I had heard that Chesterfield has an heir," Ash said. "He must be pleased."

"He is disgustingly pleased," Hawk said, with little trace of the feud Ash said had once raged between the two men. Lark was not surprised, however, for Ash had also confided that Chesterfield married Hawk's niece.

When the tea tray had been removed, Ash stood. "Ladies, you will excuse us. Hawk has experienced distinguished success with the Huntington Lodge estate and he has promised to ride the Chase property and offer some industrious suggestions, including the possible construction of a lavender distillery."

Lark watched Hawk limp from the room. "Ash told me your husband was badly injured in the war."

"And left for dead," Alex said. "We received the miracle of his return to us and now we have another, for we are finally expecting our first child, though we have been reunited for more than two years."

"Two years?" Lark cried with some distress. "Can it take that long to get with child?"

"It did for us, though not for want of trying, I can tell you. Do not be distressed. It will happen in time."

"We do not have time. According to Ash's grandfather, I must be with child before Christmas, or Ash will not inherit, which will cause him to lose the estate."

Alex's eyes twinkled. "Then you must be trying very hard to meet those requirements, which is no surprise, given the fact that Ashford is a rogue of the highest order."

"*Very* hard," Lark said pointedly.

"*Congratulations.*"

They giggled like schoolgirls, a new and heartwarming experience for Lark.

"It is wondrous to be in love and trying for a babe, is it not?" Alex said.

"Oh, we do not love each other," Lark said, aware she feared believing different, wishing she could ask Alex to explain love's meaning.

"I am sorry to hear it."

"But I like the marriage bed very much, and I like Ash, which does make it pleasant to keep to our bargain to get Ash into his grandfather's will."

"You might be fooling yourself my girl," Alex said.

"About liking Ash? Yes, well, there are times that I do not like him so much."

Alex chuckled. "About him loving you, I mean. Men rarely confess such things, you know."

Lark tilted her head, considering. "Perhaps, but I do not think he does." She smiled, wishing Alex might be correct. "Have you met all the rogues?" Lark asked, changing the subject, for she was uncomfortable with talking of her marriage and love.

"I have met every one, and you have now met three of them, did you not realize? Myles Quartermaine, earl of Northclyffe, and Hunter Elijah Wylder, marquess of Wyldborne, were both at your wedding."

Lark made a face. "I did not like those two and thought them scoundrels, not aristocrats."

"They are none of the rogues endearing when they have been drinking, especially when they are together, for then they go beyond what is prudent."

"One wonders how they won the war."

"True enough."

"What are their wives like? How many children do they have. Oh I want to meet them all," Lark said.

"Gideon is in mourning for his grandmother, so he and Sabrina will not be out in society until December, or I would suggest a house party."

Lark sat straighter. "Do people have *Christmas* house parties?"

"Of course they do. Have you never attended a house party during the holidays? There are none so special as Christmas gatherings."

Lark called for more tea and shared her background with Alex, as Alex shared a bit of her own amazing life with Hawksworth, and sometime during the course of the afternoon, the two became fast friends.

She took Alex to the nursery to meet Micah and Brian, who were, unfortunately, not on their best behavior. It seemed Micah had locked Brian in her bedchamber, and Brian did not like locks. So when she picked it and got herself out, she threw an inkwell, a full inkwell, at Micah's head. It broke, of course, the inkwell, not Micah's head, though he did have a bruise the size of an egg on his temple.

Even though Mim had basically cleaned them up, India ink stained Micah's cheek and both children's hands. Even so, they bowed, and curtsied, and gave the incorrect impression of having manners.

Lark shut the door on the nursery and rolled her eyes. "I sometimes ask myself why we want another."

"Because making babies is splendid fun?"

"I will come to see you when your own comes," Lark told Alex as they descended the stairs. "I cannot wait to hold it."

"The babe will be nearly three months by Christmas," Alex said absentmindedly, as if doing sums in her head. "I would invite everyone to Christmas at the Lodge, but it is still a heap and we have not made rooms livable yet for so many.

"Lark, would you consider holding a Christmas house party here at Blackburne Chase? This will be Gideon and Sabrina's first real Christmas without his grandmother so they will be happy for a place to go rather than remain home and feel sad. It would give you an opportunity to meet all the rogues and their families."

Lark held her fluttering middle. "I do not know what to do to celebrate Christmas, nor anything about planning a house party. I would die of fright with such a task before me."

"We could ask each family to bring the makings of their favorite family tradition. I will coordinate, so we do not duplicate efforts. We live near enough to each other, you and I, to consult on menus and preparations. Did you know that Huntington Lodge is barely twelve miles to the north?"

Lark caught Alex's contagious excitement like a

fever. "I have butterflies again. I swear I will be as sick on the day of my house party as I was this morning for knowing you were coming."

"You were sick this morning? Has this happened before?"

"I suppose a lady should not speak of such things," Lark said in response to Alex's frown. "I will never learn."

"Have you had your monthlies recently?"

"Oh yes," Lark said. "Why do you ask?"

"I thought perhaps you had been ill because you are with child, but that cannot be."

"Why can it not? Will I not know until I am as big as a prize sow—" Lark slapped a hand over her mouth. "I am so sorry."

Alex laughed, and with so much merriment, Lark feared she would birth her babe there on the indigo damask settee.

"The easiest way to tell," Alex said some minutes later as she dabbed at her watering eyes, "is that your monthlies will stop."

The men returned, and though Lark wanted to consult Alex further, she could not wait to give Ash the news. "Ash," she said, approaching him, reminding herself to remain sedate, and not gallop, as her excitement warranted, "we are hosting a Christmas house party here at Blackburne Chase, and Alex is going to help."

While both rogues regarded their wives with unspoken skepticism, neither commented further.

Lark had had the maids fasten a curtain across her small personal sitting room the day her dressmaker was due to deliver her new wardrobe.

Now Ash, Brian, and Micah sat on the opposite side of said curtain waiting for Lark to come from behind it wearing one of her new outfits.

When her first dress had been dropped over Lark's head, she regarded herself in the cheval glass from every angle, both amazed and flattered. "This cannot be me. I feel as though I am wearing someone else's clothes."

"Well you must surely be, my lady," the dressmaker said as she attempted to fasten the buttons up the back. "Because this dress is too small for you."

"I heard that," Ash said, "and I am pleased to hear my campaign to fatten up my lady is become a success. She was all bones a month ago, you must own, still is, in my eyes."

"I can hear this conversation," Lark said. "Please refrain from discussing my plump self within my hearing, if you do not mind."

On the opposite side of the curtain, Ash chuckled, Brian gave a giggle, and the additional snicker Lark heard was surely Micah's.

"Won't take but a rip and a stitch or two to fix, my lord," the dressmaker said.

"Happy to hear it."

The dressmaker whipped the first dress off and settled another over Lark's shoulders. "Here now, this one fits as it should. The empire style suits you," she said, "and the emerald-green color makes your flaxen hair shine."

Lark stepped into a pair of satin high-heeled slippers of the exact fabric and accepted a striped-silk fringed shawl the color of the blond lace on her bodice.

As she stepped from behind the curtain, her family

applauded, Brian's eyes surprisingly wistful, Micah's wide, and Ash's hot and . . . inspired.

Lark grinned, certain she understood the degree of her husband's inspiration. "I take it you approve?"

"The style suits you, and the way it looks on you suits me."

"Good, because I am fond of this style and ordered several, though I do feel like a child playing dress up. Look, my slippers match the precise color of my dress and each other." She raised her hem to show her emerald silk slippers to good advantage, and did a dance step that had the children giggling.

"You have slippers to go with every dress."

"Oh, Ash, surely not. That would be . . . extravagant."

"Nevertheless, you have them. Your order was modest, Lark. I simply made it more practical, not excessive in any way, I assure you."

Lark took a chair among them. "I wish to see Brian in one of her new dresses."

Brian did not hesitate for a moment before she stepped behind the curtain, for she was too precocious by far, now that she'd lost her fear, and almost too beautiful as well. Lark wondered if her mother had been so striking, so alive, and if Ash saw the woman he loved in Brian's perfect Irish features and fine raven hair.

Did he yearn for the woman even now? Lark almost hoped that the news about Brian's paternity, due from Ellenora's friends in London, never came, for she would as soon never know that her husband had fathered a child with the woman he loved.

Chapter 20

As the dressmaker dressed Brian in her new clothes, Ash regarded Lark. He adored her in her own new things, though he would adore her more out of them, which he believed she read in his gaze even now.

As every new day passed, he became more enamored of his bride and more torn by their goal—odd how he thought of it in terms of *their* goal now.

While Lark must soon get with child, to keep them in Grandfather's will so as to save the estate, Ash dreaded the day he would be forced to stop going to her bed.

He had wondered recently if Grandfather would accept Brian as the child Ash must produce before Christmas . . . if Brian proved, indeed, to be his. But he had realized soon enough that to claim Brian as his own would be to declare her as illegitimate and ruin her in the eyes of society.

Though Brian would not use her true name—Lark had convinced him she must have her reasons and they should keep her secret—she was legally the Lady Ashley Briana Fairhaven, legitimate daughter of the late Lloyd Harvey, duke of Amesbridge, and so she would remain.

Even if it meant losing grandfather's favor, and losing Blackburne Chase as well, come to that, Ash would not destroy Brian's future, whomever her sire might be.

All was not lost, he reminded himself now. Lark might yet conceive. Nearly four months were left to them before Christmas after all, and what better sport could be found than baby-making with Larkin Rose?

The fact was, despite his bride's guttersnipe beginnings, she had become like a sprig of fresh lavender in his life—unspoiled yet spirited—a blend he found soothing and invigorating at one and the same time.

Beneath her oft-times unbendable surface, he had found Lark to be a woman of great passion, a woman he enjoyed having as his wife, his helpmeet, his lover—a woman so rare, even his curmudgeon of a grandfather had taken a fancy to her. So rare, she would love her husband's natural child as her own.

Ash fingered the puzzling note in his pocket from Jane Hawking, Ellenora's bosom friend, asking him to come to London where she would tell him everything she knew of Nora's child. One way or another, he must discover whether he had left Ellenora carrying his child or not.

"Lark," he said, making a decision on the instant, "I must away to London soon to look into the matter concerning which I have sent inquiries." He regarded the curtain pointedly. "Do you suppose you could do without me for a day or so?"

"I think you would be missed by us all, but we would manage. What say you, Micah? Shall you, Brian, and I, become adventurers, out here in the wilds of Gorhambury on our own for a full twenty-four hours or more?"

Micah looked at Ash with fretful eyes, but he nodded

all the same, and then Brian came out wearing . . . a dress, and took all their attention.

A termagant into a swan.

The first thing Brian did was curtsey before Ash. "I believe I will be pleased to dress like a girl again," she said.

"Oh," Ash said on a chuckle, tweaking her nose, "and shall you be pleased to be named like a girl as well? Someday you will be forced to settle on one name only, you know, and be content to live with the one only for the rest of your days."

"Not yet, if you please."

"Fine," Ash said. "So you will wear dresses but still be called Brian?"

She looked at Lark, as if for reassurance, and raised her chin, much as Lark was wont to do. "I would like to be called Briana now, please."

"Briana," Ash said. "Close enough to your—to . . . Brian, and not so difficult a change to remember. It is a fine choice."

That night Lark and Ash discussed the fact that Briana did not want the world to know her first name was Ashley, so they agreed, with greater apprehension, that neither would use it under any circumstance.

The following week, a note arrived from Huntington Lodge:

Dearest friends,
    You may wish us happy. Alex and I are proud to announce the arrival of our son, Brandon Alexander Wakefield, two weeks old today, and as perfect as his mother. Alex sends her love and

bids Lark visit soon. She cannot wait to show him off.

Lark and Ash toasted Hawksworth's heir that night at dinner, and worked very hard afterward to produce an heir of their own.

Two days before Ash planned to travel to London, the Hawksworth carriage arrived promptly at nine to whisk Lark away on her adventure to visit Alex and the baby. Ash, Briana, and Micah waved her away from beside the carriage. Mim, Cook, and Grimsley stood on the steps waving her off as well, for Lark had alerted all available hands to keep the children in line during her absence.

Huntington Lodge, by Devil's Dyke, topping the steep hill beside the River Ver, was not the leaking, tumbling pile Lark had been led by Alexandra to expect. The pristine lodge stood an imposing mortared brick edifice, ruddy of face, and straight of line, with at least two score of men scrambling over its roof like ants on a hill high above them.

Everywhere Lark looked, happy, energetic men and women worked like bees in a hive. Among the tenants' cottages, home farm, and outbuildings, she saw dovecotes, granaries, even a pottery, as if the lodge were a world unto itself. Hawksworth had certainly made improvements, judging by Alexandra's description of the home she originally inherited.

The man himself welcomed Lark and helped her from his carriage with a kiss to her hand, and before bringing her to Alex, he gave her a tour of the Lodge.

"The family chambers are now livable," he said

some time later, if a bit threadbare, as are the kitchens and servants' quarters. Few of the guest chambers have been touched, because we chose to build the tenant cottages first. Ah, and here are my wife and son," he said, beaming as they ended their tour in a rose silk drawing room.

Hawk sat Lark beside Alex on the sofa and bent to kiss his wife's lips then his son's brow. "Perfect," he said lovingly cupping the boy's tiny head as he slept. "Absolutely perfect." He beamed at Lark. "Did Alex not do a fine job on this one?"

Lark smiled inwardly at the imposing Duke of Hawksworth turned to jelly by the sight of his wife and babe. "She certainly did," Lark said, reaching tentatively, and was rewarded with the smallest armful of babe she ever held. "Oh my," she said. "He is so soft." She kissed a tiny hand. "I am in love."

"And so you should be," Hawk said, kissing Lark's brow. "Again," he said, and bowed. "Welcome, and enjoy your visit." Hawk exited the drawing room and left them.

Lark cuddled and crooned to the babe and told him how fortunate he was to have such wonderful parents who loved him.

Alex beamed upon her son. "Yours will be as fortunate. When shall I hold him, or her? Did the doctor give you an approximate date?"

Lark laughed. "No, for I have seen no doctor. I am not as yet increasing, and I believe Ash is disappointed, though he says he is not, and that he is pleased to work so hard at his favorite sport."

"Oh, but you are with child," Alex said. "You bear all the signs, Lark."

Lark raised the babe in her arms to look at her belly. "I see no signs."

"Have you had your monthly flux since my visit?"

"Well . . . no."

"Aha. And how long has that been? Two months at least. You are breeding, mark my words. Your breasts are bigger too, and tender I'd warrant. Do you nap more often than not?"

"Oh." Lark held the babe in her arms closer, felt a warmth of joy and love rush through her. "The dressmaker said something on the fit of my bodice the other day, but I had not considered. And I have dropped off to sleep at the most peculiar times. Why the children dressed me in a lavender crown, as I slept in the grass beside the field one afternoon, and I awoke feeling like a virgin sacrifice."

Alex took her hand. "Before my visit to your home, when did you last have your flux?"

"I . . . do not remember."

"Do you remember the last time you did?"

"Oh, yes, for I was ever so embarrassed at having Ash see me—" Lark warmed and brought the babe up for a kiss.

"Nonsense, rogues who fought with Wellington take blood, of all things, in stride, though try and remember to have Sabrina tell you about the birth of her daughter, Julianna, and Gideon's hand in it."

"Gideon was present at the birth?"

"He delivered the child."

Lark paled. "I would not know what to do."

"Neither did Gideon."

They shared a chuckle. "We need to know how far along you are," Alex said. "Pray, liken the time of your last flux to the season, if you please. Were the lilacs in bloom? Fruit in blossom, lavender, roses?"

"Oh, I do not know. I remember that, at least a week previous, the blossoms had been falling from the apple trees."

"Dearest Lark, you must be four months gone, at least. I would wager your babe is due sometime in January or February."

"Do you think so? You think I am truly with child?"

"I think you should see a doctor."

"Perhaps I will, but I'd as soon not tell Ash until I am certain. Would you mind not telling Hawksworth yet, so Ash can be the first to know?"

"Certainly not. I adore secrets."

"Besides," Lark said, "I do not want Ashford to stop coming to my bed any sooner than he must."

"He does not need to keep from you when you are with child, did you not know?"

"I know no more of babes than begetting them. In this case, keeping Ash from my bed when I got with child was a stipulation of my own, given at the point of our original bargain." She sighed. "I now wish I had not made it, but what can I do, but stick to my own rules, if I ever expect my husband to honor my wishes in future?"

"You have got yourself into the soup with this one, my girl. Methinks that only a good seduction will get you out of it. If you need help, Sabrina has taught me some delightful tricks, which I will be pleased to pass to you. I had already planned to send you home with a jar of Sabrina's special 'oil of seduction.' It will be of use in the event you put that plan into effect. Remind me to give it to you before you leave. Sabrina has it especially made by an apothecary in London."

Lark heard a commotion outside the room.

"Oh, listen. Do you hear it? There is a babe, not my own, crying. Must be young Master Judson Chesterfield himself. Do you mind if we save our Christmas planning for our next visit? Claudia wants to meet you."

Not at all, Lark said, delighted at the prospect of another visit and of meeting Hawksworth's niece.

"I must caution you," Alex said, "before the hoards descend, that to survive a Christmas house party big enough to accommodate the rogues' families, you will need truckle beds in the nursery, triples if you are smart. We have a tenant who makes them. Remind me to give you his direction before you take your leave."

A beautiful dark-haired woman swept into the drawing room then, with a babe thrice Brandon's size in her arms and a young woman in tow.

Alex introduced them as her niece Claudia, wife to Viscount Chesterfield and mama to little Judson, and Beatrix, Claudia's younger sister.

Lark stood to curtsy, though it was difficult to stand with Brandon in her arms, and she gasped and held him tighter when Alex introduced her as the countess of Blackburne.

"Countess!" Lark said with a laugh.

"And so you are," Alex said. "Did you not realize it?"

"Oh, but I cannot be," Lark wailed. "I am not half good enough."

Alex and Claudia disabused Lark of that dotty notion that very day.

The following day, after Ash left for London, Lark took the opportunity to visit the Blackburne Chase tenants, starting at the dower house. Olga and Bud begged her to leave Briana and Micah with them while she continued her visits. Children loved spending time with Bud and Olga, and hers were no exception. Though the older couple had none of their own, they loved children and gave them every attention.

Between cottage visits, Lark took the time to stop and visit old Doctor Buckston. The man's short white hair stuck up in sparse tufts about his head, while his long beard hung full and waving. His constantly furrowed brows, both thicker and whiter than the hair on his head, gave him the look of a large gnome bearing the disposition of the curmudgeon Ash named him. His growled greeting did nothing to alleviate Lark's impression, neither did his ire at being disturbed.

He closed the door on what he called his laboratory before she could discern the nature of the haphazard projects scattered about, though at a glance the debris reminded her a great deal of Bud's woodworking shop at the back of the dower house.

"So," he said, "are you itching for a second chance at shooting me in the ballocks?"

Lark blushed. "I apologize for the nature of our first meeting. I . . . I was afraid, you see."

"Needed no medical book to diagnose that," he said. "Frightened virgins always look so, though not another in my long life has shot her lord and master in the arse on their wedding night." Buckston slapped his knee with glee.

Awed by his merriment, Lark wondered suddenly why people thought him cross.

"So what are you doing here?" he asked. "Out with it. I ain't got all day."

Ah, she thought. That was why. "I think I may be with child."

"Guess himself got his arse out of that sling you put him in, eh?" The medical man chuckled again. "Does this mean you're not afraid of him anymore?"

Lark had discovered his secret. The old charlatan was all bluster. "How do I know if I am with child? Can you tell me for certain?"

"Don't know why you'd want a brat. They're all too noisy. Best lock 'em in a room 'til they can talk sense." He winked, and asked all the same questions Alexandra did, and all but confirmed her diagnosis, based on the same evidence—enlarged and tender breasts, small hard mound of a stomach, missing monthlies.

Everything seemed quite straightforward and easy, until he asked her to lie on his table and lift her skirts.

When Lark yelped in outrage, Buckston whisked a bedpan before his ballocks.

Lark softened at his look. "Take heart," she said. "My husband has confiscated my pistol.

"Smart man. Speaking of hearts," he said. "You made mine near burst from my chest just now. I thought me worldly goods were done for." The doctor wiped his brow with a sleeve, thanked a diety Lark did not recognize, and proceeded to explain his examination.

"When did you have your last flux?" he asked again.

"In late spring," she said. "Near as I can remember." Buckston nodded.

Lark confirmed that he was a gentle man, kind and mannerly, who simply wore the guise of a curmudgeon.

"Well your husband's pistol didn't get confiscated, now, did it?" he said toward the end of his examination. "Because one of his bullets hit home. You've got one on the way for sure, mistress."

Lark walked on air as she left his office that day. She was carrying a child. Ash's child. A child conceived in tenderness, possibly even in love, on her part. She could not wait to tell Ash—

Oh no, if she told him, he would stop coming to her bed. She loved having him make love to her, even if that's not what they were really doing. She loved sleeping in his arms, waking there too. His hands soothed her to her marrow, his kiss lulled her and brought her joy. She liked warming her cold feet against his warm man-parts, another pleasure she would miss without him in her bed.

Why had she made that terrible stipulation, and how could she change her mind now that the time had come?

'Twas something she must ponder. She would wait to tell Ash of their expected child until she knew how to rescind her rule without making herself, or any future requests, seem trivial or foolish.

Once she told him, she would take Alexandra's advice and make it seem as if she were holding to her stipulation, while seducing Ash back into her bed, in such a way as to make him think his powers of seduction had won.

When the time came, she would take out that milky-green jar and ask him to apply the oil of seduction Alex gave her, and perhaps even attempt the ploy of interrupting him in his bath.

Come to think of it, perhaps *that* might be a good time to tell him that she had cheated him into marrying her.

Chapter 21

Lark hated that Ash was forced to remain in London for nearly two weeks in an effort to complete his inquiries into Briana's paternity. By the end of the second, Lark had paced herself sick, imagining the worst possible results of his findings.

Sometime after midnight, while she lay wakeful and worried, she heard a coach stop beneath the portico. She shot from her bed, never so glad of anything than to arrive at the top of the main stairs in time to see her husband—handsome in his cape and curly beaver—step into the foyer and hand Grimsley his cane. She ran down in her bare feet, wearing one of the new nightrails and dressing gowns he'd had fashioned for her.

Ash gave Grim his things and shook his head when he saw her coming. "I wonder you did not take the stair rail for better speed." He chuckled, caught her in his arms, and kissed her with speaking passion. 'Twas everything she wanted in a homecoming kiss, except for the worry he attempted to hide but she sensed nonetheless.

"Bad news," she said, stepping back. "I know you have bad news. We cannot keep her, can we?"

Because Grimsley stood nearby, holding his cape, top hat, and cane, Ash did not immediately answer

Lark. "The nights get colder as August comes to a close," he said. "Grim, tea in the drawing room?"

Ash bid his wife precede him toward the room he found most soothing with its blue damask furnishings and silk-striped walls. He sat beside her on the settee, where he took her into his arms and kissed her again, because he'd missed her so much; then he kept her beside him so he could hold her as they talked.

"Pull your feet up and tuck them under your dressing gown," he ordered. "We cannot have you becoming ill."

"Can we not? Why?"

"Because you have children to raise."

"More than Micah?" she asked turning him toward the subject troubling her.

"Perhaps," he said.

"Oh Ash, tell me."

"Nora and her friend, Jane, lost touch after Nora married Ames and went to live in France, so Jane knows nothing but gossip about Nora's last years, and it is not pretty. Word is that Ames's temper got the better of him, more often than not, and that he was responsible for Nora's illness. When her lover called Ames out, Ames was killed in the ensuing duel."

"Her husband's rising temper could be the reason Nora sent Briana to you then, could it not, rather than your paternity?"

"I thought the same, but Jane says Briana *is* my natural daughter. Nora confided as much when she was frantic to find her unborn child a father."

Ash sighed and chafed his wife's cold hands. "I am sorry, Lark. I know you wanted to bear my first child. I could see it in your face. But you love the one I already have, despite your disappointment, do you not?"

"Yes, Ash, I do. Yes," she repeated, initiating another kiss, one filled with a meaning Ash could not discern. "Tell me, then," she said when he would have continued. "What is the problem with our keeping Briana, if she is yours?"

"There is a man claiming to be Ames's uncle searching for Briana. He claims also to have a letter from Ames naming him the girl's guardian. He has made inquiries as to her whereabouts of Carstairs, our family solicitor."

"Oh no," Lark said. "Is Carstairs not the man who sent Briana to us in the first place?"

"Yes. Arranging an appointment with him is what kept me in London. I felt the need to meet with him myself, though I never used Briana's real name, not even with our own solicitor. Good news, though. Carstairs has not as yet told this 'uncle' where to find Briana, and he has promised to look deeply into the matter and put the man off for as long as may be within the law. Meanwhile, I have applied to Hunter to have the man's activities investigated."

"Does Hunter do such work?"

"Yes, he does, has done since the war, though the fact is not widely known and should be kept between us."

"I understand and appreciate whatever he can do. I would do anything to keep Briana from being taken from us."

"We, both of us, would." Ash rose to gaze out the night-black window. "My father was right. I hurt so many with my selfish flight to war. My mother lies helpless, while Nora, forced to take such a man, was cut down in her youth."

He turned to regard Lark, innocent and caring. "I do

not deserve you, nor do I feel worthy enough to bring a new child into the world."

Lark smiled at what she likely perceived as a jest, Ash thought, though he was serious. He wasn't good enough for her.

"You are a good father Ash. We have two children, not even our own, who would attest to it."

"As they would to your mothering. I have applied for their guardianship, Lark, Micah's and Briana's. I know we should have discussed such a step beforehand, but it seemed imperative of a sudden to sign the documents. I have written to Reed Gilbride St. Yves to speed the process. He has friends in high places after his service to the crown, and if any man knows how to obtain swift and legal custody of children, he is the one."

Lark threw herself into his arms. "I am so pleased, Ash. You will see that they have a future. A real future. Come." She took his hand and led him from the drawing room as Grimsley made to enter with the tea tray.

"His lordship is no longer thirsty, Grimsley," his audacious bride announced as she led him willingly up the stairs.

Ash hauled her up short half way there. "You are a heavy-handed one this evening. May I ask what you are about?"

"I am about to fill my hands with something even heavier." She glanced askance at the evidence of his interest. "Shall we make another attempt at a baby? The task has been deuced difficult without a potential father in attendance."

Ash barked a laugh. "I have missed you, saucepot."

"Come," she said, "and show me how much."

Ash happily complied.

* * *

In September, Lark and the children went lavender gathering, so she and Cook would have the supplies to make soaps, sachets, and lavender wands as Christmas gifts for her guests.

Another day, they went apple-picking in the orchard. After they filled several baskets of the shiny red fruit, she was tired, so she spread a blanket in the grass. For tea, they ate the bread, cheese, and the apple tarts she had brought. Then Lark bid the children lie down and rest before they picked more apples, and she did the same.

She had no sooner closed her eyes than someone was attempting to rouse her. "Aunt-eee, Aunt-eee, wake up, wake up. Briana is crying."

"Micah!" Lark sat up with a rush of dizziness. "How long have I been asleep?" She touched her brow to stop its spinning, and then she took in her surroundings and assimilated her nephew's . . . words? "Micah, did you speak to me?"

"Briana is in the tree crying."

Lark rose then, with no more thought to the miracle that had just occurred, and every thought for Briana's safety, and followed her nephew toward a grandfather of a horse chestnut tree.

Micah pointed upward and Lark was forced, with trepidation, to shade her eyes with a hand, against the glare of the setting sun. There she saw Briana, so far up, as to appear the size of an ant amid the chestnut's full shirred leaves.

"How did she manage to climb so high? Never mind. Micah, run and fetch his lordship, and hurry. Bring him back. Oh, and tell him to bring a ladder."

As soon as Micah left, Lark began climbing toward Briana. "Are you all right?" she called, for the child had said nothing since she appeared.

"My foot is stuck and I am afraid to tug it and fall."

Lark thought she must be sixty feet up, she seemed so far away. "Can you see a safe place to sit and wait for help?" Lark called.

Briana looked about her and found a stout limb on which to perch.

"That's my girl." Lark climbed forever, while a score of ripe, spiny chestnuts dropped around her, sometimes hitting her, until she reached the child. Not that reaching her meant either of them was safe.

It took several minutes to extract Briana's foot from the crook of the tree, and even then, they were forced to leave her shoe behind.

"Listen, darling, I am going to help you get down one limb at a time. You will go down one, then I will get down one, and then you will have your turn again. Do you understand?"

Briana nodded and heeded Lark's every instruction, no matter how minor, and in that way, they managed to descend the better part of the distance, until Lark slipped, teetered, clung, and fell to the ground.

"I am all right," she called up. "'Twas barely thrice the length of my own body I fell." She heard men shouting, and running feet, then Ash was lifting her into his arms, muffling his scold with kisses.

One of the tenants got Briana the rest of the way down and carried her, as Ash carried Lark, to the farm wagon she had brought to haul the apples. The tenant rode his horse to the village for the doctor, while Ash drove Briana, Lark, and Micah, straight to the Chase.

Mim put Briana to bed and Ash put Lark to bed;

then he paced and raged around the perimeter of her bed while they awaited the doctor.

Buckston saw Briana first and pronounced her fit, Mim reported, and then the doctor came to examine Lark.

To her relief, Buckston sent Ash from the room while he examined her. "My baby?" she asked, after the door shut.

The doctor only grunted in response to the question and remained silent throughout his examination. Finally, he pronounced her and her baby fit, but for her twisted ankle.

"You had better take life easier and no more tree-climbing until this little one of yours appears, if you wish to keep him from harm," he said.

"No more tree-climbing," she said, "I understand, but as for taking life easier. . . ."

"Yes?" Buckston looked incredulous as he gazed at her above his spectacles.

"I am to have a Christmas house party," she said. "A rather large one."

"Nearly three months from now? You'll be big-bellied and no mistake by then. Society doesn't usually approve a woman of an interesting condition showing that much in company."

" 'Twill not be a society gathering, close friends only, with a great many children. Micah never had Christmas. Please Doctor Buckston, I could do without it, but poor Micah and Briana."

That seemed to soften him as nothing else had. "How many children?" he asked, almost warily, as if he must put up with the lot of them himself.

"Two of ours, ten of Reed and Chastity's . . . oh my, fifteen or twenty, I'd guess, all ages. I can hardly wait."

Buckston rolled his eyes then shook his head as if he couldn't understand, though the charlatan could not keep his big old eyes from twinkling. "Unless something happens in the next week to say different, I can't see any reason why you should not have your Christmas house party, providing you rest until the very day."

Lark grinned and covered her babe protectively, more grateful than she could say. As she was about to warn the doctor that she had not as yet given her husband her happy news, Ash stepped into the room, his jaw set. He would not be turned away again.

"Well, how is she, Buckston? May I take her over my knee now and beat her for her foolishness?"

"Not if you want a healthy babe come February."

Ash paled. Lark had never seen the like. He looked so pallid of a sudden, so without color, that Buckston pushed him down to sit on her bed with a mere finger to his shoulder. The grinning medical man picked up Ash's wrist as if to test it for life. "Gonna swoon on us, old man?" he asked with a chuckle.

"Do not be ridiculous," Ash said, but his words held no bite.

"Rogues are the most skittish of men when it comes to dealing with their increasing wives," the doctor told Lark as she watched her husband with worry.

"Why is that?" she asked.

Buckston shrugged. "Perhaps they know they're perpetuating trouble, or can envision the problems they'll face raising terrors like themselves. Difficult to say."

Lark laughed, but when she did, Ash turned on her, accusation lacing his look. He might be surprised about the babe, but she was *not,* and he knew it.

The doctor saw it too and packed his leather satchel

with no little dispatch. "No, no need see me out. Grimsley is like to be waiting just beyond the door. He'll set me down the stairs just fine and send me on my way with a dollop, besides." Buckston regarded Ash pointedly. "Meet her halfway."

Ash nodded, opened the door for the medical man to depart, and shut it again.

Lark closed her eyes, suddenly exhausted.

"Won't work," Ash said. "You'll have to face me sooner or later."

Lark took in the thunderous set to her husband's brow. "Did you honestly mean to beat me?" she asked.

"You frightened ten years from my life, not to mention Micah *telling* me Briana was in trouble and you were trying to save her. I could not think beyond the amazing sound of his voice, while the situation he conveyed scared the bejesus out of me."

"The same happened to me," Lark said. "Except that I had fallen asleep and thought I must be dreaming."

Ash sat on her bed. "You've been sleeping so much because you're carrying our child."

Lark smiled tremulously, uncertain of his reaction, and her eyes filled. Angry or not, she was foolishly pleased to be sharing this moment with her husband, not that there seemed any joy in *him*.

Rat's whiskers, she wanted this to mean more to him than the securing of an inheritance. "Fancy that," she said. "It seems I have fulfilled my end of our bargain."

"How long have you known?"

Presented with the question she dreaded, Lark raised her chin. "Do not fret; a delay in your knowledge makes no matter to your place in your grandfather's will."

"Why did you not tell me?" he asked, so in control,

she might have imagined his fleeting grimace of pain at her words.

"I was waiting for the right time."

"Last night, as I made love to you and spoke of having a babe of our own did not seem like the proper time?"

If they *had* been making love, Lark thought, 'twould have been the perfect time. She turned on her side, facing away from him, because she did not want him to see her tears.

He slipped into bed behind her and wrapped his arms around her. "Do not, Larkin. I know increasing women tend to weep, but do not be sad. Be happy. You have made me so."

She rolled to face him. "Of course you are happy. You are now your grandfather's heir."

Ash raised a chiding brow and wiped her tears with his fingertips. "I am happy because none of you were hurt, not Briana, nor you, nor our babe. You were foolish, Lark, and gave me a fright."

"Briana needed me."

"The termagant. She should have sat in that tree until I arrived. 'Twould have done her good to cool her heels a bit."

Lark did not suggest that he take a good look at the height of that particular horse chestnut at any time soon for he might become as pale as when he heard her news.

She thought he might kiss her then, but someone knocked at her door, so he rose to answer it.

Briana and Micah stood framed by the door, contrition clear on their fresh-scrubbed faces. Ash let them in, and they stepped to her bed as one, like salt-and-pepper twins, one raven-haired, one flaxen. "We're sorry for leaving the blanket while you slept and for climbing the tree," Briana said.

"So you both climbed it, did you?" Lark stroked the lazy curl from Briana's temple while she raised a chiding brow her nephew's way. "I am happy you were, neither of you, hurt. Your ankle is not hurt, Briana?"

"Not like yours, but I am missing a shoe." She raised a stockinged foot, wiggling her toes.

Micah sniggered.

Lark caught his collar and tugged him closer. "And you," she said. "Why did you wait so long to speak to us?"

Micah kept her from combing back *his* hair by claiming her hand. "I did not mean to make you sad," he said. "Where I grew up, they strapped me when I 'blathered.' He shrugged. "I stopped. When I got here, I waited, and when I saw I might talk safe, I did not know how to start."

"I am sorry I put you with that family," Lark said. "I did not know they were unkind. Did they treat you very badly?"

Micah shrugged.

Lark brought him down for an embrace, swallowing against his untold pain.

"I remember you," he whispered against her hair, and she wept.

Chapter 22

Four weeks after Lark fell from the chestnut tree, she ran out of patience. Since the event, Ash had kept to his own bed by night, while acting as if she should be wrapped in cotton by day. Though Doctor Buckston visited a week after her fall, and pronounced her fit and healthy, Ash continued to avoid her bed.

Was he honoring her foolish stipulation that once she got with babe he should stop coming to her? As a man of honor, he must be, and yet, 'twas not his choice, for his body seemed to rise to the ready whenever she stepped near.

As a matter of pride, she tested the assumption and discovered he rose at the least provocation—the brush of a breast, a whisper at his ear, an intimate reference. She had even tripped and ended in his lap the other night, almost by accident, and took heart in the hard throbbing way she affected him.

She had given him every chance to make his needs known to her in some way, but he kept his peace, so now she must take matters into her own hands.

Lark placed the milky-green jar of seduction oil on her bed table and remembered everything Alexandra taught her about seduction. She learned her lessons well: she had an ache at the base of her spine. Women in her condition often did. She needed her husband to knead the ache while employing the soothing "liniment" from the jar. *She* could not reach the spot, not without intensifying her pain.

First, of course, she would need a soak in a hot bath.

Lark chose this evening because she saw enough water boiling in the kitchen to fill the huge copper slipper bath.

In preparation, she donned a confection of a dressing gown, a diaphanous pale rose silk trimmed in a deeper rose velvet at the plunging neck, but silly her, she forgot to don its matching night rail beneath.

When she heard Ash dithering in the dressing room—he often dithered, especially at baby-making, which she found satisfactory—Lark listened for the splash that meant he was stepping into his bath, before making her entrance.

As she waited, she pulsed in anticipation just knowing the moment was near. Lord, she had missed his attentions this past month, though God knew she had made good use of her time. Had anyone ever slept this many hours?

Ash's eyes grew large when Lark wandered into the dressing room, her hand at the base of her aching spine, as if she sought surcease from pain.

When she noticed him, she started, which took no skill, for his roguish handsomeness astonished her anew. His hairy, water-slick chest, near enough to touch, made her fist her hands so she would not . . . yet.

She must appear truly startled by the sight of him, while he regarded her as if he had never seen her before.

Lark knew her dressing gown clung to her rounded

belly and revealed the larger crests of her milk-full breasts, for she had begun truly to increase in recent weeks, and Ash had not seen her naked in some time.

"Motherhood becomes you, Larkin," he said, as she stood over him. "You fairly glow with good health."

Lark caressed the scope of their child, soothing the babe as well as herself. "If not for my back, I would feel rather brazenly fit."

He sat up. "Are you unwell? What is wrong with your back?"

" 'Tis nothing. It simply aches, which Alexandra and the doctor say is normal for a woman in my condition. I thought a soak would do me good when I heard the tub being filled, and foolishly hoped 'twas for me."

Lark suspected from the sound deep in her husband's throat that he fought some inner battle. He looked set to invite her in, and knowing him, he must be in full physical arousal. But as a gentleman, he might, under the circumstances, suggest that he leave first.

Poppycock, she was taking no chances. Lark unfastened her sash and allowed her dressing gown to fall the slightest bit open. "May I join you?"

Ash groaned inwardly when his neglected manhood leapt to vital and unfortunate life as his saucy bride dropped her wrap to the floor and bared her beautifully rounded body for his awestruck admiration.

Lord, but she was breathtaking in her maternity.

As if that heady tease were not enough, she stepped into the tub, splashing water mercilessly over the sides and onto the floor, and sat right down to join him in his bath. She smiled as if 'twere an everyday occurrence, tangling her legs with his, silk to sinew, soft to hard . . . maternal contentment oblivious to raging need.

Ash spared a lamentable thought for his deliriously happy manhood—all dressed up with no place to go.

Or could he be blissfully mistaken? Did a seductress regard him across the breadth of his bath? Did motivation drive her innocent pose? Loose hair of sunlit gold cascaded to his bride's alabaster shoulders. Heavy breasts rode the waves that lapped at them—making his mouth water, his tongue jealous—finding its level upon her swollen rosy-ripe nipples.

Did the siren who held his gaze call to him in the silent way he imagined? "Is this not a bit . . . unorthodox?" he asked with a last grasp at self-preservation.

"You mean soaking in a hot tub in my condition? Not according to Alexandra."

"And she is the expert, is she, after one child?"

"She is the only expert I know, though she garnered her advice from Sabrina who has borne five, you understand."

"Of course. Forgive me. It is just. . . ."

Lark fished about beneath the water, skimmed his calf, his thigh. "What?" she asked.

Ash about died of anticipation. "You are my wife."

"I know." She raised the soap like a trophy and grinned. "I have a babe in my belly to prove it."

The crux of the matter, Ash thought, shifting to accommodate his thickening manhood.

What would she do if he claimed her? What would she do if he pulled her toward him and impaled her now, this minute, here in their steaming bath?

After a month of celibacy, Ash near spilled at the thought.

"My back feels better for the heat," Lark said, purring like a lazy cat, head against the tub, a smile about her heart-shaped lips, her cheekbones high, his hornpipe higher. "Will you rub it for me, down low?"

Ash started. "Excuse me?"

"My back. I think it would feel better if you rubbed it while the hot water soothed it. Will you?"

Ash released a shuddering breath. "Turn about, then."

Just like that, Lark scooted his way and turned her back on him, too quick and willing by half. Did she have seduction in mind, this bride who'd shot him in the arse the first time he made to go near her? Was she attempting to lure him back to her bed, despite the stipulation she might also regret, *please God?*

Ash spread his legs to accommodate her, her back against his front, and he began to make soothing circles at the base of her spine with his fingertips. As he did, Lark moaned, squirmed, and rubbed against him, until he thought he might burst, but who cared? This was the closest he'd gotten to Lark, to ecstasy, in weeks, and he wanted more. He wanted everything of her that he could get.

Her complacent sighs became a trial of sensual pleasure. Memories flooded Ash, her riding him, him riding her, learning him in the lavender field, measuring his rod against a parsnip, the parsnip coming up short.

Ash grinned as he kissed a bare shoulder. She tilted her head so he could better reach her neck.

With his free hand, he began to stroke her midriff while he continued soothing her back. She relaxed against him, aware surely of his hard reaction.

He cupped a breast and she raised it, as if for his delectation. Taking that as a sign, he fingered her nipple, and she failed to stifle a throaty moan of rapture, stiffening him the more. Ash went for broke—he'd always been a gambling man—and removed his hand from her back to play her at her center.

When he breached her and knew, as well as she, that she wept there to receive him, she turned her head to regard him, her gaze open, knowing. "Your hornpipe wants playing."

Ash opened his mouth over hers, swallowed her grateful sob, and tasted the salt from her tears in the kiss. He had not been wrong. His wife wanted him as much as he wanted her.

He played her as he kissed her, until she reached a climax of incredible duration and proportion, judging by her keening song of joy.

"Hush," he said. "Grim will come looking to see what I need."

"Then I will send him away, for I know what you need." She rose like a mermaid from the sea, wet and glistening, and turned to stand before him, proud in her expectancy, offering the gift of herself.

Ash stroked her belly, kissed her, every inch, laving and adoring her with his lips and tongue, awed anew that his child grew, there, beneath her tight white skin and fast-beating heart. Then he placed his mouth at her woman's center and made his pearl-bright fairy sing again.

Before he sensed her wicked intent, she swooped and impaled herself in a rush, swallowing, and capturing his manhood within her tight silken glove.

"Have mercy," he said and became her willing slave. He devoured her mouth, skimming her every crest and hollow in the same way she stroked and stoked him.

When she closed a talented hand around his ballocks, he thought she would bring him to climax, for he had never been so rushed to frenzy; yet he knew he should not be surprised at any sensation his Larkin Rose evoked.

He begged her not to move, thanked the gods for her seduction, kissed her until he could not keep from moving. And when he did begin, he could do no more than help her milk him—there was no other way to describe the earth-shattering coupling.

Which of them led the charge was arguable, but his money was on Lark. Ash cared not; he knew only that he had found the portion missing from his soul for a long month's time and that he would not be severed from her again.

She reached her peak three times more before she let him spill his seed, leaving him laughably grateful and damned near dead.

A full five minutes passed before either of them realized the water had chilled.

Ash stepped from the bath first and helped her out, wrapped her in towels, and carried her to his bed.

"Why not my bed?" she asked when he joined her.

"Because I have lain here too many nights alone to bear. I craved the feel and scent of you here. We will change beds on a whim, shall we, for we are bedmates, you and I, come what may, from this day forward."

"You *admit* that you missed having me in your bed?"

"Not as eloquently as you admitted as much."

Lark tugged on his forelock. "I wish you would make a try at eloquence."

Ash chuckled, leaned on an elbow, and toyed with her rosy nipples. He even toyed with the notion of telling her he loved her, but feared the possible rejection, or breach, that a lone revelation might engender.

"Let me admit that when you stepped into my bath, I prayed, like I have never prayed before, to the angels and saints on high, that you came to me with the express purpose of seducing me."

Lark bit his ear. "I admit . . . *nothing.*"

Ash chuckled and relaxed in a way he had not for weeks. "Do you know how many nights I sat beside your bed and watched you sleep? I knew such joy that you carried my child, but such loneliness at our resultant separation."

Lark bit her lip and Ash knew that as a woman of her word, she would not, after all, admit to anything, not even to missing him. "What about your stipulation that I stop coming to your bed now that you are with child?" he asked, unable to leave it unspoken.

"You have just declared my stipulation null and void," she said. "I make no quarrel with your pronouncement."

"I honor my contracts, madam. If you wish such a separation, you will have it, but you must tell me so."

"And will you take my every future request at naught, if I rescind this, my first?"

"Your first was made at pistol-point, you must remember, though I'd as soon not, at which juncture you carried through with your threat. Bearing that in mind, and elsewhere, which remains scarred and tender, I shall never make the mistake of taking any of your requests at naught."

Lark seemed to ponder some high mathematical equation; then she nodded, as if satisfied with her account. "I did not tell you about the babe, for I disliked the notion of you leaving my bed. There. Make sport of me, if you will."

Ash crushed her to him, pleased he'd brought her

that far. "I am sorry you could not bring yourself to share your concerns, Lark, though I understand, for trust has always come hard to me as well." He hoped the confession would set them on a path to trust, but as he awaited her reaction, he saw that his sated bride had fallen asleep and likely heard not a word.

Six weeks before Christmas, ten triple truckle beds arrived, which Lark ordered placed in the nursery, and adjoining bedchambers, for the rogues' children and their assorted nursery maids.

Ash watched astonished as the beds were carried inside. "Good God," he said. "How much did all this cost?"

"We will pay a quarter the cost. Each of the rogues with children will. Those are community truckles. We are likely to take turns at house parties, Alex said, and 'twould be foolish for us all to make the investment, so the truckles will be sent to whichever house hosts the next gathering."

"Alex is a quick one, but you're catching up, by God."

"She had to be quick, did she not, carrying the burden of her entire family while Hawk was off fighting Boney?"

"Yes," Ash said, kissing his wife's brow and stroking his growing child with a possessive rush. "You are kindred spirits, I don't doubt, which is why you like her so."

"She is my first and best friend."

"Take care that you and your friend do not plan us out of house and home. Do not mistake me, for I am looking forward to Christmas, but as it stands, I must slaughter enough livestock for beef and pork to feed them all, and likely sell one of our few remaining paintings as well."

"Save the painting, for I have a notion about feeding them. Early each morning, you must make up a hunting party. We will eat whatever you shoot. Just take care to bag a variety—goose, swan, hare, pheasant, partridge—whatever you will. You should fish the lake as well."

"Will you require boar and venison too?"

"For boar's head?" She grimaced. "I pray you will not. As for venison, that would be lovely."

"And supposing we have ill luck in our sport?"

"If we eat bread and butter or toasted cheese, if our pudding have more flour and suet than meat, then so be it, for we will all be together for Christmas."

"A bride with all the answers," Ash said, kissing her brow. "When is Alex due to arrive so you may make your plans? I think I may have to be away."

"When you do not even know the day?" Lark scoffed. "Tuesday week," she said, "and see that you are to hand."

When Alex saw Lark, she hesitated. "Good grief," she said as they embraced, her babe between them, "you are as big as I was the first time I visited, and with all of three months to go, you poor thing."

"Fat, I know." Lark patted her belly with pride.

"As a prize sow," Alex said with twinkling eyes.

Lark's face warmed as they walked arm in arm up the steps to the house.

They began by looking over the wooden toys Bud crafted as gifts for the children in attendance. In trying to make certain they had enough, Alex and Lark were forced to make a list so as to count their numbers.

Lark sat with quill and parchment, while Alex paced the drawing room with a fussing Brandon. "Gideon and Sabrina have two sets of boy twins, and Julianna."

"*Two* sets?" Lark said.

"Three-year-old Caleb and Josh are Gideon's own, though Gideon adores Julie, Damon, and Rafe. Beware, Hawk calls the older twins Demon and Rapscallion, for he is their uncle by blood, having been half brother to Sabrina's first husband."

"I will never get any of it straight."

"You will in time. Mark two children for us, Brandon here, rooting for nourishment, and Beatrix, and your two. That makes how many, nine? As for Reed and Chastity. . . . Alex searched her reticule for a list she snapped open with a flick and handed to Lark; then she unfastened her bodice for her son to suckle.

Lark scanned the list. "Matthew, Mark, Luke, Rebekah, Harry, Sidney, Brenna, Clarice, Jillian, and Meggie. Chastity must be a saint. How old are they all?"

"Lord, no one knows. Their own twins, Jillian and Meggie, are six months old now. As for the rest, none are older than thirteen, as close as anyone can guess."

"Are twins rampant with rogues?"

"Reed himself is a twin, so 'twas no surprise he and Chastity produced a set. Gideon's Sabrina has borne twins for two husbands, so the fault must be hers."

"I am anxious to meet Chastity and Sabrina," Lark said.

"They will love you." Alex tried to rouse her son to resume his meal, but it was useless. "There, you," she said kissing his milky lips, "asleep again, and only two drops taken." She closed her bodice to put him to her shoulder.

"I am envious," Lark said, her arms wanting.

"Not for long. Soon, you will simply be tired."

Lark perused her lists. "Nineteen children, six rogues, four wives—and a score of nursery maids and servants—all here for Christmas." She paled. "What have I got myself into?"

Alex soothed her fears before they determined the traditions they would observe, who would occupy which chamber, and who would need cradles. "I brought bed linen to lend you," Alex said. "Claudia lent us extra as well for she and Chesterfield will go to his family for the holiday."

"We should sit with Cook while you are here," Lark said. "She is hopeful of direction."

Alex organized meals in a trice, while Cook took to the notion of feeding so many with an air of anticipation. "Too long since we did Christmas," she said. "Can't wait to fill my kitchen with scents of roast goose and plum pudding."

"You may not realize," Lark said to Alex as they left the kitchen, "but you taught me a great deal today about organizing a house. I will be a better manager after this."

"Do not tell Hawk. He says I will manage him into his grave."

Over tea, Alex began a new list. "Which decorations will we find outdoors?"

Lark frowned. "The decorations are in the attic."

"No, the fresh decorations—holly, ivy, mistletoe, rosemary. . . . Collecting them is entertainment at a house party. Have you never gathered Christmas greenery?"

"I will be a dreadful failure," Lark wailed.

"Sit," Alex said. "Put your feet up. "You do not do this alone. Chastity will lead the children in a Christmas theatrical. Sabrina will oversee decorating the house. For my part, I will stand beside you in all things, though I cannot wait to decorate your Christmas tree. It will be my first, but not my last."

Lark could only shake her head.

"This will not be as bad as you perceive," Alex promised. "Besides, Sabrina plans to put the rogues themselves to work, even as regards to the children."

"Hah! This I would like to see."

"Oh, you will."

Chapter 23

Lark could not believe that Christmas and her house party were upon her. She and Alex stood watch at the drawing room window, the frolicking babe in Lark's belly keeping her from getting as near to the glass as she wished.

Anticipation and trepidation rode her in turn. "Who should introduce who?" she asked again.

"Forget the rules," Alex said. "No formalities are to be observed among friends this Christmas. Everyone will be excited and speak at once, introducing themselves, kissing and embracing. Oh, and backslapping. The rogues are fond a good backslap. They consider it manly."

"If you were not beside me, I would die," Lark said.

Alex squeezed her hand. "I would not miss your first Christmas."

A rare snow had begun to fall well before the first set of carriages clattered up the drive. When they did, Lark and Alex went to wait on the steps. Ash stepped out a minute later to place Lark's wrap about her shoulders.

He chuckled when he saw the same crest on all three carriages. "I cannot believe it takes so many to carry the St. Yveses' brood. You will not credit it, Lark, but

I remember a time when Reed disliked children of all things."

Nevertheless, too many to count poured from the second and third carriages, one each bearing a woman too well-dressed to be a nursery maid. Alex told Lark 'twas Reed who stepped from the first carriage, and accepted two bundles, likely so Chastity could alight.

Ash ran down to offer Chastity his hand and greet them; then Lark and Alex ushered them from the cold in a trice.

Lark should not be surprised that even at first meeting, formalities were dispensed with embraces between rogues' wives. Between the rogues themselves, handshakes and backslaps.

Reed bowed to Alex and Lark. "May I introduce my sisters, Pegeen and Sunny, who give a great deal of loving care to their nieces and nephews."

Pegeen and Sunny curtsied their silent greetings.

Lark admired Chastity at once. She organized her children with a word so they stood like stair steps; then she rattled off their names down the line and laughed at Lark's uncertainty. "Do not try to remember names. Soon enough the brigands' quirks will single them out." She had unwrapped both baby girls, hers and Reed's, while speaking.

Lark relaxed. "If Sabrina is as efficient as the two of you, I may as well stop worrying about anything going wrong. I do not think any of you would allow it."

Reed put an arm about his wife's shoulders. "You are right there, but do not ask her to cook you anything."

Chastity tossed a frown her husband's way, amusing their brood, but for the babes who howled.

Lark led Chastity with the babes toward the red-papered winter parlor, and clapped her hands near its entry for attention. "Ladies and children only in this room, for feedings and such," she announced. "The tower library will be your retreat, gentlemen, though you will not be allowed to hide, as the women *will* be permitted in there."

Ash and Reed protested vehemently, but the wives banded together. Men and women alike knew there was no hope for the rogues. Not a one of them would step into a room where another rogue's wife might bare her breast, and no wife would think twice about invading their male sanctum.

Before Lark and Alex finished assigning bedchambers and nursery rooms, the second two carriages arrived, each bearing a different crest.

Hawk and Beatrix stepped from the first, and Alex sighed in relief. "I was afraid the snow would delay them. Gideon and Sabrina occupy the carriage behind them," she added, before accepting her husband's kiss and passing him their son.

Lark barely exchanged greetings with Hawk and Beatrix before she was looking up into the eyes of one of the most handsome men she had ever beheld, barring her husband, of course.

"Gideon St. Goddard," he said on a bow and kissed her hand. "Gad, Ash you got yourself a beauty." He took his petite wife's arm and led her forward. "Larkin Rose, my wife, Sabrina."

"Lark."

"Bree."

Another new friend. Emotion tightened Lark's throat. She had never had a family, never friends, and suddenly she felt as if these strangers were both.

Sabrina bore raven hair and porcelain skin . . . and

all five of her children hung about her husband's legs, not her skirts. Lark meant to ask later how she managed it. "Shall I show you to your bedchambers now or later? Chastity is in the parlor feeding the babes."

Sabrina removed her bonnet and extended her hands to her smallest twins. "Let us greet Chastity first. When are you due?"

"February, or March, perhaps. I am not certain."

"You are a brave one to take us all on."

"Shh, Bree," Alex said. "Do not frighten her. I promised 'twould be easy."

Sabrina raised a dubious brow Alex's way as they entered the salon where Chastity nursed her twins simultaneously, one at each breast.

Sabrina chuckled. "So that's what I looked like." She bent to kiss Chastity's cheek and stroke a soft baby fist.

As Lark rang for Grimsley, she attended to their discussion of nursing babes, for she had much to learn.

She heard a knock a moment later. Not even Grim would breach the sanctum. Lark rose. "Should we have tea now to warm us, then a formal tea in the drawing room later? We can send for the rogues then," she said. "They will be warming themselves with something stronger about now, at any rate."

"Sounds perfect," Sabrina said. "Even with hot bricks, the carriage was chill."

Lark left to give Grim instructions.

"Where have our men disappeared to?" Sabrina asked when Lark returned.

Alex explained the house rules for ladies and gentlemen.

"Oh no fair," Sabrina said on a chuckle.

"You will *not* admit that you think so" Alex said.

Sabrina and Alex seemed to share the familiarity of sisters, Lark saw, while she and Chastity were fairly new to this club of rogues' wives. "Alex, Sabrina? Were you acquainted *before* you married your respective rogues?"

"Caleb!" Sabrina took a vase from one toddler's hand and began placing breakables beyond reach. "Alex and I lived together once," Sabrina said. "Before I married Gideon, Alex cared for her family and Hawk's, and housed me, Damon, and Rafe, as well. We owe her a debt of gratitude."

"Nonsense. You make of it more than it was," Alex said. "Besides, I liked the company. I like being needed." She hooked her arm through Lark's, as if to show she meant it. "Wait until you see the Christmas Lark planned."

"But I planned nothing. You did it all."

Their laughter set Lark at ease. She reached for Chastity's babe who had done with nursing to keep her from swatting her hungry sister. "Chastity," she said. "Tell us how *you* came to be a rogue's wife."

A minute later, Lark stopped patting the babe's back. "You were a nun?"

Chastity grinned. "And now I am the mother of ten."

Beatrix came in then and gave Alex her fussing son.

"Bea, send Sunny and Peg down for a light tea," Alex said, "Unless you care to remain and I will fetch them?"

"No, thank you," Beatrix said. "I discovered a diversion of interest in the nursery."

"Oh? And his name is?"

Beatrix blushed. "Matthew."

Chastity squeaked and clapped a hand over her mouth.

* * *

If their wives but knew it, Ash thought, the library sat empty, while he, Gideon, Hawk, and Reed introduced the children to each other and generally attempted to reduce the havoc in the nursery.

"Uncle Hawk," Damon said, or at least Ash thought it was Damon, and not Rafe. "Tell us a story."

"Oh yes, do," Beatrix said coming in. "It has been an age since you did. Alex says Sunny and Pegeen should go down for a bit of informal tea."

The two women happily escaped. They might be comfortable in a room full of children, Ash thought, but never in a room of military men.

"Story," Beatrix reminded Hawk, tugging his sleeve.

Hawk looked about as if for an escape of his own. "Where is a Frenchie when you need one? Why me? Gideon is the storyteller."

Ash regarded the waiting children. "Are they all accounted for?" he asked, a bit nervous at keeping track of so many.

Reed, Gideon, and Hawk looked about and counted heads.

Ash winked at Micah and Briana, who appeared quite interested in so many playmates.

"All but toddlers and suckling infants accounted for," Gideon said. "As should be." As he said it, a little one, barely beyond toddlerhood—to Ash's mind—climbed into his lap. "Here's my sweet pea," Gideon said, kissing her nose.

"His shadow," Hawk explained.

At that, a girl with a single blond braid leaned against Reed's chair, called him Papa, whispered in his ear, and made Reed grin. Two little ones occupied his knees, while several sat at his feet. Rather amazing, Ash thought.

"*I* have a story to tell the children," he said. "Except that the story is true."

"What?" Briana asked.

"You know." Micah nudged her. She nudged him back.

Ash rolled his eyes. "Those two are mine," he admitted to his friends before turning to the circle of children. "Have any of you ever heard of Father Christmas?"

Several pairs of eyes widened. Most looked quite interested, except for a boy of about ten or eleven who scoffed. Nevertheless, Ash continued. "This very village is famous, because Father Christmas is known to live among us. People have caught sight of him delivering gifts on Christmas Eve to all good little girls and boys."

"What does he look like?" one of Reed's youngest asked.

"He wears a long, hooded velvet robe, like a bishop of old, with a sprig of holly in his buttonhole. He has white hair and a long white beard and carries a sack of gifts. If you behave while you are with us, he will bring a gift for each of you."

"No such thing as Father Christmas," said the scoffer in a cockney accent.

"Harry!" Reed snapped.

"There is too," Micah said, stance defensive, almost as if he were defending Ash, which made Ash proud.

Harry stepped briskly forth, matched Micah's stance, and popped him a good one, smack in the nose.

Briana shrieked and charged Harry, in defense of the brother she usually fought.

Other boys got into the fray—Briana was the only girl, but she was streetwise, was his Briana, and game for anything. Ash beamed.

"What is the meaning of this?" Lark shouted over the din.

"They're fighting," Ash said.

"I can see that. Stop them!"

"Why would we stop them?" he asked. "They're getting to know each other, becoming friends."

"That's not how you become friends."

Ash regarded the rogues. "It's how we did."

They, each of them, nodded in turn, regarding his wife as if she might be daft, though, truth to tell, their own wives looked as horrified as Lark.

"What is wrong with you?" Lark said. "You think beating each other to a pulp is sporting?"

"Right." Ash grinned, and Hawk nodded.

"Exactly," Reed echoed.

"Glad you understand," Gideon said.

"You're in trouble," Hawk told Gideon, who turned to regard his narrow-eyed wife.

Reed took one look at Chastity and separated Harry and Briana—the only two left fighting—before his own wife beat *him* to a pulp.

"You let him pummel a girl?" Chastity said, turning the military war hero's ears scarlet.

"She's no ordinary girl," Harry said, wiping the blood from his nose.

"Thank you!" Briana beamed then licked her bloody lip.

"See?" Ash said. "They're friends now."

Lark raised her arms then dropped them to her skirts. "Wash up, children," she said, "and that includes the ones who fought Boney. It's nearly time to dress for dinner." She turned back to regard him rather pointedly, Ash thought. "We're having parsnips," she said. "*Mashed* parsnips."

Myles Quartermaine and Hunter Elijah Wylder arrived fully five hours late, at about the time everyone congregated in the drawing room after dinner. Even the rogues had finished their brandy and cigars and joined their ladies by then.

As the two rogues Lark recalled from her wedding night entered her drawing room, all smiles, Grimsley formally introduced them.

They had surely been carousing, she thought, for they smelled like the Pickled Pigsty and appeared as foxed and oblivious as she remembered them. Fact was, they reminded her too much of her low beginnings for her to like them any more now than she had that night.

Nevertheless, she smoothed her royal velvet gown over the mound of her child and rose with Ash to step forward and welcome her guests into her home.

When she offered her hand, the two stood as addled as the last time she had seen them. Again she wanted to beat them bloody, the both of them, a heathen urge she thought she'd long since conquered, though it reminded her how shocked she'd been over the children's brawl earlier. Had she come so far she forgot who she was?

Lark supposed there was good and bad in that.

"Couldn't take the guttersnipe, eh, old man?" Myles said, belatedly slapping Ash on the back. "Can't blame you. This one's not only beautiful, she smells better."

Lark curled her hands into fists.

Hunter eyed the mound of their child. "Looks like you finally managed to 'insert yourself' into your grandfather's will."

Lark shot out and bloodied his nose.

Her guests gasped.

Blood dripped from between Hunter's cupping fingers as Chastity brought a handkerchief to stem the flow.

A heavy silence followed. Now *everyone* knew who she really was, Lark thought. Wilting, she turned to face them. "So much for making a good impression," she said, but rather than censure, she saw mirth in every expression.

Alex and Sabrina rose to applaud, Chastity grinned, and Myles stepped behind Hunter's coattails. "That you, Arky?"

"Well done," Hawk said, and Gideon winked.

"You really *did* shoot Ash in the backside on your wedding night, didn't you?" Reed said.

Lark raised her chin, feeling a rush of freedom. "Yes," she said. "I did, and I beat the daylights out of him before the wedding as well."

"Perhaps that's why we're such good friends," Ash said, taking her into his arms, and claiming her before all and sundry, making Lark feel cherished, and happy, and turning Myles Quartermaine and Hunter Elijah Wylder into a pair of rueful, red-faced rogues.

Chapter 24

After a successful hunting party the next morning, as everyone sat down to a hearty breakfast, Hunter and Myles made public and formal apologies to Lark, and were as publicly forgiven and welcomed to the Christmas celebration.

Later, Ash concurred with the other rogues that for the sake of safety, only the children five years and older should be allowed to accompany them into the woods for the gathering of the Christmas greenery.

Ash also insisted that several carriages be made available for the ladies to deliver them to the spinney, and return them to the Chase, as needs be, for tending to babes and such.

He and his fellow rogues, and whichever offspring were allowed to accompany them, set off half an hour earlier than the women to make the brisk, invigorating trudge over hillock, and through orchard and field, to the spinney.

Ash managed to meet the first carriage when it arrived so as to offer Lark his arm. "I do not know why you persist in accompanying us this morning. You could slip and endanger the babe." He placed his arm firmly about her waist as they walked.

"I will not miss my first expedition for Christmas

greenery, nor am I likely to slip with you holding me so tight. No, do not let go. I take pleasure in your solicitous attention."

After that flirting remark, Ash could do nothing but kiss her for some few minutes, before she could be allowed to follow the rest of the ladies deep into the spinney, where three competent military men stood beside the coveted Christmas plants, awaiting wifely direction.

The small wood boasted enough holly bushes to satisfy even Sabrina's salacious greed for the crimson-berried stalks with spiny, variegated leaves. Immediately they arrived, she put the children to work gathering sheaves, piling, and tying them to the sleds they had dragged along.

Above and around them, birds and other forest creatures squawked, scurried, and chattered at the brazen human invasion.

Ash and Lark watched as Sabrina tugged on Myles coat to snap him from his boredom and direct his gaze upward. "Mistletoe," she said, in the way she might have said, "fetch."

Myles sighed. "Gathering mistletoe is a tedious boot-beating business," he said, as he looked despairingly high into the tree from which the parasitic clusters of pearl berries and pale green leaves hung. "Do we really need mistletoe?"

"Get into the spirit, man," Hunter said, slapping Myles on the back. "Ladies have always been encouraged to kiss beneath mistletoe."

Myles regarded Pegeen as if with speculation. "I'm for mistletoe," he said, and began to climb, shaking the hemlock to which the mistletoe clung, dislodging snow on all their heads.

A collective groan rose, though no one seemed actually to mind.

"Mistletoe is also known to increase fertility," Gideon said, tongue in cheek.

Reed chuckled and indicated the frolicking children. "Does this look like we need help with fertility?"

Hawk shook his head. "Not you two. You keep producing doubles."

Gideon and Reed regarded each other with wide grins.

"What else do we need in addition to the holly and mistletoe?" Ash asked, supporting Lark.

"Laurel, ivy, and rosemary should do," Sabrina said. "Oh, and children, fill a sack with the horse chestnuts you see scattered on the ground, preferably the ones that have shed their spiked pods. Your younger brothers and sisters may paint them gold later, and we can hang them on the tree."

"What a brilliant notion," Chastity said.

Alex shook her head. "Bree will always have brilliant notions, though some of them get her into more trouble than others."

Hunter took Sunny's arm. "Shall we go deeper into the wood to forage for laurel, ivy, and rosemary?"

Myles chuckled from above. "He'll find mistletoe, mark my words. Come to think of it, I could use some help up here. Pegeen?"

To Ash's surprise, Pegeen began to climb.

"Wait a minute," Reed said, following his sister's upward progress with his gaze.

"We're in a tree, Reed," she said. "What can happen in a tree?"

Ash and Lark regarded each other, remembered the possibilities, and slipped away.

"Come down, Peg," they heard Reed say.

"Mind your own business, Reed," his sister responded.

Slinking off like naughty children, Ash urged Lark to move as far away from the group as he could get her. Still directing her toward the carriage he believed she should take home, he kept to the concealing thicket, so as to steal an intimate minute alone with her.

Last night, they had teased and played each other in bed, like tuning instruments for the grand performance, until she had fallen suddenly asleep. He knew that her condition exhausted her, that she had expended a great deal of energy with her guests, but Lord, she'd left him aching.

"I want you," he said, now backing her against a tree.

"What? Here? There are people everywhere."

"They are far too distant to come upon us," he assured her.

"Not far enough."

Ash slid a hand over her belly, and beneath it, until she closed her eyes and sighed. He tugged up her gown, bit by bit, found her warm and ready, and brought his babe-ripe bride pleasure, there with the snow falling all about them.

Though he'd been left rod hard and randy, 'twas still a most memorable experience.

Lark slept in his arms all the way home in the carriage. When they arrived, he carried her up to her bed, where she continued her much needed rest.

When Lark awoke, she found that her guests had returned from greenery gathering and that her house had been transformed into Christmas. Alex, Chastity, and Sabrina had directed the children's changing into dry clothes and the doling out of hot chocolate and iced gingerbread.

Employing varying amounts of the greenery they collected, Sabrina made the kissing boughs, Chastity the wreaths, and Alex the garlands. They had also added holly to the baskets and vases of dried lavender about the Chase, which made everything more festive.

"You do not mind that we took it upon ourselves to decorate for you?" Alex asked Lark later, as they admired the drawing room's garland-festooned mantel.

"What? Sorry that I missed all the hard work? Of course not, I am delighted with the results, and grateful. I do not have my old energy. This is beautiful and good, and the sight fills my heart to overflowing. Thank you."

"You missed nuncheon and tea, and I feared you would miss dinner as well," Alex said.

"Which explains why I am ravenous. Oh, did anyone decorate Grandmama's room?"

"We did not even think of it."

"Let us do so now, all hands to the task," Lark said, aware she could not, for the life of her manage it alone, and she was grateful when they rose to her aid.

Every man woman and child worked to decorate Ash's mother's room for Christmas, her gaze following it all.

"Do not tell me she does not realize it is Christmas, Ash. Look at the sparkle in her eyes," Lark said.

Ash regarded his mother and moved toward her bed. When he arrived, he bent to kiss her brow, which he had not done in an age, and thought he caught a hitch in her breath.

"Lark wanted you to have Christmas," he said. "She is a good lady, my wife."

Did his mother attempt to agree by offering so slight an eye movement as to make it seem unlikely. "Mama?" Ash said, comprehending Lark's avowal that his mother might be aware of more than he thought. He gave in to all her urging then and took his mother's hand. "Mama, squeeze my hand if you understand me."

When she did, Ash was forced to sit on her bed so as not to fall to his jellied knees—the rogues and their ladies talking and laughing about them as if a miracle had not just occurred.

Christmas surged to breathless life, sped Ash's heart, opened it to every foolish possibility.

He leaned nearer. "Mama," he all but whispered. "I am sorry I ran off to war rather than remain and face my responsibilities to you and the estate. I did not mean to hurt you with my departure."

His mother squeezed his hand twice then, frantic and . . . hopeful? Ash looked deep into her eyes and he knew, of a sudden, the meaning of Christmas peace.

Was her gift to him forgiveness or simply the knowledge that his father's judgment had been incorrect? Either way, Ash felt released from the weight he'd borne for so long. He felt . . . absolved, and for the first time in his life he understood the need, the power in forgiving.

Lark came up behind him and placed her hands upon his shoulders. "I never knew Christmas could be so wonderful," she said.

He took her hands, kissed each in turn, and smiled *with* his mother. "Neither did I."

* * *

The following morning, while Bud St. Nick brought the huge cedar into the picture gallery where it would be set up and decorated, Chastity held a private rehearsal for the children's Christmas theatrical in another room of the house. "It is a secret," she said, forbidding anyone to enter. "I will have no spoiled expectations, but simple enjoyment, however our cherubs perform."

Olga St. Nick had accompanied her husband and brought several splendid handmade gifts. They included a Christmas stable with the carved figures of the holy family, a toy farm wagon for Micah, and a lady puppet and stage for Briana.

For the new babe, they brought a white cradle, built by Bud and painted with the Blackburne family crest by Olga. She had also made the baby blankets, bonnets, and the littlest sleeping gowns Lark had ever seen.

Lark invited the couple to come for Christmas Eve supper but they declined in favor of dinner Christmas Day.

The snow had continued falling steadily for days and so the children begged to put the sleds to better use than hauling greens.

Sabrina looked to the ladies and held up a cautioning hand. "This is the tradition I brought and I know how to go about it."

She regarded Damon who begged the loudest for a sledding party. "I do not wish to go outdoors and become cold and wet," she said. "Go and ask your father."

"You may do the same," Chastity told Mark and Luke.

Lark shrugged and sent Micah and Briana to ask Ash.

After the men gave in to their children's pleas, as Sabrina predicted they would, the rogues came looking for their wives to set the event in motion.

"Lark," Ash said, "the children are to go sledding."

"I am glad to hear it. I wish you will have a wonderful time."

Reed reared back and furrowed his brow at Chastity.

Gideon turned on Sabrina. "I see *your* hand in this."

Hawk chuckled. "You are right." He looked to his own wife for confirmation.

"Do not look at me," Alex said, striding past. "I have a babe to feed."

"No!" Myles said when he realized the men had been outfoxed and were to take nearly twenty children out to play in the snow, but it mattered not, because that was the plan.

The women remained inside and made decorations for the tree—ribbon rosettes, parchment snowflakes. Lark filled lace circles with lavender buds and tied them with bows to hang on the tree.

They worked beside the huge bay window in the portrait gallery so as to keep watch over the sledding party.

Lark noted the camaraderie among the rogues, the way they must have worked together to defeat the common enemy. With the children they laughed; shouted; and made snow caves, snowmen, and snow angels. They hauled little ones on their shoulders uphill; took them on fast rides down; wiped noses; carried laggards; and doled out cocoa, hugs, and kisses. More often than not, they also replaced mittens, hats, and scarves.

"Do you see that some of our older children have paired off?" Chastity said. "Matthew and Beatrix for instance, and Micah and Rebekah."

Alex admired a rosette then looked up. "Harry and Briana as well," she added, "for I heard them discover that they had both survived the London streets."

Lark was not surprised to hear as much about Harry for there was an edge to him that could only be earned one way. She was lucky Briana had not acquired quite so brittle an edge.

"Reed seems to be counting heads more often than the others," Lark said.

"Old habits," Chastity said. "He is a good father."

"Gideon is more likely to get down and play with the children, rather than organize them," Sabrina said, shaking her head. "As if I have six, not five. Ah, there he goes. See, he and Micah are about to . . . tip." Sabrina rose as did Lark while the two flew through the air, Gideon's arms firm about Micah, Gideon landing them so Micah never touched ground.

Lark sighed in relief.

Sabrina smiled. "He does make for a fine pillow."

"The children are enjoying his antics," Alex said. "Hawk is less apt to play and more likely to teach them to build or repair something, like the snow cave he is overseeing. What about Ash, Lark?" Alex asked. "What is he likely to do with the children?"

"Ash reminds me of a lost soul," Lark said. "As if he does not yet know where or to whom he belongs, but he gives instinctively to each of our children what they need most, whether it be responsibility, or a hair ribbon."

"He is a good man," Alex said, "and you *do* love him after all."

Lark's eyes filled. "How should I know if I do?"

Chastity looked up from her work. "It sounds as though you are two lost souls, or two halves of one," she said. "Perhaps you will be whole only when you both know the answer to that question."

Lark turned to look out the window oblivious to the happy scene before and about her. "How can we be two halves of a whole if a lie stands between us?" she asked, but no one answered.

A stranger came to the Chase that afternoon, a man who introduced himself as Drummond Amesbridge and asked to be brought before the earl of Blackburne.

Lark had Grimsley show the man into a small receiving room off the main foyer, while she sent the retainer for Ash. She did not enter on her own but waited for her husband.

She met Ash in the hall and they clasped hands. "Where is Briana?" she asked.

"Well protected," Ash said. "One of us will have to go for her, or our friends will keep her hidden. I half expected this. Ready?"

She kissed him. "For luck."

He nodded for Grim to open the door and they went inside.

Ames's "uncle," Drummond Amesbridge, a worm of a man, slimy and underhand, lacked the ability to meet any eye. With dispatch, he claimed legal custody of Briana and insisted on getting her "home" for Christmas.

When asked to prove his claim, he handed Ash a sheaf of signed and sealed documents. "You have no choice," the worm said, "but to hand the girl over."

"The papers look real enough," Ash said. "But I must confer with Hunter for a minute then have Reed come and peruse them. Reed has experience in such matters."

"Bring the girl," the man said.

"You will be all right?" Ash asked Lark before he left, and she nodded.

As soon as Ash quit the room, Lark swooned into the arms of the worm, however distasteful the experience.

When Ash returned, he introduced Reed as the earl of Barrington, to impress Ames's shoddy fake of an uncle, and handed Reed the documents.

"The problem is," Reed said, after reading them, "they are all based upon a letter and record of birth, conspicuous by their absence."

Lark rose and handed Reed the paper she had picked from the man's pocket when she swooned. "This might help," she said. "Read the name if you please."

"Briana Fairhaven," Reed said, lost as to its significance, though Ash and Lark grinned.

"And do you know where Briana Fairhaven was born, Mr. Amesbridge?" Lark asked, not expecting an answer. "France," she supplied. "So why do you suppose her proof of birth is written in English?"

The man blustered. "I have no notion."

"Ash," Lark said, "can you get Briana?"

"She is here," Reed said opening the door and ushering her in.

Briana went to Lark and Ash, and they claimed her, Ash with a hand to her shoulder, Lark by tidying her hair.

"Briana," Lark said, "do you know this man?"

Briana regarded her, not the worm. "He was a friend

to Amesbridge. My Mama was afraid of them. They wanted her money."

The worm snorted and denied as much, while everyone ignored him.

"Of course," Ash said. "Why did I not think of Nora's fortune?"

Briana regarded Ash with trust. "I did not know when I should tell you, but my Mama said I would be a woman of property after she died, and when she did, the servants were to send me to you, so I would be safe."

"And so you will be." Ash squeezed his daughter's shoulder and narrowed his eyes upon the worm as if he might rip him apart. "I have jurisdiction in this village, and friends in high places. The girl remains here. You had best return to Seven Dials, or better yet, sail for the colonies, for you are under investigation as we speak and the stink of your reputation is foul."

The worm turned crimson and spluttered, even as Reed "escorted" him out by the seat of his pants.

Reed took up the certificate when he returned. "What amused you about this?"

Ash lifted Briana into his arms. "Tell him your real name, sprite. He will say nothing until you give permission."

"My name is *Ashley* Briana Fairhaven."

Lark knew by the look on Reed's face that he saw the truth in the matching expressions of father and daughter regarding him.

Chapter 25

On the afternoon before Christmas Eve, the children's excitement reached fever pitch as they dressed for their Christmas performance. Chastity had the rogues set up chairs for the audience and hang a curtain at the far end of the portrait gallery, beside the huge Christmas cedar hung with plump crimson apples, lavender balls, small gold pears, ribbon rosettes, pinecones, gilded chestnuts, and fine-cut snowflakes.

The audience sighed in appreciation as the curtain opened to reveal a nativity tableau. Matt, hooded, as St. Joseph; a blue-veiled Beatrix as Mary; Brandon Alexander as baby Jesus; Sabrina's Caleb and Joshua, twin lambs in white wool; Mark, Luke, and Micah, wise men all, in capes of silver, copper, and gold.

Christmas filled Lark's heart and tightened her throat.

Chastity read a short version of the nativity, then the heavenly hosts in parchment wings appeared. "Lully, lulla, thou little tiny child," they sang, accompanied by Rebekah on her flute.

"To end our tableau," Chastity said, "each of the children who wishes, may step up and tell us, in their own words what love means to them." Chastity and

Lark exchanged glances; Lark knew that her new friend was attempting to help answer her question.

"Children," Chastity said, "you may begin by saying, 'Love is,' and then tell us what love is to you."

A moment of hesitation ensued before Luke stepped forward. "Love is Mama stealing us from the workhouse."

Luke's sister Rebekah followed. "Love is Papa braiding my hair."

A speaking look passed between Reed and Chastity.

Damon rose next. "Nurse says love is when Mama and Papa nap in the middle of the day."

Sabrina squeaked, and Gideon leaned close, whispered in her ear, and kissed her cheek.

Lark and Ash sat forward when Briana rose and curtseyed. "Love is being able to admit who you are. My name is *Ashley* Briana."

Lark covered her mouth with a hand.

She had her answer. Love was the ability to be oneself. . . . Love was a kiss, a whisper, intimate moments, speaking looks, shared years, tears, hurts and sorrows, good times and bad, raising children, loving them, a reaching hand . . . Ash's own now taking hers, clasping it, speaking without words, his eyes bright—as if he too had just recognized love for the first time.

Lark turned the concept over in her mind. The rogues and their ladies all shared love, but to hear them tell it, love had not come easy. They had traveled rutted roads and fought their destinies. Before they had accepted their fates and acknowledged love, to a one, they had hurt, then forgiven, each other.

Was that the final secret then? Forgiveness?

If so, she would be doomed, for Ash forgave little. He would never forgive a deception that forced marriage. No matter his grandfather's will, he should have taken to wife a bride freely chosen.

Could a one-sided love inspire forgiveness for a deceit so vile? Did so dishonorable a cheat deserve the hand of forgiveness? Lark feared not.

Nevertheless, as she soothed her child with a stroking hand, she knew that before he or she entered this world, the truth must be spoken, however harsh the results.

'Twas nearing midnight and all their guests had long since retired to their beds before Ash was able to take Lark, in her wine velvet pelisse, out in the horse-drawn sleigh. He gave the horses their heads, for they knew the moonlit path well after so many turns had been taken that evening.

"I feared Reed would bloody Myles's nose," Ash said, "the way you bloodied Hunter's, when Myles took Peg in the sleigh."

An owl hooted as they shushed slowly past. "I do not see why," Lark said. "Pegeen is a woman grown."

"Because Reed was afraid Myles would employ his roguish charm and Peg would succumb, of course."

"But Reed is as dangerous as any of you."

"Yes, so he knew what might happen."

"What might? Stop the sleigh and direct your roguish charm my way, if you please. Let me see if I have the will to resist you."

Ash regarded his pregnant bride twice before guiding the horses toward the trees. "Keep your blinders on," he said to the matched pair as he took his wife into his arms.

'Twas not long before they played their lavender-field game, hands in each other's clothes, seeking all manner of sport, despite the nip in the winter air, and the iced white flakes drifting about them.

"I see what you mean about rogues and sleighs," Lark said, sitting up, breathless, some time later. "I want what you want, but the babe makes it difficult in so closed a space."

Ash grinned and rode the movement of their child with his palm. "Little Isobel is energetic tonight."

"Little Zachary, you mean."

He kissed her icy nose. "What say you to a nice warm bed?"

"Not yet, I like it out here. I want to do all the naughty things the rest of the rogues and their brides did."

"What naughty things?"

Lark took off her gloves, moved the carriage blanket aside, and took his hornpipe out to play. She chuckled wickedly at his hiss of appreciation. "Now that I have it, what *should* I do with it?"

"I do not know that it will perform at all well. It has never been so stiff from the cold."

"Let me warm it then." Lark bent to do so, with her mouth, of all things.

Ash gave a shout of shock and pleasure. "Good God, woman? How did you know to do that?"

"The wives have been talking."

"All the wives?"

Lark shrugged. "Some have more to teach and others more to learn."

Ash thought he should protest the intimate exchange of information, but Lark did it again, closing her lips over him this time, taking him full in her mouth, and his every thought fled. He knew nothing but her lips on his sex, milking him, suckling him, as if she would devour him. When he thought he'd expire from holding back, she took him into her hand again, as if to make him spill.

"You have to stop." He covered her hand with his. "Lark, stop, or I will ruin the blankets."

To his surprise and delight, she loosed her bodice and removed her lace scarf to glove him. While he suckled her cool breast, she worked him with skill, and he found her center, and brought her pleasure with his own.

When they got back to her room, Ash found a sprig of holly on her dresser and picked it up. "What is this?"

"You were to show me what rogues did with their buttonhole sprigs, remember?"

Ash grimaced. "While once that might have seemed a fine notion, I do not think, under the circumstances—"

"What? Can we no longer speak of such things? What has changed between us except that we are more intimate? Is your reticence based upon the fact that your roguish ways involved your many conquests?"

Ash sighed. "They were naught but naked women wrapped in red ribbon," he said, "a sordid past I would as soon forget."

"So . . . tell me what you did then with the holly sprig?"

"I tucked them into the ribbon's bow."

"How disappointing. I thought surely you tucked them elsewhere."

"Ouch." Ash grimaced. "Have you not noticed, my love, how spiny holly leaves can be? Though now that

I think on it, I might gently place that sprig between these lovely milky breasts."

Lark stepped away and gave him a seductive pose in profile. "Can you not see me clad in naught but a red ribbon with a magnificent bow?"

Ash took her in his arms. "Do not mock what I hold dear." He placed the sprig in her honey hair. "Perfect," he said. "Though I have long since thought you beautiful, you are to my eyes, at this moment, only to be revered."

"Oh no, never say so. Maternal perhaps, saucy yes, but never to be revered. I am your still your guttersnipe bride, make no mistake. Shall I be forced to beat you to remind you?"

"I had rather you took me to bed."

"Yes," she said. "Yes."

They undressed each other there, beside her bed, but when they met in the center, and teased and kissed, as they were wont to do, their need escalated to a degree that could not be satisfied.

"We are a fine pair, are we not?" Ash said falling back against the sheets. "Me, hard as a pikestaff, you slick and pulsing. But you are too full and round with the babe to make it possible." He kissed her hard naked belly. "Not that I am complaining, mind. I am awed and grateful."

Lark closed a hand around him, though 'twas not what either of them sought. Still, he spoke her name in the rush of frustrated pleasure at her touch.

"I want you inside me," she said, "deep and deeper still. Nothing but you thrusting into me will do. Hard. I want you hard and fast, Ashford."

Ash regarded his raging manhood, aching to be gloved, as much as she ached to pull him in, and he shook his head. "I aim to please, madam, but I dare not."

"Let us try against the wall again?" she suggested. "Have we a sturdier footstool?"

"And take a chance on hurting you or the babe? I think not." But Ash remembered what Buckston had said about meeting her halfway and it gave him an idea.

"Lark," he said, tossing aside the blankets and moving to the head of the bed. "I have an absurd notion that just might work. Do as I say and do not argue." He knelt, and urged her to kneel facing him, closer, then closer still, her legs parted, her knees on either sides of his.

He placed pillows beneath her bottom to prop her up and position her, held her almost astride him. She leaned forward, yet away, so as not to crush their child, but at exactly the right angle to receive him.

With a shout of joy, Ash gloved himself in his wife's willing warmth, and while she arched and leaned back against his bracing arms, Ash moved in her.

"Do nothing," he said. "I will do all the work and bear your weight. Just open for me, love. Welcome me."

"I do, Ash. More than you know."

Their passion turned wild and unruly. Her intense frenzy shivered his spine, as if she were driven, as if there might never be such another coupling, or another chance to express what they'd never dared.

For his part, Ash wanted more, many and more couplings, and he hoped Lark did too.

Neither spoke the thought, not in words, but in the merging of their flesh they avowed it with eloquence—two as one, victorious, and secretly, shockingly, in love, for his part at least.

Ash barely acknowledged the insight when Lark cupped his ballocks and brought them against her; he rejoiced in the sensation, and called her name with heightened rapture.

"I am flying, Ash, flying away from you, from myself." She opened her eyes and looked full at him. "This is wonder. I cannot bear it—"

"Bear it, love, a Christmas union always to remember, like naught in my experience. My wife, belly ripe with child, taking me so deep, I ride bliss to the stars. I never knew such wonder."

"Make it last," Lark said.

"You will kill us both," Ash said on a gasp. Nevertheless, he slowed his pace, ground his teeth, and placed his hands between them to make her to rise again.

And after she reached her pinnacle, three, maybe more, times, Ash embraced oblivion, fearing nearly for their safety. But when he questioned her, some minutes later, she laughed, with the little breath she could muster; purred; and curled against him to sleep.

Unlike his ill-used and fatigued self, she woke looking radiant, as if she would take on the world, and her first Christmas Eve besides.

After nuncheon, while her guests either finished their personal Christmas preparations or spent time with their children in the nursery, Ash surprised Lark by urging her up the stairs toward her small sitting room.

Ashley Briana—for so everyone had taken to calling her since her announcement—arrived shortly thereafter wearing a claret velvet dress to match Lark's own, Christmas gifts for both of them from Ash. Surprised and pleased as Lark to see it, Ashley Briana went to Ash, curtsied, accepted his compliments, and stepped into his embrace.

"Thank you," she said simply, her least number of words at once since her first. Then she came to stand before Lark and fan her skirts. "Look, Mama, I am almost as pretty as you."

Christmas when you least expected it, Lark thought, but Micah rose and shouted, "No!" and Ash hauled the boy on his lap.

Ashley Briana placed her arm about Lark's shoulder and raised her chin in challenge.

Micah ignored his sister's gauntlet to regard Ash, as if he might like to make a similar statement.

Ash looked to each of the children in turn and reached for Lark's hand. "Micah, Ashley Briana, only you can grant *our* most fervent Christmas wish, which is that you consider yourselves ours, equal in our love, with equal right to call us Mama and Papa."

Micah threw his arms around Ash; Ashley Briana grinned, as if she expected as much; and Lark accepted her husband's handkerchief.

Children's excited voices drew them to the main staircase where the party congregated, including every one of the nineteen children. Alex and Chastity waited, each at the base of a stair rail, and those children old enough stood in two rows at the top.

"What the dev—er, what Christmas tradition is

this?" Ash asked, as he took his wife's arm and they made their way down the stairs to the foyer.

"It is a new tradition, a banister race," Alex said. "For children ten years and older. Hawk and Reed are to be the judges. Was there ever such a banister to be seen? Such a long low stair, the rail arched like a chair, a base that kisses the floor, as if the carver had such a sport in mind when he designed it. I tried it myself last night to be certain it was safe."

"She did. After everyone retired," Hawk said, "and more than once, I might add."

"I say the winner gets to stay up and wait for Father Christmas," said Rafe.

"There is no Father Christmas," Harry said, repeating his litany.

"Is too," Damon argued, and I am waiting up for him to prove it, whether I win the race or not."

"So he thinks," Alex said.

"Where is Bree?" Lark asked.

"She is . . . indisposed," Gideon said, looking pale, culpable, and shock-struck.

Alex raised a speaking brow. "I believe next year's baby Jesus has been chosen."

Gideon lifted his two-year-old twins in his arms with the ease of practice and kissed each brow. "Poor Mama."

Lark saw that Gideon loved his children, welcomed the notion of more, but felt frustration at his wife's suffering. "Who has had the fastest slide so far?" she asked, changing the subject for Gideon's sake.

"Micah," Damon said, "but that is not fair because he has had weeks to practice."

"Mama can slide down faster than me," Micah said.

"You, Lark?" Chastity asked. "You have tested the banister as well? In your condition?"

"She slides all the time," Ashley Briana said with pride. "Come, Mama, show us."

"No," Ash said, "Mama is not up to a slide today," but Lark started up the stars.

"Larkin Rose Blackburne, I forbid you to slide down that banister. Think of the ba—" Ash regarded the eager listening children. "Larkin, heed me for once."

Lark faltered in the stairs when a spasm tore through her, but she hated giving in to her husband's orders. Not that she would slide, or do anything to endanger the babe, but she would climb the stairs if he ordered her not to. "Allow me to be the judge, if you please," she said, turning to regard Ash as she shook off her discomfort. When she made to take another step, a new pain cut her, doubling her in half, so she gasped, one hand to her splitting middle, one to her aching back.

"Ash, get her," she heard Alex say from a distance, but Alex needn't have bothered, because Ash was there, and Lark felt herself slide into the darkening security of his waiting arms.

"Continue the races," Ash called back, but Alexandra followed him as he carried Lark up to her bed. When Ash put Lark down, Alex elbowed him from his wife's side. "Get her some water. Is it her stays, do you think?" She freed Lark's buttons as she spoke. "They may be too tight."

Ash returned from the dressing room with a cup of

water, feeling his chest clench with fear. "She never wore stays in her life. Is she all right? The babe?"

Alex pulled Lark's dress free and passed a tiny amethyst vinaigrette bottle beneath Lark's nose.

Lark roused, coughed, and turned away.

Alex took the cup of water from his frozen hand, held it to his wife's lips, and Lark drank. Ash had never been so grateful for anything.

He and Alex worked together to finish undressing Lark as she moved in and out of consciousness.

When Ash turned with her night rail in his hand, he saw Alex staring at Lark's petticoats. "What?" he asked.

Chastity slipped into the room. "The men have the races in hand. What can I do?" She saw the petticoat, looked at Alex. "Her labor has started."

"Too soon," Lark said, rousing and drifting away again.

Ash felt his heartbeat treble. "Two months early?"

Alex looked at him, but he needed no word of confirmation.

"No," he shouted, not certain what he denied. He shook himself, regarded the women. "Tell me that whatever happens, Lark will be safe," but neither Alex nor Chastity seemed inclined to make him that promise.

Chapter 26

After having borne five babes of her own, Sabrina was sent for, and when she examined Lark, she confirmed their worst fears.

Lark accepted a sip of wine, but a new pain tore into her, and she pushed the glass aside. Afterward, she remained conscious, looking as frightened as Ash felt, though he attempted to mask his emotions for her sake.

"Ash," she said, "we must talk."

Chastity, Alexandra, and Sabrina rose as one and left the room.

Ash was grateful for the opportunity to touch his wife again. He sat on her bed, took her hand. "Rest," he said.

"No, there are things I need to say and you need to hear."

Her words shivered his spine, portending a finality he would not accept. "Lark, do not—"

"Ash, you must listen to me. Let me explain the least of my sins so as to prepare you for the worst of them."

"The worst? Are you saying you came to me with chil—No, I knew you for a virgin. I felt myself tear your barrier."

Lark gave him a half-hearted smile, her expression filled with so much yearning Ash swallowed a quick rising sob. She cupped their child, revealing how much she loved the babe in her womb, their babe. "He is yours," she said.

"Ours. I know."

"Will you let me speak now?"

Ash sighed and bowed to the inevitable, for she would not be silenced.

"I have done many terrible things for which you will disdain me."

Ash firmed his jaw for he wanted none of this confession business; then he remembered his mother and her frantic forgiveness, his own peace as a result, and he wanted to give Lark the same peace, to ease her labor and bring forth their child in safety. "Tell me," he said.

"There is no need to secure Micah's guardianship," she said. "When he was born, I went to the country, found a family to care for him, and signed the parish register naming myself as his mother. I did it so no one could take him from me. Though I lied, in the eyes of the law, I am his mother, and you, as my husband, are his legal guardian."

Another pain tore through her. "This is bad," she said riding it out. "The babe coming so soon." She looked at him with concern. "Do not hate me."

She would believe herself dying for certain, Ash knew, if he professed his love at this juncture. "Why would I hate you?"

"Because you dislike deceit, of all things."

"But I like you *above* all things."

"For the moment," Lark said. "Remember that I have loved Ashley Briana as my own, tell her so. It matters not that you loved the mother. I love the daughter. *Your* daughter."

"Oh, Lark no." Ash took his wife's hand. "You mistake the matter. I never loved Nora. She was hard, calculating. I—we used each other. I am ashamed to admit it, but 'tis so. Then, in the way of society, we became betrothed because her inheritance would complement mine. 'Twas back when I thought I had one, of course."

He kissed Lark's brow, her sweet lips. "I speak true Lark. I considered love a dreadful risk, back then, something to be avoided at all costs, but—"

Another pain. He took her hand. She asked for Alex.

Ash kissed her brow, feeling useless and dismissed, and left to fetch the women.

He sent Gideon, who needed action, for Doctor Buckston, and then he paced and awaited the summon to return to his wife.

Her labor continued all afternoon and into the evening. By then, the ladies were certain there would be no keeping the babe from making its untimely appearance, however dangerous.

Buckston could not be found, either at his residence or his surgery. Every rogue mounted a horse and drove from house to house in all directions to search for the good doctor, all except Ash.

Finally allowed back into his wife's room, alone with her again, praise be, Ash could hardly bear the sight of her suffering without shouting his frustration. He wanted to take her pain to himself. He wanted to push his fist through a wall, break something, fix everything.

Lark roused and saw him, beckoned him close. "Another sin," she said. "One of many. Go to my dresser and withdraw the packet wrapped in a figured scarf, tied with a gold ribbon."

Ash did as she requested, despite the seeming foolishness of it, and brought her the packet.

"Open it," she said.

"Lark this is no time for—"

"Open it."

To humor her, Ash did as he was told, then he stood staring down at his silver snuffbox and missing leather glove. "I thought I had misplaced these."

"I took them from you before you played that fateful game of cards with my father. 'Twas the least of my sins. Soon you will know my worst."

"Lark stop. No more. It matters not."

"I am a thief. Thievery is how I supported Micah. Not da. He would not spare the boy a farthing, so I supported him, in whatever way I could. Your wife is a thief, a liar, and a cheat."

"A pickpocket, I know. You pinched these the way you pinched my grandfather's will and the false proof of Ashley Briana's birth. So be it. See, there is nothing to confess that I do not know, but if you need absolution so much. . . ." Ash shuddered at the finality of the implication, hated to take the step for that reason, but for her peace and safe delivery he would do anything.

"You are absolved Lark. Now let it go. You did your best for your sister and her son. He is ours now, and safe. You are safe." He stroked the mound of their child with a possessive hand. "We will see this one safe born as well."

"Absolved but not forgiven," Lark said wetting her lips. "Water, please."

Sabrina had warned that if he gave Lark water, she might be ill, which would do her no good. Ash moistened her lips with a finger, and felt such a rush of love that his chest ached. If he told her now, she would think he was trying to ease her way into eternity.

She about broke his knuckles with her next pain. "I deceived you on our wedding night," she said between clenched teeth.

"What?" he said, smiling so he would not break down and weep. "You shot me in the arse then slept with another man?"

Lark screamed, a mixture of pain and frustration, Ash suspected.

"No, damn it! Listen to me. You did not *lose* the card game that bound us. Or you should not have lost if . . . But for me, you would have won, Ash."

"Certainly n—"

She nodded, and watched as if awaiting his comprehension. Ash wondered how she'd managed it. Why? Why, when she'd not wanted him any more than he'd wanted her? Ah, not for herself. Never for herself.

"You dropped your cards on the floor," she said. "Remember?" She nodded. "I see you do. Before you could retrieve them, I switched your ace for the two of hearts. Pickpockets are fast and I am the fastest."

"Tell me why."

"For a big house and fancy dresses, of course."

Ash denied her words with a shake of his head. "For Micah," he said, but Lark's scream drowned his words and the women came rushing in.

Sabrina began putting a cloth beneath Lark, and Alex pushed Ash from the room as Chastity slipped in with blankets. The door shut behind him.

He didn't know if Lark had heard him or not. He knew she had not cheated for herself. He knew her heart, by God.

To his surprise, he found his grandfather pacing outside Lark's room.

"It is Christmas Eve," the tired old man said when their gazes met.

Ash shook his head in incomprehension. "What are you doing here?"

"You invited me for Christmas, remember?"

"Christmas . . . I forgot."

"According to our old bargain, if she lost the babe before Christmas, you would fail to meet the stipulation in my will."

With a roar, Ash gave vent to the pain inside him. "I do not want your blasted money," he shouted. "I care naught for your bloody will. I want nothing—*God please hear me*—nothing but my wife safe in my arms. I love her. Do you hear me, Grandfather? I love my wife! I want her safe. I want our babe . . . if Lark is not the cost." Ash looked to the heavens. "Please let Lark not be the cost."

He looked back at the broken old man. "From you, Grandfather, I want nothing." Ash's ire rose again. "Keep your money. Give it away. If I have to remove my wife and children from this house, so be it. I will gladly pay the price. Any price. Much as my mother loves the Chase, she would pay the price as well to see my wife safe. Even she loves Lark."

Sabrina slipped from Lark's bedchamber into the hall. "We can hear you shouting Ash. The whole village can likely hear you."

Ash turned, focused on Sabrina, and found himself in a place he barely recognized; he was so lost to fury, until he remembered his words to his grandfather. "Did Lark hear me?"

Sabrina grinned. "You have renewed her strength. She sobbed when she heard your declaration."

Ash stared at the closed door as if he might see through it. He placed the flat of his hand against it. "Lord, this was not the way I wanted to tell her."

He heard her scream again, felt her pain to his soul.

"Where the devil is that doctor?" Ash ignored his grandfather's renewed bid for attention and ran down the stairs calling for his horse. He would ride to hell for the blasted doctor, if he must.

He would do anything to keep Lark safe.

The rogues congregated in the library, midnight upon them. Reed and Hawk paced, sometimes into each other, while Gideon stared into the fire. All awaited news of Lark and the babe.

Ashley Briana sat alone awaiting Father Christmas until Rafe and Micah, then Damon and Harry, joined her. That no parent saw, and forbade, their insurgence as the nursery stairs filled with children became a surprise in itself. That they were breaking such exalted rules became the subject of whispered discourse and delight, until Matthew warned that silence would go undetected, noise caught out.

After that, silent as lambs, they watched the strange comings and goings in reference to her new Mama's bedchamber, all of them waiting for Father Christmas . . . and perhaps something more.

Sometime after the church bells rang for the midnight service in the village, they heard the low jingle of sleigh bells, and the muted clop of horses hooves, the shush of runners through snow.

Ashley Briana watched as some of the children sat straighter. A few of the little ones stood for a better view and some cowered in fear, until the man they awaited came running up the stairs—hooded, robed in crimson velvet, white of beard, buttonhole of holly, and carrying a fat sack topped by a drum, a trumpet, and a porcelain doll.

"In here," her Papa said, opening her Mama's door and letting Father Christmas inside.

The children became more silent, more hopeful.

Ashley Briana was not alone in sensing that something momentous was about to take place, for Micah took her hand, squeezed it, and Ashley was grateful.

"That was him," Damon whispered a few minutes later.

Harry swallowed his pride and allowed his wonder free rein. "I think it was."

Damon's gloat was halted, Ashley noted, by a rush of mysterious muffled sounds from her Mama's closed room. A scream, a cry, a shout of triumph, a lusty wail.

Ashley regarded Micah, certain her eyes must be as large as his.

Some while later, Father Christmas stepped into the hall across the landing bearing the blanketed proof of Ashley's rising hope, all kicking legs and fighting arms.

"I wonder what else he has in that sack," little Julianna said.

A stooped old man stepped up to Father Christmas and touched the babe's fingers with reverence.

"Your great-grandson," Father Christmas said, handing the mite over. "Small but hearty, and not near as early as everyone surmised."

The old man wept and held the babe as if it were a fine porcelain treasure. "I only wanted to grow him up," the old man said. "Burned the will yesterday. Wanted him to know."

"The earl will be glad to hear it," Father Christmas said and then he saw the children, and Ashley started, as he winked before he took the babe back into her Mama's room.

Several minutes later, Father Christmas returned to the hall, fat sack in hand, and made for the picture gallery.

Taking his wink as a sign of acceptance and permission, the children followed at a goodly distance and watched as the proof of Christmas placed toys beneath the moonlit Christmas tree. When the robed man finished and started in their direction, they scampered up the nursery stairs, muffling squeaks and giggles, and ran to the big window overlooking the yard.

Oohs and Aahs abounded as a bright red sleigh, pulled by two matched pairs, disappeared down the drive.

"Happy Christmas," floated, as if on the air behind it.

"Did you hear that?" Ash asked as he slipped gratefully back into his wife's room and stopped at the sight before him.

Larkin Rose, his wife, safe, sitting in her bed, smiling, radiant, so beautiful she made him ache. Their Christmas babe was suckling at her breast, blanketed and tied with a red bow, a sprig of holly in its center.

"Happy Christmas, Papa," she said.

Ash's heart leapt. "Happy Christmas, Mama."

He shed his shoes and shirt, climbed into the bed beside her, and touched his son's soft silk fingers. "Welcome to the family, Zachary."

Lark placed her head on his shoulder and regarded their child asleep at her breast. "Ash," she said. "I beg you will forgive me."

"Lark." He kissed her crown, placed his cheek upon her hair. "I received forgiveness from my mother, and never knew its power until I did, so I gladly give you mine. But where is forgiveness necessary when there is such wonder to be met?

"Rather, let me thank you for our new son, and a life as joy-filled as Christmas, for you saved me when you switched those cards. *You* are everything I never knew I wanted for Christmas, and for as long as we both shall live—you, Micah, Ashley Briana, and our sleepy little Christmas baby."

Lark raised her head, caught his gaze with brilliant eyes, and met his lips, while gratitude and love rushed Ash in tides too wild to be borne.

"I love you, Ash."

"I love you, my lady Blackburne, though I am not half good enough for you."

About the Author

Annette Blair is the Development Director and Journalism Advisor at a private New England prep school. Married to her grammar school nemesis—and glad she didn't know what fate had in store—Annette considers romance a celebration of life. She especially enjoys crafting a new romance, hearing from her readers, and collecting glass slippers. Contact her at P.O. Box 302, Manville, RI 02838 or go to www.annetteblair.com.

More Regency Romance
From Zebra

Discover the Romances of
Hannah Howell